WHO . . . OR WHAT . . .
IS THE ECOLOGIC ENVOY?

"Admiral, we can no longer control the elections on Hernando. A mutant form of A-damp virus wiped out the entire Popular Front planning force ten days ago."

"An Accord system action?"

"Exactly, sir. A lone agent from Accord's Ecolitan Institute. We can't prove it, but all signs point that way. First: the security guards were taken out by hand—broken neck, crushed windpipe. Second: it was done quietly, no guns, no traces. Imperial Intelligence believes that only Accord has the capability to deploy individualized weapons—"

"Was this really a *weapon*?" snapped a senior Admiral.

"Admiral," answered the Commodore, "have you ever run across a swamp fever virus that affected only a private banquet hall in an open public restaurant, killed an entire room full of people simultaneously, within seconds, while killing a squad of armed guards by hand?"

L.E. MODESITT, Jr.

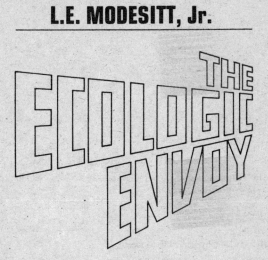

THE ECOLOGIC ENVOY

TOR®

A TOM DOHERTY ASSOCIATES BOOK
NEW YORK

THE ECOLOGIC ENVOY

Copyright © 1986 by Leland E. Modesitt, Jr.

Edited by David G. Hartwell

First printing: September 1986

A Tor Book
Published by Tom Doherty Associates, Inc.
175 Fifth Avenue
New York, NY 10010

Cover art by Wayne Barlowe

ISBN: 0-812-54584-2
CAN. ED.: 0-812-54585-0

Printed in the United States of America

0 9 8 7 6 5 4 3 2

For Susan,
gymnast, supporter, and daughter,
who liked this book from the first draft.

"You get what you can, and you call it honorable."
L. deLewis Spragg, *Politics of Trade*

"Trade is too important to be left to politicians."
Variation on Twentieth Century (A.D.) saying

"Politics is too important to be left to the traders of votes or to the traders of tangibles."
G. Wu-Reginald, Farewell Address to the
S. A. Guild

"Trade and Commerce are merely another form of war. At least, the warriors admit their calling is war."
Fleet Admiral Gorham, *Memoirs*

"True trade is honest, but not merciful. Politics is dishonest, no matter how merciful ... and war is neither honest nor merciful ... therefore, choose trade above politics, but politics above war. ..."
Anonymous

. . . I . . .

The needle-boat blinked out into norm-space. Both high and low wave detector plates flared.

"Flame!" The pilot scanned the board, jabbed a series of control studs to put all energy radiating equipment into a passive mode, and waited for the picture to build on his screens.

Energy concentrations peaked around the fourth planet, Haversol, then spread to a standard picket line and deep warning net typical of an Empire operation.

Whaler's fingers flickered over the control studs as he took in the information flowing from his receptors. While all the material would stay on tap for the Institute to dissect after his return, his own survival might depend on a nearly instantaneous understanding of the tactical pattern.

"Ten stans, max," he muttered to the controls, eyes darting from screen to screen. The needle-boat itself was a single pilot craft, jammed with sophisticated sensors and communications equipment, and made possible only through a combination of thin hull, minimal support and backup systems, and overpowered drives.

At the upper left of the board in front of Whaler, a flat panel flashed amber twice, then settled into a steady glow.

He touched the panel and listened to the direct feed of the Imperial comm net through his own implant.

"Seven . . . clear on grid november five . . . interrogative . . ."

"That's negative."

"Angel four . . . negative on survivors . . . send the junkman."

"Hawkstrike! Hawkstrike! Gremlin, Arthur class, vector zero eight five, radian one three three, ecliptic plus two."

"Hawkstrike, gremlin acquisition, closing."

The Imperial Fourth Fleet was obviously mopping up the scattered remnants of the Haversolan system defense forces.

"Class four on radian two five seven. Hotspot three. Interrogative waster. Interrogative waster."

"Waster's down. Negative."

Screeeee!!!!

"Unscramble, Northwave. Unscramble."

"Gremlin secured, Hawkstrike. Repeat, Gremlin secured."

The needle-boat pilot shook his head and touched the pale green panel to start the power-up for nullspace reentry.

The return coordinates for his out-space base flashed across the display. The Institute maintained its own forces independent of the Coordinate. So independently, thought the Ecolitan who was the needle-boat's pilot, captain, and crew, that the government itself had no idea of the Institute's strength.

"Sooner or later, they'll need us again," murmured the pilot. "Sooner, if this is any indication. Much sooner."

Nathaniel Firstborne Whaler, sometime scholar and full-time practicing Ecolitan, automatically squared himself within his seat cocoon and cleared the board readouts, returning all the data to the coded master disc in the center of the boat.

As the bell chime sounded in his ears, Whaler tapped the sequencing plate, and the needle-boat vanished from the norm-space where the Imperial detectors had failed to notice the discrepancy in the energy levels that had been the only sign of its presence.

. . . II . . .

The Admiral glared around the conference table that circled an empty space, then tapped the flat control panel.

The panel flashed twice before settling into a steady amber glow to signify that the full security screens were on-line and functioning.

A tap on another panel stud brought the holo star map into being in the once-vacant center of the encircling table.

The Admiral lifted the light pointer from the console and rapped the table. Once. The low murmur from the dozen senior officers died.

Guiding the pointer into the holo map, the Admiral focused the tip on a G-type system on the far side of the Rift.

"Accord. You can see how it controls the trade lines. Particularly since the Secession."

The pointer tip moved from the holo and jabbed at the Commodore.

"Let's have your isolation strategy report."

The Commodore stood stiffly and gestured at the blank wall to the right of the senior officer. A segment of the holo, blown to larger dimensions, appeared. On the inner edge of the Rift, the Imperial side, three stars appeared in red.

"Haversol, Fonderal, and Cubera. Until the success of our recent operation, Haversol was the largest out-Rift trade staging point on the Imperial side dealing with the Coordinate traders. The economics dictated that we hit Fonderal first, and that was completed before we even planned the Haversol campaign. The embargo on Fonderal was a simpler matter, of course, because of its lack of an internally supported infrastructure. Even *they* couldn't tackle that kind of rebuilding job, not in the short run, and especially with Haversol still open.

"Next came the flanking movement. We managed to get adequate support to the statist insurgents, who, in turn, were able to topple the monarchy. Of course, the new provisional government asked for Imperial assistance, and the Fourth Fleet was close enough to provide the necessary support."

"That left Hernando and Haversol along this corridor, and we've just about completed the establishment of the military support agreement with the new government of Haversol."

Another system on the holo blowup began to alternate flashing white and red.

"That leaves Hernando."

The Commodore coughed twice, reached down, and took a sip from the tumbler before returning to the presentation.

"Obviously, this is all just a sketch, but the next step will be harder. Hernando is considerably more stable than the other systems. Still . . . if we can get a more favorable government in the upcoming elections or, failing that, generate enough civil unrest to demonstrate a certifiable lack of control, we would have the basis for another control action, citing the threat to Imperial commerce. That would just about close down Accord's access to the Limber line."

The Commodore looked back at the Admiral.

"Any questions, Admiral?"

"What's the best possible time line?"

"The midterm elections on Hernando are more than a standard year off, and to generate any real results will be hard in such a short frame, but we intend to try. Certainly, by the next elections after the midterms—"

"Aim for the midterms. Giving Accord time to react could put us on the defensive."

The Commodore nodded. "Full speed ahead on Hernando it is, Admiral."

. . . III . . .

Tipsy, that the man definitely was.

Otherwise he would not have staggered down the hallway and elbowed his way through the heavy wooden door into the private party in the second dining room of the Golden Charthouse.

Twenty people, fourteen men and six women, sat around the two rectangular tables, enjoying the first course of dorle soup and the thin and genuine wheat crackers and anticipating the days of power to come. Only six weeks remained before the upper chamber elections.

A tall man, clean shaven and attired in a formal, deep blue tunic and contrasting cream sash, was standing to make the first toast.

"To the people of Hernando and to the Popular Front, the government to be."

The drunk, a sandy-haired fellow, lurched inside the room.

"Sir, this is a private party." The guard moved away from the curtained archway to block the intruder. His partner approached from the other side.

Neither thought to reach for the illegal freezers in the belt holsters they flaunted.

"So . . . want to join the celebration . . . see the new masters . . . see what kind of government the Empire bought . . . how much the sellout cost . . . "

The sandy-haired man stood almost as tall as the two guards. All three were nearly half a head taller than the men seated around the tables, even than the toastmaster.

"Sir!" protested the lead guard, stiffening.

The interloper stumbled backwards, then kicked the heavy door shut. The toastmaster jerked his head toward the noise.

"Sorry, friends!"

With his right hand, the intruder launched an aerosol into the space between the tables. Simultaneously, a backhand slash casually broke the neck of the guard on his left.

The right-hand guard grabbed for his freezer, too late, and had no second chance as he doubled with a crumpled windpipe and a smashed kneecap.

Even before the aerosol had landed and come to a full stop, the Ecolitan had returned his full attention to the diners, with a small dart pistol in each hand.

The toastmaster in blue was dragging a stunner from his waistband when the first dart caught him in the throat.

"Help!"

"Security!"

"Flamed greenie!"

"Get him!"

"You do!"

A black man with flaming golden hair dove from the top of the nearest table but fell short of reaching the attacker, and was rewarded with a dart in the neck and a kick snapping his collarbone.

The shouts and sounds, already muffled by the private dining room's heavy insulation and rich hangings, began to dwindle under the effects of the darts and the aerosol.

The Ecolitan calmly continued to shoot anyone trying to reach him or to escape until there were no living figures in the room. None had escaped. Then he checked the bodies, methodically studying each face and comparing it against his memory, and insuring that every member of the Popular Front present was indeed dead.

The sometime Ecolitan professor who bore the unlikely name of Nathaniel Whaler disliked the necessity of the assignment but continued to move with measured and deliberate speed, touching nothing except with his gloved hands as he turned each still form. Last, he replaced the aerosol in his tunic, concealed the dart guns in his boot sheaths, and opened the heavy wooden door, staggering out as he closed it behind him. Weaving back and forth, he stumbled back down the hallway and out into the main corridor from the hidden Charthouse.

Three levels down, he disappeared into a public fresher stall. In time, a blond man in a dark blue business tunic crisply strode out.

After descending yet another level to the open square, the Ecolitan/businessman sat down beside a fountain on an empty pseudo stone bench, apparently admiring the interplay of the golden water with the crimson spray curtains.

In time, a young woman, low-cut blouse revealing her profession and assets, sat down next to him, thrusting her chest at him with an artificially inviting smile.

"Complete?"

"All but Zeroga," answered Whaler. "Not at the dinner. You try the firm. I'll hit his quarters."

As he spoke, Whaler let his eyes range over the woman, as if appraising what she offered.

She rolled her eyes in exasperation.

Whaler shook his head vigorously, and the woman pouted publicly before standing with a flourish and mincing her way from him and the fountain.

The Ecolitan shook his head again and stood.

Finally, with a last look at the fountain, the blond man who had been sandy haired and would be again walked down the corridor to the flitter stand, where he dialed for public transportation.

. . . IV . . .

The Commodore stood more stiffly than usual, waiting to report to the Admiral and the other members of the Ministry's strategy board.

"I understand we've run into some difficulties on Hernando, Commodore."

"Yes, Admiral. A major stumbling block, though you will recall that my last report to the board indicated the lack of time facing us."

"I recall that. However, would you please provide a fuller explanation for the record." The tone of the request sent shivers down the back of the senior Commanders in the briefing section. Several others shifted their weight quietly.

The Commodore turned to face neither the audience nor the Admiral and pointed at the lit screen, which displayed a chart.

"As you can see, the Conservative Democrats, with the help of the seven seats held by the Socialist Republicans, control the Upper Chamber, and thus, the executive branch of Hernando's government. The Popular Front, with some outside technical support, had identified the most vulnerable Conservative Democrats and targeted them.

17

We also targeted those strong opinion leaders opposed to a greater Imperial presence along the Limber line.''

The chart shifted.

''This indicates the probable election outcome, including deaths and retirements, which we had predicted last month.''

''That doesn't look like a problem,'' commented a junior Admiral to the Commodore's right.

''It wasn't . . . until some mutant form of A-damp virus wiped out the entire Popular Front planning group and the ten leading candidates—all on the same night ten days ago.''

''Accord?''

''The Institute. No way to prove it, but the signs all point that way.''

''Such as?''

''First, both security guards were taken out by hand. One had a broken neck and the other a crushed windpipe.'' The Commodore cleared his throat before continuing. ''Second, it was done quietly. No guns, blaster bolts, slug throwers. And virtually no traces left.''

The Admiral studied the faces around the conference table. Several expressed open doubt.

''Why do you think those are enough to point at Accord and at the Ecolitan Institute, Commodore?''

''Well . . . we don't deal with biological weapons, especially tailored ones. Imperial intelligence, as well as the Ministry's teams, indicates that only Accord has a capability sophisticated enough to develop and deploy individualized weapons—''

''Was this really a weapon?'' snapped a senior Fleet Admiral.

''Admiral,'' answered the Commodore, ''have you ever run across a swamp fever virus that killed an entire room full of people within a unit or two, simultaneously? At the same time when two armed security guards were killed by hand?''

The silence dragged out. Finally, the Commodore turned back to the Grand Admiral.

"That brings up the hand-to-hand ability. We might have a dozen men with the ability to disable a pair of two-meter-tall armed guards in seconds. Several other terrorist groups might have a handful spread across the Empire. None of us have anyone with that ability also immune to swamp fever, mutated or not, or with the ability to walk through a crowded restaurant into a private dining room and assassinate twenty people and then leave without even being noticed."

"Not even noticed?"

"Not so far as we can determine."

The Admiral surveyed the faces again. "You might ask why this all points to Accord. I'll tell you. What the Commodore has not said is that all members of the Institute are either naturally immune or immunized against swamp fever and a number of other fast-acting diseases. He also has not mentioned that the Ecolitan Institute maintains the most intensive hand-to-hand combat training in the civilized worlds, along with a special corps that is little more than a crack terrorist unit."

"Can we prove any of this?"

"That's not the point. Accord wanted to send us a message. They sent it, and we've received it. It doesn't change a thing. Single individuals, no matter how gifted, cannot stop the massed force of history that we will bring to bear."

The Admiral frowned slightly after finishing the declaration, then touched the control console. The holo star map and the wall charts vanished.

"We can't wait for another set of elections on Hernando, not with this kind of a challenge. How soon can we go with Plan B?"

The Commodore cleared his throat. "That's already underway, but the flagship won't be ready for about three standard months—"

"See if you can make it two."

The Commodore nodded.

The Admiral touched the amber stud, and the security screens winked off.

"Adjourned."

. . . V . . .

Restinal paused outside the open door.

"Come in, Werlin. Come on in."

Restinal didn't recognize the voice, but it was apparent from the cheerful tone of the invitation that the speaker recognized him.

He shrugged, took a tighter grip on his datacase, and went in.

The room was paneled in lorkin wood. The desk and chairs were all carved from it as well. Restinal noted that the furniture all matched, each piece done in the spare style termed Ecolog.

Behind the desk, which was really a wide table with a single drawer, sat a silver-haired man, laugh lines radiating from the bright green eyes. Restinal mentally compared the face against the ones shown him by Delward before he'd left Harmony. He struggled momentarily before realizing that the man was the Prime Ecolitan himself, Gairloch Pittsway. For some reason, Restinal hadn't expected to be met by the Prime himself, much less in an empty office without aides.

"You wonder about the absence of subordinates?"

"Exactly," responded the Delegate Minister for Interstellar Commerce.

"You shouldn't, not if you've followed the precepts of the Institute. Unnecessary subordinates are a sign of weakness. Our fault that most no longer know the precepts, no doubt, since the Iron Rules are no longer popular in the schools' curricula."

Restinal didn't have the faintest idea what the Prime was talking about. He kept his face blank.

"I realize you don't understand what I'm jabbering on about, Werlin, but don't worry about it. If you don't understand it instinctively, it would take more time than either of us has for me to explain what I mean. Power is the question now.

"Neither the Orthodoxists nor the Normists have the power to force their choice for Trade Envoy to New Augusta upon the other. The Supreme Justiciary passed the choice back to the House, ruling that the selection has to be made by the political arm of the government. You're stuck. And you don't like the Institute all that much, since we are the sole remaining traditional structure still respected by the masses you professional politicians cultivate so assiduously. Both you and the Orthodoxists would like to reduce the influence of the Institute more than the passage of time and the ravages of peace have already done.

"Forcing a choice upon the Institute, with the attendant publicity, solves all your problems. Neither party has to take responsibility for the choice. If our selection succeeds, then you will take credit, and if he fails, we take the blame."

"That is conjecture, respected Prime," responded Restinal.

"Gairloch or Prime. None of that 'respected' hypocrisy, please." The Ecolitan smiled, the open smile of a man at peace with himself or as if at a child's joke, before he went on. "The Institute attempts to minimize dealing with speculations or conjectures. I doubt that my analysis is anything but factual. I respect, however, the position in which you have been placed by the operation of the political machinery."

The Prime Ecolitan stood and walked from behind the table toward the still-standing Restinal.

"Please sit down. I forget that politicians all too often stand on ceremony."

Restinal's knees felt rubbery, and he eased himself into one of the carved high-backed chairs. Although the chair was not upholstered, the flowing curves of the wood seemed to welcome him.

The Prime poured a cup of water from a crystal pitcher and placed it on the table next to Restinal before he returned to his chair behind the desk.

Restinal picked up his case, placed it on his lap, opened it, and pulled out the carefully drawn list the Elders Quaestor and Torine had hammered out in the short hours before he had been dispatched.

"Keep the list. The names on it are predictable. They begin with Tormel, Reerden, and Silven."

Restinal kept his mouth shut. The list began with Tormel, Reerden, and Silven. But there were only two copies of the list—the one he had and the one Torine had kept. He, Restinal, had handwritten both.

"I can see you haven't had that much contact with the Institute, Werlin, and I'm afraid that will make your acceptance of your role that much more difficult.

"In answer to your unspoken question, none of us has seen the list, but we do know the personalities of the individuals who made the choices and the parameters for selection. I'll admit, in candor, that I would be hard-pressed to name the next person in order on the list, although we could probably pick eight out of ten."

Restinal allowed his features to express mild interest. "Perhaps you have already made a choice, then?"

"As a matter of fact, I have. But the name is not one on your list."

The Minister for Interstellar Commerce suddenly felt sticky in his formal blacks, as if he had been placed squarely in the Parundan Peninsula rain forests.

"If you would explain—"

"Werlin, the Institute is not obligated to explain anything, but since you are intelligent and informed, I will put it in simple terms. The same reason why the House of Delegates cannot select any Envoy is why anyone chosen from that list will not succeed."

"I fail to see that. Most governments select their Envoys." Restinal was beginning to see why Elder Torine had delegated the job to him and why few of the older Delegates cared much for the Institute.

"Most Envoys fail. We do not care to be associated with failure. The question is not political. The question is power. Politics is a system of using nonovert force to work out an agreeable compromise that does not lead to violence. The more equal the base of power, the more political the means of agreement can be."

Restinal was lost, and he knew his face showed it.

The Prime shook his head.

"Let me attempt to explain by analogy. When two torkrams contest for superiority, do they fight for blood? Of course not. They fight until one loses his footing. In fact, the amount of violence is minimal. If a prairie wolf should wander into the hills, however, the torkram becomes a merciless attacker. The first is an example of near equality of force, as well as an example of similar social behavior which allows what might be called a negotiated settlement. The second is a struggle for survival.

"You and the other Delegates are assuming that in negotiating with the Empire the basis of force is equal and the social behaviors behind the political structures are alike. Both are questionable assumptions."

"Are they really?" questioned Restinal. What did torkrams have to do with the picking of Envoys anyway?

"As a consequence," continued the Prime, "we have picked our own nominee."

Restinal repressed a whistle. Elder Torine didn't like being crossed, and neither did Elder Quaestor, and the Prime was blithely crossing them both.

"Do you honestly think the Delegates will agree?"

"Yes. They have no choice. They don't want to take the blame if things go wrong. Elder Torine knows that. Did you ever ask yourself why you were chosen to present the list and bring back our reply?"

Restinal had wondered but had dismissed it in the face of Torine's encouragement and insistence. He nodded at the Ecolitan.

"We are not unaware of the impact this could have on your career, Werlin," continued the Prime. "But you should be able to surmount any difficulties. If not, it is doubtful your career would have lasted much longer."

Delegate Minister Werlin Restinal was getting the picture, and though the outlines were blurry, he didn't like the view. The Delegate Minister for Interstellar Commerce was about to become Elder Torine's scapegoat unless he could turn the announcement to his own advantage.

"Who is your choice?"

"Nathaniel Firstborne Whaler."

The name meant nothing to Restinal.

The Prime lifted a thin folder from his desk and slid it across the flat surface to where the Delegate could reach it.

Restinal opened it and scanned the background on Whaler.

Nathaniel Firstborne Whaler—senior fellow of the Ecolitan Institute; 38 A.T.U.; 191 centimeters; fluent in the eight leading tongues of the Empire, plus Fuardian and ancient English; Class B scout pilot; combat master; Class C energy tech; noted economist and recognized authority on infrastructure economics.

His single previous tour with the government had been

as the Ecolitan Special Assistant to a previous Minister of Commerce.

Restinal was impressed, in spite of his skepticism.

"Are you sure he's the best choice?"

"Do you have anyone who can match half his qualifications?"

Restinal repressed a sigh. There it was, in green and black. Take Whaler or go without the blessing of the Institute . . . and anyone to blame things on if the talks fell through.

. . . VI . . .

The tall woman was the Special Assistant. Although the meeting was in her office, she waited for the Admiral.

"The Admiral, Ms. Ku-Smythe."

The Special Assistant acknowledged the faxscreen with a curt nod and stood to await her visitor.

"You look very professional, Marcella."

"Thank you." She gestured to one of the two chairs in front of her desk.

The Admiral sat, erect with the military bearing that could only have come from years of training.

"Have you reconsidered your position on the Coordinate issue?" The Admiral's gray hair glinted in the indirect light. Although, as Defense chief, the space officer could have obtained the best of rejuve treatments, the gray added yet another touch of authority.

"Commerce will support the Emperor. That has always been our position."

"I know that. You know that. What other official position could you have? Why all the reservations?"

Marcella shifted her weight before answering, then coughed softly to clear her throat.

"Sooner or later, you'll push Accord to the point where

the Institute will gain control of the situation. That point is
closer than anyone on your staff is willing to admit. It's
almost as if they're pushing you toward military action.
On the other hand, we've worked to make trade the tool
for expansion. Without the right kind of legal background
and the impression that Imperial commerce is jeopardized,
you're taking the unnecessary risk of pushing the independent out-systems to support Accord.

"And that's totally unnecessary. None of them really
like the Coordinate. You want to act before we can neu-
tralize Accord, and right now Halston and the Fuards, at
the very least, will regard your plans as a danger to all the
out-systems—"

"Since we're being candid," interrupted the Admiral,
"aren't they?"

"Why broadcast it? If we can get Accord to agree to a
trade agreement with Commerce, that becomes a legal
document admitting greater Imperial sovereignty—the very
sort of legal sham that the out-systems will buy." The
Special Assistant frowned, pursed her lips, and waited for
the Defense chief to reply.

"Why did you support our action on Haversol?"

"Because we had a previous trade agreement and because Haversol was stalling on renegotiating to avoid com-
plying with the terms. That provided the justification the
Emperor needed."

"What's the difference for Accord?"

"You know the difference very well. We don't have a
trade agreement with Accord, and, currently, we recognize
the Coordinate's full independence. Unlike Haversol, they've
the means to fight, possibly to cost you a great deal more
than you expect."

"With what? Three small fleets that don't total the
Fourth Fleet?"

"Remember how we lost the Rift in the first place?"

"That was nearly four hundred years ago."

"After four hundred years, we still haven't repaired the

damage to Terra, and we still don't have all those systems back. You have ten major fleets and are building another. With all those ships, we only get systems back through the combination of trade and force. And here you are, trying sheer force again. It hasn't worked before, and it won't work now."

"Marcella, we've discussed this before."

"You asked—"

"I know. I know. I asked. You still feel that the urgency of the situation is not great enough?"

"Not nearly great enough."

The silence grew as both looked away from each other.

"Well . . ." began the Admiral. "I do value your opinion."

"I understand." The Special Assistant's voice lowered, softened. "Enough so you make your staff wait outside. You've always listened, ever since . . ." She paused, then continued, "but you do your job the way you see it, and you're usually right. Not always, but usually. And we'll support you, whatever you decide."

"I know. I wish I had your personal support as well." The Admiral stood and turned to leave, then half faced the woman again. "Take care, Marcella."

"Thank you."

The Special Assistant looked across the wide and empty office at the closed portal for a long time before returning to her console, where the panels flashed, each light clamoring for her attention.

. . . VII . . .

"Best simulation results indicate forty percent probability of successful trade negotiations; twenty percent probability of failure; ten percent probability of direct armed conflict; thirty percent unquantifiable." Despite the pleasant sound of the terminal, the evenness of the word spacing rendered the report mechanical.

The Director turned to the three people at the conference table. "Forty percent chance that the situation can be resolved without war. If we can come up with these figures, so can the Admiral's staff. What's the chance of success if the present Envoy is removed?"

"Personality profile not a major component of success probability. Personality profile is a major component of unquantifiable component."

The Director frowned.

"What that means," offered the dark-haired woman across the table from the Director, "is that the personality of the Accord Envoy will shift the unquantifiable component into other areas. The current success probability is based on the structural situation. In short, we could still get a peaceful solution, though that could change at any time."

30

"What would happen if Defense could assassinate the Envoy?"

"Probability of war rises to fifty-five percent," answered the computer.

"Probability of Imperial victory twenty-four percent. Probability of significant loss to Empire approaches unity; probability of destruction of Accord approaches unity."

"Any other significant probabilities?"

"Probability of loss of Rift and Sammaran Sector approach unity; probability of survival of Ecolitan Institute approaches unity."

The Director leaned back in her swivel.

"So . . . if Defense is allowed to force the issue, we're all likely to get blackholed."

The man in the group cleared his throat.

"That assumes one thing . . . that Defense can successfully operate a covert assassination. How likely is that if we oppose it, and if External Affairs is opposed, and if their Envoy is warned?"

The Director tapped the table to still the quick rustles.

"You forget that we cannot officially oppose Defense. Nor could we directly ever feed that kind of information to an Envoy from Accord. That sort of behavior would have even the Senate slapping riders onto our authorization, and we've avoided that for too long to go back to that sort of interference again."

"Could I have an answer to the probability questions?"

"Yes. Let's have the readout on those," the Director agreed.

"Probability of successful assassination not quantifiable under first order assumptions. Under second order, probability twenty percent, with a standard deviation of not more than twenty percent."

The Director smiled.

"All right," she said. "You've got the verification that to warn their Envoy will alter the probabilities along the lines we think would be desirable. How can you warn him, clearly, and yet in a way that will convey the absolute seriousness of the situation?''

"That's simple. We try to assassinate him first.''

. . . VIII . . .

Nathaniel Whaler took another full step in front of the Imperial Marines to survey the entrance to his Legation.

The New Augusta tower corridor was nearly as wide as the average street back on Harmony but without the more elaborate facades that graced the capital of Accord. On New Augusta, each address within the towers or tunnels merely seemed to have a standard portal. The portal to the Accord Legation, aside from its green color and gold letters proclaiming the LEGATION OF ACCORD, differed little from the others he had passed.

As high as he was in the Diplomatic Tower, there was considerable foot traffic, along with numerous automated delivery carts.

Nathaniel half turned toward the bystanders who watched his honor guard with a mixture of boredom and indifferent curiosity. As he did, the sight of an all-too-familiar object coming to bear on him sent him into a diving roll behind the still-standing guards.

Scritttt!

The splinter gun fragments shattered across the portal facing and skittered along the corridor.

"Spread and search!" snapped the Marine Lieutenant.

"He's gone already," observed Nathaniel, dusting himself off.

The Marine officer ignored the Ecolitan's observation and sprinted down the corridor. Two ratings closed up next to Nathaniel, each scanning the corridor in a different direction.

"Sir? Don't you think you should get under cover?"

"Little late for that."

Most of the bystanders had scuttled out of the path of the onrushing Marines or had found they had business elsewhere.

Nathaniel scanned the faces that remained. Two of the handful still in the corridor struck him as possibilities, and he committed their faces to memory before turning his full attention to the narrow scratch on the portal.

"Hmmm . . ." he murmured. The splinter had barely scratched the permaplast. He checked the corridor floor and tiles for nearly twenty meters but could find no trace of the splinter fragments he had heard.

What with the apparent attack and all the Imperial Marines, the Ecolitan felt more like he had been leading an expedition through Accord's southern forests than arriving in New Augusta.

Finally, he touched the Legation entry plate, and the door slid open. The two Marines marched in and stationed themselves in front of the entry desk. Nathaniel followed.

The decor of the receiving area that was supposed to represent the decor and ambience of Harmony didn't. The gargoyled lorkin wood hanging lamps were Secession Renaissance. The woven wheat grass entry mat was Early Settler. The inlaid blackash tea table was pre-Secession, and the likes of the long maroon and overupholstered couch had never been seen in Harmony or even in the depths of the Parundan Peninsula.

As Nathaniel refrained from staring at the mismatched furniture, three more Marines quick-stepped in with his field pack and datacases, deposited them next to the entry desk, and marched away to reform outside the Legation.

The Lieutenant stepped up and gave the Envoy a stiff salute.

"Further instructions, sir?"

"Dismissed," Nathaniel responded in Panglais.

"Yes, sir. Thanks to you, Lord Whaler, sir."

As the door noiselessly closed, the Ecolitan turned his attention to the woman at the desk. She wasn't from Accord, and his change of attention caught her intently studying him.

That was to be expected. The Empire supplied, without charge, space in the Diplomatic Tower and paid up to twenty assistants or technical specialists for each Legation. A planetary government, hegemony, federation, or what-have-you could send as many or as few nationals as it desired for Legation staff, and use any or none of those paid by the Empire.

The catch was the cost. If the Legation were located in the Diplomatic Tower, the Empire paid for the space, the power, and the Empire-supplied staff. If any out-system government chose to put its Legation elsewhere in New Augusta, then the Empire paid none of the costs. While the richer or more militaristic systems, such as Olympia or the Fuardian Conglomerate, had separate Legations staffed strictly by their own nationals, most non-Imperial governments availed themselves of at least the space in the Diplomatic Towers.

The House of Delegates of Accord, not known for its extravagance, had accepted quarters in the Diplomatic Tower and had sent only three people to New Augusta: the Legate, the Deputy Legate, and an Information Specialist.

Just prior to his arrival at the circumlunar station, the copilot of the *Muir* had handed Nathaniel a stellarfax.

WITHERSPOON EN ROUTE ACCORD FOR CONSULTA-TIONS. WHALER CONFIRMED ACTING LEGATE DURA-TION. sgn. RESTINAL, DM, IC.

The rest had been confirmation codes.

So now he was standing in the entry of a Legation he was in charge of, looking at a clerk/staffer/receptionist who had never seen him but who worked for him, theoretically, but who was paid by the Empire. And just before that, the message had been delivered by splinter gun that someone wanted him dead.

Hardly the most encouraging beginning.

Nathaniel drew out his credentials folder and presented it to the young woman.

She took it, with a hint of a smile, studied it briefly, then greeted him more officially with a gesture that was nearly a half bow, half curtsy.

"At your service, Lord Whaler." Her greeting was in the old American of Accord, but with an accent and a stiffness that demonstrated practice, but not fluency.

"And I at yours, in the service of the Forest Lord and the Balance of Time," he returned in the archaic format that was no longer used, even in the deepest forests of Accord. While he spoke, he studied the woman's face. She did not understand.

"I don't speak Old American as well as I should," she admitted in Panglais, the standard tongue of the Empire. With her long red hair, freckles, and boyish figure, she might have reached his shoulder.

"I understand. You are called?" asked Whaler in the accented Panglais he had decided to use.

"Heather Tew-Hawkes, Lord Whaler. Would you like to see your quarters?"

"Shortly."

He took another look around the entry hall. Small and crowded with the three hanging lamps, the long couch, an imitation strafe chair, the tea table with the faxmags on the lower shelf, and the entry desk itself before the closed interior portals which presumably opened onto the rest of the Legation.

"The rest of the staff I would like to encounter," he announced.

"Yes, sir. You know that Legate Witherspoon has returned to Harmony. The Deputy Legate, Mr. Marlaan, had already taken leave. And Mr. Weintre is out for the day."

Forest Lord! What was going on? All the natives from Accord were fleeing like troks at his arrival.

"I see. The rest here will I see . . . and my office . . . before I go to my quarters. Can you arrange for my . . . my . . ." Apparently struggling with the Panglais word, he pointed to the field packs.

"Yes, sir. We can take care of them."

Heather gave him a questioning glance before speaking again, tossed her flowing red hair back over her shoulder with a flick of her head.

"Will you be having any assistants coming from Accord?"

Odd question right off the bat, reflected the Ecolitan.

"Final arrangements will I announce shortly," he temporized.

Heather handed him a small folder.

"You might want to look through that first, Lord Whaler."

The file was scripted in the Old American of Accord and outlined the names and functions of the staff. At the end was a map of the Legation spaces.

He glanced through it quickly, storing the information for full recall later.

"Read this later, I will. You may begin."

Heather touched a stud on the console at her desk, and one of the doors behind her opened.

Nathaniel stepped through after memorizing the location of the panel stud that actuated the entry.

The Accord Legation occupied half the three hundredth level of the Diplomatic Tower.

Heather led the way through the spaces.

The tower was divided into four wings joined by the central lift/drop shafts. The official working spaces of the Legation were in the west wing of the tower. Nathaniel's office and the trade talks section had been placed at the right, almost into the north wing of the tower. A spacious private suite adjoined his office, and both were on the outer edge of the tower, with floor to ceiling windows overlooking the hills to the west.

In turn, the trade talks staff suite adjoined his office. His private quarters could be entered from his office or through a separate door, since the private apartment was actually in the north wing.

Because the tower was actually a square, the north, east, south and west designations really indicated onto which public corridor an office or private quarters opened. All the Accord natives from the Legation had their quarters on the three hundredth level, but the local staff lived elsewhere. Wherever they could or wherever they wanted? Which? wondered the Ecolitan without asking.

"This is the travel/visa/quarantine/health section," stated Heather without taking a breath.

A man and a woman, obviously high-paid professionals, looked up from their consoles.

"Harla, Derek, this is Lord Whaler, the Trade Envoy and Acting Legate in the absence of Legate Witherspoon. Lord Whaler, Harla Car-Hyten and Derek Per-Olav."

"Pleased am I to meet you," announced Nathaniel in Panglais.

"And I you," the two chimed in ragged unison.

"How long for Accord have you worked?"

"Three standard years."

"Just over a year."

"Why for a foreign Legation do you work?"

"The Empire itself has a limit to the number of, if you will, travel generalist professionals that it can use," answered the woman, Harla Car-Hyten, "and takes only the most experienced. Working for Accord provides a solid foundation. We have to work somewhere.''

"Accord is far enough out on the Rift,'' added Derek, "that we get to learn more than with an inner system.''

And, thought Nathaniel, with the small number of tourists and the restrictive policies of the Delegates and of the Empire itself, the work couldn't be all that demanding.

"I thank you,'' he finished politely as he turned to continue the tour of the official spaces.

"Lord Whaler, Ms. Da-Vios.''

Mydra Da-Vios was the Empire-supplied and paid "office manager" who had been Witherspoon's personal clerk and who would supervise the staff of his trade talks section, according to the briefing file which had been dictated by Witherspoon himself before he had left. That was the same folder Heather had handed Nathaniel right after he'd arrived.

Mydra looked up at him from her console openly but did not attempt to stand. Brown eyes so dark they verged on black, short dark brown hair, and a plain brown tunic piped with yellow, cloaked her with an air of competence.

"Any questions you might have?'' he asked.

While his question was partly a pleasantry, her answer might give him a lead. So far everyone was acting as if he were to be humored, not that he'd done much to discourage the impression.

"Mr. Marlaan did not convey how the talks would be structured or staffed. While I have detailed another assistant, I do not know if this is the proper arrangement nor with whom I should coordinate further.''

Nathaniel kept his mouth shut, while nodding gently.

Heather's question about staff made sense, too much sense. So did Marlaan's position as Deputy Legate. The briefing officer at the Institute had concluded that Marlaan's psy-profile wasn't suited to being a mere executive officer type. Yet Marlaan had stayed in New Augusta through a second tour, against all odds.

Mydra was asking politely who was going to do the real work, implying that it couldn't be Nathaniel.

"Lord Whaler?" prompted Mydra.

"The current arrangement is proper." He smiled again.

"Would you like to see your office and quarters, Lord Whaler?" interrupted Heather softly.

"That would be pleasing."

The corner office was bigger than he had expected from the plans in the folder Witherspoon had left, with a large reclining desk swivel surrounded by an impressive communications console. The recliner easily could have swallowed a man twice Nathaniel's size.

On the inside wall of the office, away from the panoramic window, was a conference table flanked with upholstered chairs. The far interior corner contained cabinets and counters, including a fully equipped autobar.

The casements to the portals, one to the office, the other to the private quarters, were the heavy-duty type, indicating that the doors were likely to have endurasteel cores under the wood veneer.

Interesting, thought Nathaniel. Is that to keep someone out or me in?

Heather pointed to the far door.

"That's to your private quarters. The locks will key to your palm print, if you'll just touch each of them right now."

Heather gave him a quick tour and explanation of the near-palatial quarters—separate private den/library with comm console, bedroom complete with oversized bed and sheensilk sheets, a guest room, a compact kitchen, two complete hygienariums, a dining room with space for eight at table, and a living room centered on a full wall window overlooking the lower towers of New Augusta.

"If you need anything, Lord Whaler, just let me or Mydra know. If I'm not on desk duty, whoever is will take care of you. If you want to eat here, just order up dinner from main service. The number is in the folder, but tower

information can also provide it. If you feel more adventur-
ous, you might try the Diplomat's Club in the dining
area. It's reserved for Legates, Ambassadors, and Envoys.''

Nathaniel nodded.

''Tomorrow's the last day of the week, and some of the
staff had already arranged leave, since you weren't expected until next week. But I'll be in early if you need
anything.''

''Too kind you are, but if I question, I will call.''

Heather left through his private office.

Really make you feel like some kind of idiot, don't
they? Are all Empire women like that?

He wandered through the rooms, apparently just taking
it all in, looking at this and that, occasionally picking up
an old-fashioned book, a miniature fire-fountain, touching a
cushion, his fingers straying to his old style wide belt from
time to time.

The multitector in the belt registered four snoops, but
from the energy level and the pattern, all but one were audio.
The one in the living room was video as well.

Probably more sophisticated equipment on the way, not
ready because I arrived early, he mused. Or snoops good
enough that I can't detect them.

Nathaniel put the datacases in the study, lugged the field
pack into the bedroom and began to unpack. Some of the
diplomatic blacks he'd never even worn, except when
they'd been fitted at the Institute. Several of the outfits
were special, but not in any way an Imperial would suspect
from either a visual inspection or an energy scan.

In theory, all he had to do was present some terms of
trade, bargain a bit, and see what developed, while staying
alive and in one piece. That was theory. Practice usually
required a great deal more effort.

. . . IX . . .

The screen buzzed twice.

"Corwin-Smathers," answered the Staff Director, as she tapped the acceptance.

The faxscreen remained blank, but the green signal panel lit. The dull gray of the screen indicated either a blank screen call or the caller's inoperative screen.

"You alone?" The mechanical tone signalled that the caller was using a voice screen.

"Yes."

"The Senator should take an interest in the Accord affair. External Affairs is outgunned, by those who control the guns especially."

"The Accord affair?"

Too late, the director realized that the connection had already been broken.

Why Accord? Why a blind call?

Virtually anyone could make such a vidfax call. More interesting was the fact that it had come in on her private line, unlisted and unregistered either in the official listings or the office's confidential listings.

The I.I.S.? Or could it be a double blind, with someone trying to set up the Senator? Or discredit Courtney herself?

42

She frowned, then tapped a call panel.

The portal at the far end of the office irised open and shut behind the woman who entered. "Yes, Courtney?"

"Would you please dig up anything that's pending with regard to Accord, probably something to do with Commerce or Defense, I would guess."

"The Senator's off on another crusade?"

"No . . . trying to figure out whether he should be."

The dark-haired woman turned to go.

"Sylvia," added the director, "you might ask some of your former colleagues if they've heard anything. Nothing classified, you understand, just rumors, odd information."

"I'll do that. How soon?"

"Yesterday, if you can."

The portal closed behind the staffer, and Courtney Corwin-Smathers leaned back in the swivel, ignoring the softly blinking lights on the console that had automatically prioritized the pending messages.

She wondered who Sylvia really worked for. Certainly it wasn't just for the Senator, for all the salary she drew. Still for the I.I.S.? Halston. The old devil Admiral?

She tapped her fingers on the genuine gorhide antique blotter.

Should she key in Du-Plessis?

Shaking her head in response to her own question, she touched the top console stud to call up the messages awaiting her.

. . . **X** . . .

Standing in front of the hygienarium mirror, Nathaniel straightened the collars of his formal dress blacks. The uniform displayed no ornamentation. Buttons, belt, and boots were all black. The square belt buckle bore a green triangle, and his formal gloves were a paler shade of green.

He half wished that he had some sort of insignia to put on his collars, as so many of the military and diplomatic personnel from other systems seemed to have.

The irony of it struck him even as he thought of it, and he grinned at himself in the mirror. Not in New Augusta an eight-day and wanting some tinsel to dress himself up.

With a last look at his wide-angle, full-length reflection, he turned and waved off the lights.

Once out of his private quarters and into his office, he palm-locked the quarters' portal, then walked across the dark green carpet to the console. The message light was unlit.

Outside, through the window, he could see dark and swirling clouds, scarcely much above him, and some of the towers' tops were lost in the mist. Hoping that the rain wasn't an omen of the day to come, he marched through the portal into the staff office.

"Good morning, Lord Whaler." Mydra greeted him as the portal whispered open.

"A good day also to you," he replied, trying to remember to keep his syntax suitably tangled.

"The honor guard should be here shortly."

"An honor guard for me? Unbelievable that seems, for a poor fumbler of figures such as me."

"A matter of protocol."

"I know, but for a professor unbelievable it seems."

At the far side of the office sat Hillary West-Coven before her console, industriously plugging figures in. Nathaniel hadn't figured out what she did, unless it was some sort of backup for Mydra.

Waiting in the silence that had followed his last remarks, Nathaniel looked over the staff office again. Three consoles: one which was vacant, one for Mydra, and the last for Hillary. All the consoles were pale green, which toned in with the institutional tan fabric covering the walls and with the deeper green of the carpet. The office retained a faint scent of pine, or a similar conifer, though no greenery was in sight.

No pictures hung on the walls, unlike the other staff offices in the Legation.

He shifted his weight, looked down at Mydra, and asked, "What did you before I arrived on New Augusta?"

"I'm in charge of Legate Witherspoon's office normally, but we didn't see any sense in doubling up on personnel, since he will be absent for some time, or so I was told"—she paused—"and since you will be assuming some of his duties."

Nathaniel nodded, his eyes lifting as Heather stepped through the portal from the corridor leading back to the receiving room.

"Mydra . . . oh, Lord Whaler." With a flip of her long red hair back over her shoulder, she finished, "Your escort has arrived."

"Thank you."

Nathaniel swung the genuine black gorhide folder containing his official credentials under his arm and marched across the staff office to follow Heather, bunching the pale green gloves in his left hand to give the impression he was clutching them tightly.

He reached the reception area right behind Heather.

"Tenhutt!" snapped the squad leader. Four Imperial Marines in their formal red tunics and gold trousers stiffened even straighter.

"Lord Whaler, sir?" questioned the leader, who couldn't have been as old as most of the first year Ecolitans Nathaniel had been training less than two standard months earlier.

"The very same I am."

"Yes, sir. Would you please, sir, please allow us to escort you to your audience with the Emperor?"

"Honored I would be."

From that, Nathaniel decided he was the one to lead the parade and marched out.

The Imperial Marines, caught by his sudden departure, slipped into quick-step and fell in behind him before he was ten meters down the corridor to the drop shaft.

Not too bad, he decided. But he wondered how they would have held up in the outback of Trezenia.

Nathaniel marched right into the high speed drop lane without hesitation. The four Marines angled themselves into a hollow square above him, allowing each to cover a quarter of the shaft.

They carried stunners, and each wore a belt commpak.

Two electrocougars waited in the private concourse. The first was crimson and displayed the Accord flag on a staff over the left front wheel panel. The second car was, surprisingly, a dull brown.

One of the escorts held the rear door of the crimson vehicle open for the Ecolitan. After seeing him seated and closing the door, the Marine eased into the front seat across from the driver, a woman Marine. Belatedly, on noting the driver, Nathaniel realized that at least one of his escorts had been female.

The squad leader and the other two escorts used the brown car to follow his into the tunnel.

"How often this do you do?"

"About eighty systems with Legations here, I'm told," answered the nondriving Marine. "I'm new, three weeks here. This is my second assignment for escort duty. Some of the other teams have had five or six in the past month."

"Just for diplomats seeing the Emperor?"

"No, sir. All sorts of functions—parties, reviews. You name it, and we're on call."

The driver glanced at the escort Marine. The young man stopped talking.

"Many functions and reviews there are then?"

"I really don't know about that, sir."

"What after this duty will you do?"

"That's up to the assignment branch, sir."

"No desire for other duty have you?"

"Whatever the Service needs, sir, that's where I'll be."

Nathaniel leaned back into the cushions. Information wasn't likely to be any more forthcoming.

He recalled the map he'd called up on his console. The Imperial Court had been placed on the high plain east of the main part of the underground city and towers, while the Port of Entry was to the south.

Had he been the Emperor who'd set it up, Nathaniel would have put the court and palace in the hills to the west.

As the tunnel car swept up from the depths into the concourse of the Imperial Palace, Nathaniel leaned forward to get a better look.

Fully fifteen different tunnels merged into the entry area, though he could see only two other limousines.

When the electrocougar glided to a stop, the escort snapped out of the front seat and had the rear door open for Nathaniel instantly. The other three squad members were formed up and waiting before Nathaniel's black-booted foot touched the golden tiles.

A red-coated woman, a striking figure with black hair, black eyes, and a deeply tanned face, stood at the head of the ramp from the concourse.

"Lord Whaler?"

"The very same."

"I'm Cynda Ger-Lorthian, the Emperor's Receiving Auditor. Would you be so kind as to accompany me to the receiving and waiting room?"

"That is where the Emperor receives?"

"Oh, no. That's where you will wait until the Emperor is ready to receive you and where you will be briefed on how the presentation of your credentials will be conducted."

"Sounds like this is done most regularly," the Ecolitan observed as he fell in behind the Receiving Auditor.

"Really quite simple, but we do like to make sure there are no misunderstandings and that everything goes according to plan."

The receiving room, about the size of his office at the Legation, featured a semicircular table surrounded on one side by comfortable padded swivels. The table and chairs faced a blank wall.

"If you would sit there, Lord Whaler, we'll go through the procedures."

Nathaniel's fingers flicked to his belt. The chair was snooped to the hilt, with virtually every kind of gimmickry that could be crammed into it. He turned toward the chair beside the one he'd been offered. It was rigged the same way.

Nathaniel kept the smile from his face. One purpose of the room wasn't exactly to impart information. He eased himself into the larger chair.

Cynda Ger-Lorthian sat next to him and pulled a small panel from the drawer of the table. She pressed a stud.

The mist of a holoscreen appeared on the other side of the table.

"Here's the way the receiving hall looks from the portal."

Nathaniel watched the view, as if he were looking into

the enormous room, a gold-tan carpet leading from his feet out toward the throne of the Emperor.

"This is the actual floor plan," continued the Receiving Auditor as the holo display changed. "You can see you have almost fifty meters to walk before you reach the bottom step of the throne.

"You're scheduled for a ten minute presentation. That's longer than average, which means that the Emperor will have something more than the formalities."

"When starts all this?"

"At the time the previous appointment is complete, I'll give you a signal. You walk in the portal and stand. After you are announced, the Emperor will recognize you, and you walk to the throne. Stop at the bottom and make some acknowledgment to the Emperor, a bow, head inclined, whatever is customary for you, which the Emperor will return. You climb to the fourth step, and the Emperor will come down to meet you."

"Here's the way it will look. He is addressed as 'Sovereign of Light.' "

The holo projection showed a still version of the Emperor greeting someone on the wide steps below the throne.

"Do you have any questions?" she finished up with the rush of someone who has repeated the same words time after time.

"When is the audience completed?"

"The words used to signify closure will be something like 'May you enjoy the peace of the Empire.' It is never quite the same. The Emperor enjoys minor deviations from the protocol."

Ger-Lorthian checked her timestrap and stood up.

Nathaniel followed her example, and the two of them were rejoined outside the briefing room by his escort of four Imperial Marines.

The portal to the receiving hall extended high enough to admit a full-sized combat skitter, and the closed, gold-plated portal was obviously backed with endurasteel. With the depth of the casements, Nathaniel doubted whether that Imperial combat skitter could have dented the surface of the portal.

"When the chime sounds, Lord Whaler, the portal will open. Please step through and wait."

A deep bell echoed from the top of the portal casement. The doors recessed into the massive casements without so much as a whisper.

Nathaniel stepped through and placed himself squarely in the middle of the ribbon of carpeting that ran toward the throne block.

Five portals studded the immense circular hall of equidistant intervals, and a similar carpet ran from each toward the circular stepped structure on which rested the Throne of Light.

In all probability, the throne rotated to face whatever portal the Emperor wished or protocol demanded.

Empires need Emperors, and the bigger the Empire, the more impressive the Emperor should be. As a practical matter, reflected the Trade Envoy for the Coordinate of Accord, Emperors only came in one size—human. At least, human emperors did. His Royal and Imperial Highness Jostan Lerann McDade N'troya, while white-haired and close to 196 centimeters, was only human.

The Emperor of the Terran Empire, the Hegemony of Light, the Path of Progress, compensated for his mere humanity by wearing an unadorned and brilliant white uniform that cloaked him in light, making him the focus of the receiving hall in which a full-sized Imperial corvette could have been hangared.

A crowd, gathered around and on the lower steps of the throne pedestal and large enough to comprise several subotta teams, was lost under the sweeping lightstone buttresses, and the height of the ceiling swallowed the pulsing beams emanating from the Throne of Light.

Nathaniel waited on the tan carpet, as he'd been briefed by the majordomo, Receiving Auditor, whatever she was called.

Several of the group gathered below the throne, a good stone's throw away, glanced at him and pointedly turned their heads.

The Imperial hangers-on all affected light-colored clothing. Only the Emperor wore out-and-out white, and no one wore a predominantly dark outfit.

Nathaniel wore Accord's diplomatic blacks. If he had worn the greens of the Ecolitan Institute, the effect and impact would have been the same. In the bright universe of the Imperial court, two colors were absent. Solid green and solid black—the colors of Accord, the colors associated with the Ecologic Secession.

"The Lord Nathaniel Firstborne Whaler, Trade Envoy from the Coordinate of Accord. Presenting his official credentials to His Imperial Highness, Provider of Prosperity and Sovereign of Light."

The announcement stilled the hall for less than an instant.

"We await your arrival." The Emperor's voice filled the hall, overtoned and benevolent.

Nathaniel marched up the tan carpet, which gradually lightened into gold as it neared the Throne of Light. The throne itself stood higher than he'd realized from the holo projection.

Stopping before the bottom step, the Ecolitan bowed once.

"Lord Whaler, the Empire is pleased at your presence."

Nathaniel climbed four steps. The Emperor stood and descended.

From the corner of his eye, the Ecolitan could see that the Empress, who had remained in her seat below and to the left of the Emperor's, was not in the slightest interested in Accord or in credentials. She continued her conversation with a blond man dressed in a peacock blue tunic belted in scarlet.

"Lord Whaler." The Emperor addressed the Envoy.

"Your Highness."

A minor murmur circled the crowd on the throne pedestal. Protocol required the more formal "Sovereign of Light."

But, thought Nathaniel, we provincials can't be expected to know everything about the delicacies of court etiquette.

Nathaniel handed him the credentials case.

"My credentials, my writ to the Empire. May we all live in peace and prosperity."

"On behalf of the Empire and its peoples, I accept your credentials and your wishes for peace and prosperity."

The smile the Emperor N'troya gave the Ecolitan was genuine enough, and so were the tiredness and the thin lines radiating from the corners of his dark eyes.

"Was your trip pleasant, Lord Whaler?"

"To reaching New Augusta, I looked forward. Seeing your receiving hall, disappointed I am certainly not. Most impressive and suited to you."

The Sovereign of Light chuckled.

"I gather that's a compliment, Lord Whaler, and in our position as royalty, so shall we take it."

The royal chuckle effectively stilled conversation around the Emperor for several instants, except for the fragment of small talk which drifted upward.

". . . so devilish in that outfit, but what could you expect from Accord—"

The speaker, a lady in rust and yellow with a neckline which barely cleared her ample breasts, broke off in mid-sentence.

"Lord Whaler," continued the Emperor as if he had not heard the interruption, "your frankness is refreshing. What do you really think of the Empire? Honestly now?"

Nathaniel could sense the indrawn breath from those listening around the throne.

"Your Highness, large groups of systems organized must be. People accept the government they deserve, and many systems accept the Empire. Wise is the Empire to accept and govern wisely those who wish such governing. Wise too is the Empire which only extends its rule to those who wish it."

He bowed slightly to N'troya as he finished.

"Well chosen words, Lord Whaler. Well chosen."

"Your service, and looking forward to these talks on trade I am."

"So is the Empire. We trust you will fulfill our confidences." The Emperor straightened. "During your stay in New Augusta and thereafter may you enjoy the peace of the Empire."

The Emperor nodded dismissal.

Nathaniel bowed and waited.

The Emperor turned and climbed back to the Throne of Light.

At that, the Ecolitan marched back down the carpet toward the massive portal. Before exiting, he faced back to the throne and bowed again.

When the portal opened, he exited the receiving hall.

"Lord Whaler, your escort."

The same Receiving Auditor waited as the portals shut behind the Envoy. The same four Marines swung in behind him as he walked back the way he had come.

"I didn't catch your conversation with the Emperor, Lord Whaler, but you must have a way with words. That's the first laugh I've heard during an audience in months."

"Truth only I spoke."

He didn't offer more, and Cynda didn't ask as the short procession made its way back to the Imperial concourse.

Once more the charade with the guards was repeated as he entered the crimson electrocougar. The car whisked him back into the depths and to the Diplomatic Tower.

Nathaniel sank into the red cushions.

Smoothly as things seemed to be going, he had the feeling that pieces to the puzzle were missing. Which pieces? That was the real question.

. . . XI . . .

A muted brown tunic, slashed with irregular gold stripes, and matching brown trousers—with a sigh, the Ecolitan pulled the outfit from the closet. The clothes were common enough not to draw attention, and his utility belt was compatible.

Once he had the outfit on, he checked himself in the hygienarium mirror. The looseness of the tunic gave him an informal appearance, almost touristlike.

He straightened the belt before heading for the private exit.

Probably Mydra or someone would wonder where the Envoy had gone for the afternoon, but a little mystery would brighten their lives, if they even bothered to check. Besides, he was bored. Bored with waiting for things to happen.

He laughed. "With one take-out aimed at you, you're bored."

All told, the trip from his quarters down the drop shaft to the tunnel train level took less than fifteen minutes. Best of all, no one had given him a second look.

Like virtually everything else he'd seen, the tunnel train level was immaculate, sparkling and shimmering in the indirect light.

All the same, he missed the outdoors, the scent of rain or dusty air, the openness of a horizon stretching into the sky.

The second train was the one he wanted, running south toward the shuttle port. The short train—only four cars—whispered into the concourse so silently it nearly caught him by surprise.

Each car contained twenty-four individual seats and twice that space for standing room. Roughly half the seats in his car were full.

Nathaniel sat opposite the rear portal, where he could observe the entire car without seeming to.

Two seats away, carrying a slim folder, sat a blond Imperial Sublieutenant with her eyes fixed on the panel at the end of the car.

She had not looked up when he had taken his seat, nor did she move a muscle until the second stop after Nathaniel had boarded. At the Ministry of Defense concourse, the Sublieutenant snapped out of her seat, walked past Nathaniel and through the portal before it was fully open.

Nathaniel stretched, ambled to his feet, and barely escaped the train before the door shut behind him. The train was whispering its way out of the concourse toward the shuttle port within instants of his departure.

Muted brown with scarlet trim struck the color scheme for the Ministry of Defense concourse.

Unlike the Diplomatic Tower, the Defense Tower had two lift/drop shafts, one guarded by a full squad of armed soldiers, the other apparently unguarded and open to the public.

Nathaniel watched as the Sublieutenant marched toward the guarded shaft, flashed something, and was waved through. Then the Ecolitan settled down on one of the scattered wall benches, one that had a view of the approaches to both sets of lift shafts, with a faxtab in hand, giving the impression of scanning it while waiting for someone.

Within minutes, he could sense the pattern.

Younger Imperial citizens drifted in and out, seemingly at random, and took the public lift shaft. For all their leisurely appearance, a certain tenseness underlay their casualness, showing in a quietness, a lack of chatter.

Scarcely a handful of individuals presented themselves to the brown-clad guards at the smaller lift/drop shaft, and of that scattering, Nathaniel saw only one other person in uniform, another woman. Two other civilians were quietly turned away.

After a quarter of a standard hour, one of the guards glanced over at Nathaniel, studied the Ecolitan, and returned his attention to the console.

Nathaniel did not react, but kept his nose in the faxtab, with an occasional look around for his "appointment" while he continued to track the comings and goings.

Another quarter hour passed. The guard who had first noted Nathaniel looked him over again, this time giving him an even closer scrutiny and keying something into the console.

Nathaniel went on recording the arrivals and departures into his belt storage.

A quarter hour later, almost to the second, the guard at the console looked up and toward Nathaniel. At the same instant, one of the patrols turned toward the console operator.

The Ecolitan dropped the faxtab and folded it. Unhurriedly, he rose, stretched, peered around, looked at his wrist, shook his head, and finally crumpled the faxtab in apparent disgust.

He stalked away toward the tunnel train stage.

It hadn't been necessary to stay quite so long, but he had been looking for a reaction.

Once in the train, decorated in pale golds and off whites and filled with the low murmur of music, he again took an end seat, this time to see if he could spot a tail. The train was half full, about as crowded as he'd seen any public transport in New Augusta, and he decided, since no one else had joined the small group waiting on the stage, that a tail was unlikely.

Back in the living room of his private quarters at the Legation, he first dialled some juice from the dispenser, then settled himself into the deep chair facing the window. He felt more at ease in the living room than in the expanse of the official office of the Envoy.

People assumed that you had to get inside a building to find out what was going on. Not always so. Sometimes a fairly good picture was painted just by who came and went.

Item: Very few military personnel arriving.

Item: Fewer still in uniform.

Item: Virtually all public access was by young Imperials—student age—and on a continuing basis, as if by appointment.

Item: Military access more tightly guarded than anything else seen in New Augusta.

Item: No discernible patterns in sex of either military personnel or students.

Item: Guards not only tracked loiterers, but maintained voiceless communications with the central communications point.

What conclusions could he draw?

Despite the low profile the military seemed to have assumed on New Augusta, they possessed a great deal of real power.

Further, the "student" appointments implied one of two things: either the military career was respected and desirable or it was required of at least some of the population. The lack of uniforms also intrigued the Ecolitan.

New Augusta, in spite of all the apparent freedom, was a tightly controlled society.

How tightly remained to be seen.

. . . XII . . .

The man in black stepped into the drop shaft, angled his body out into the high speed lane, and watched the levels peel away.

Mydra had told him what she thought of the idea.

"After someone shot at you . . . going out alone, unescorted, Lord Whaler, is foolish. Very foolish."

Foolish perhaps, but a Marine escort with crimson uniforms would have been like dropping a location flare.

On the way down, he smiled faintly as a Fuardian Military Attaché tripped over his dangling sabre and pitched headfirst into the slow drop traffic, almost colliding with a Matriarch from Halston.

Accord didn't have lift/drop shafts, or the towers with hundreds of levels running from deep in the ground up into the lower cloud levels. For the scattered communities of Accord, such towers would have been an energy waste. Harmony was the only city of any size throughout the Coordinate, and the capital had fewer people than any single one of the New Augustan towers.

As the Ecolitan dropped toward the concourse level, he edged himself into the slower lanes, finally swinging off onto the orange permatile of the exit stage.

He walked briskly toward the private side of the concourse where the official tunnel cars and diplomatic vehicles waited. His eyes never stopped their continuous scan. His ears listened for any untoward sound.

"Lord Whaler?" called a young driver.

"From whom?" he asked noncommittally, still scanning as he approached.

"Lord Rotoller at Commerce." She gestured toward the car and the seal on the open passenger door.

As he bent to enter the vehicle, he checked the energy levels but could find nothing overtly suspicious.

He settled himself into the overpadded seat as the electrocougar dipped noiselessly into the tunnel on its trip from the Diplomatic Tower to the Imperial Ministry of Commerce.

"How long have you worked for the Commerce Ministry?" he asked the driver.

"Two standard years, sir."

"Like it do you?"

"It's part of training. If you're a student at one of the professional or nonmilitary service schools, you're assigned a part-time job as well."

"What school for you?"

"Government Service Academy."

"A specialty you have, a favorite course of study?"

"Political theory's the most interesting. But I like economic history the best." The young woman half turned in the seat, without taking her eyes totally off the controls and guidelights. "Do you think the Ecologic Secession was based more on the imperatives of Outer Rift trade or on the political restraints imposed by the Empire?"

"An interesting question," temporized the Ecolitan. "The factors which to the Secession led as in so many conflicts were doubtless many. Some of them are lost, I would suspect, and today scholars and politicians focus on what they see as important, not on what those involved saw as important."

"That's what Professor Har-Ptolemkin says, that we project our own motives back onto history too much." The driver stopped talking, waiting for a response.

"Trade, the political reasons, the personal heritages, all factors have to be considered. No one sat down and said, 'For these reasons will we rebel.'

"No . . . doubtless said they something more like, 'We are tired of the Empire and want to be free.' And each had a somewhat different reason."

"Do you think they really knew that clearly what they wanted?"

"People say they know what they want, but often when they must choose, they choose not what they asked for."

The student driver did not continue the conversation, and the electrocougar began to slow and climb. After a sharp turn, the vehicle came to a halt. A man clad in a gold jumpsuit opened the door, and four others, wearing identical metallic uniforms, stood by the underground carved stone portal, ramrod straight in the artificial light.

At 191 centimeters, the Ecolitan didn't consider himself particularly tall, but he stood nearly a full head above the five gold-suited guards. Two were women, and all wore long knives in silver scabbards and silver-plated stunners in gilded holsters.

A man and a woman near his own height waited for Whaler inside the portal. Both were dressed in the maroon of the Imperial Commerce Ministry. The man stood in front of the woman and, abruptly, raised his left hand in the open-palmed symbol of greeting used on Accord, almost as if he were being coached.

Whaler returned the greeting.

"Alden Rotoller, at your service, Envoy Whaler. May I present my Special Assistant, Marcella Ku-Smythe?"

"At your service," Whaler returned stiffly in Panglais.

As he acknowledged the introduction with a slight bow and a direct look at Marcella, he was struck by the contrast between the two. Marcella was not beautiful, though her features were clear, clean, and attractive in a strong way, with a nose more aquiline than pert. Her eyes focused with an intensity common to few. Rotoller's face was essentially dead by comparison.

"Your staff?" inquired the Lord Rotoller.

"The full disposal of the Legation for the purposes of any negotiation has been accorded me."

"Of course," responded Rotoller. He turned and motioned toward the ornate private lift shaft.

The dimness of the shaft surprised Nathaniel as he followed the Terran Minister, since the public shafts in New Augusta were so brightly illuminated.

Beyond the white tiled exit stage was a stark, semicircular hallway decorated with a maroon and white tiled chessboard pattern. The walls were white, trimmed with thin maroon molding that shimmered.

Two guards, facing the lift exit, wore stunners in black functional throw holsters and tunics and trousers of solid maroon.

Off the hall were four portals, but only the one on the far left was open. As soon as Marcella Ku-Smythe stepped onto the exit stage tiles, Lord Rotoller turned and walked through the open doorway.

Nathaniel followed. So did Marcella and the guards.

Did they think he was an ogre left over from the Ecologic Secession?

The chamber they entered resembled a private club in Harmony far more than a meeting room for the Deputy Minister of Commerce. Three deep chairs, each with a side table, were drawn up around a light fire, itself contained within flux bricks in the middle of the room. Each side table contained a napkin, real cloth, and a mug holder.

Rotoller suddenly dropped into one of the chairs.

"Take your pick."

Nathaniel bumped into the one closest to him, trying to see if the furniture was either anchored or snooped. Neither seemed to be the case, and he eased himself into the maroon cushions.

The room was decorated in shades of cream and maroon, and the light fountain flared maroon intermittently.

"Would you care for something to drink? Some liftea, cafe, perhaps some Taxan brandy?"

"Liftea, it would be fine."

Rotoller tilted his head at Marcella.

"Cafe," she ordered.

One of the guards disappeared through another portal that had opened from a seemingly blank wall, to return a moment later with three beverages and three identical plates of pastries.

The guard, a woman with closely cropped brown hair, offered the pastry tray to Nathaniel first, letting him choose one of the three plates. She placed his liftea on the table, then served the Taxan brandy to the Deputy Minister before finishing up with Marcella.

Silence stretched out before Whaler realized that the other two were waiting for him.

He picked up the heavy mug and lifted it toward his host.

"For your hospitality and courtesy."

"And for your kindness in coming," the reply came automatically.

The Ecolitan took a small sip of the steaming tea and set the mug back in its holder.

"Such courtesy, for one such as I, most overwhelming is."

"No more than you deserve, particularly when it is you who do us the honor of coming so far."

"And on a small courier at that," added Marcella.

"How was your trip?"

"As expected." Actually, he had enjoyed it and the chance to compare the courier with similar class ships of the Institute. His enjoyment had been heightened by seeing the Imperial battlecruiser tagging along as an official escort.

"Long trip, I imagine," responded Rotoller. "Can't say I've been out to the Rift. In this job, you get tied to the faxwork, in the details, not that it all doesn't have to be done. Marcella does all the real in-depth work, though, and I don't know what I'd do without her."

The Lord smiled faintly at his assistant, who smiled faintly back.

"Lord Mersen will be pleased to know you have arrived safely and will take great interest in what you have to offer."

"Most kind, most kind," returned Nathaniel.

"Did you bring any staff with you?" Again, it was Marcella.

"Ah . . . the question of staff. Such a joy, and so helpful are they, and so determined. A thousand pardons to you, Lady. Would I not mean to offend, in any circumstances."

"No offense, Lord Whaler."

"But your question . . . no . . . answer it I did not. Staff, besides that of the Legation, as you meant, have I none at this moment."

Before the growing silence became totally oppressive, Rotoller jumped in.

"Guess something like New Augusta must be a new experience for you. Understand your government isn't fond of large bureaucracies or diplomatic establishments."

"Our government has not the numbers or the systems with which to deal as does the Empire. Our Envoys are not numerous but deal with more than diplomacy we do. Some other cities and systems have I seen, but none so large and impressive as your capital."

He inclined his head toward the light-haired Special Assistant. "And none with officials so enchanting."

Nathaniel took another sip of the liftea and began the last pastry, interposing nibbles with broad and idiotic smiles.

"Haven't spent the time we should have," continued Rotoller, "since matters between Accord and us have been going so smoothly recently. This trade imbalance thing sort of crept up on us, and I gather that's been the same sort of feeling in Harmony, from what our Legate's reported."

"True. One hesitates to rock a boat floating with a smooth tide, not when so many other disturbances evident are. The Delegates were not aware of the extent of the problem facing the Empire and so the request caught many unprepared. Trade can be the lifeblood of an outer system, and what is a small imbalance to the Empire reflects more heavily for us."

"Do you think some of the other systems are waiting to see what happens?"

"Trade affects us all, and Accord understands such effects, as do you and others in your Ministry. One thing does lead onward to another. That is known. Most important will be these talks to those affected."

The pattern continued.

"Can't tell you how pleased we are to have a chance to chat before the talks get underway . . ."

"Is your Legation here much different from the people back home, really?"

"Understand Accord hasn't changed too much lately . . ."

"Is the Ecolitan Institute an all-around university now?"

Nathaniel responded in kind.

"Pleased am I to have such opportunities . . ."

"People they are people, and much help can be anyone."

"The changes, they happen. Everywhere are changes, but on Accord we take the best of the old, we hope, and the best of the new . . ."

"Ah, the Institute . . . not exactly what you would call a university . . . nor even a training school . . . more an experience, a way of combining a look at the past and the knowledge of today."

The atmosphere changed ever so slightly, and while Nathaniel couldn't pinpoint it, the tête-á-tête was over.

"Regret we couldn't talk all day, Lord Whaler. You've

given us a most fascinating insight, but there's far too much waiting for both me and Marcella at our consoles.''

The guards stiffened as the two Commerce officials rose from their chairs.

Nathaniel followed.

"So kind have you been in your courtesy, and much too much of your time have I taken today."

"Our pleasure, Lord Whaler. Our pleasure."

While the guards were alert as the three drifted to the drop shaft, their hands poised near their stunners, the Ecolitan almost found himself shaking his head at the sight. If he'd really wanted to dispose of the pair, holding their hands near their weapons wouldn't have done them a bit of good.

"Hope to see you soon," finished off the Deputy Minister as Whaler climbed back into the electrocougar.

"And I you."

Ignoring the frescoes in the tunnel and the driver, an older woman who seemed to want to ignore him, Nathaniel leaned back in the cushions and tried to think.

Why had the two Commerce officials wanted to meet him?

He shook his head and waited until the limousine came to a stop in the private concourse. Rather than using the front entrance of the Legation, he took the back side exit from the lift shaft which led to his private quarters.

The corridor was nearly deserted. He passed a woman and two men on the way to his private door. The belt detector showed the snoops on the portal were still operational.

From the entry, he walked to the study where his datacase had been left. As he half expected, someone had been through the material, despite the privacy seals on the suite locks and on the datacase itself.

What surprised him most was that only a rudimentary effort had been made to replace the case and the material within in the same positions where he had left them.

On the one hand, great technical sophistication had been involved in analyzing the palm-print codes to open the doors and the datacase without destroying the locks or triggering any alarms. Yet the material had been replaced carelessly.

By angling his belt light at the smooth surfaces of the cases, he could tell that fingerprints remained, without any evidence that the intruders had attempted to wipe them off.

That confirmed the general identity of the intruders as government operatives of some sort or another.

He shrugged.

At the moment, there was little enough he could do.

. . . XIII . . .

Nathaniel set his mental alarms for 0700. The switch to Terran standards hadn't affected his own internal timing. He was awake at 0659.

Once in his office, he tapped several studs on the massive desk console. He hadn't figured out all the possible button combinations yet, but with the aid of the local directory he'd called up into the console memory, he was managing to make direct calls without having Mydra or someone else place them.

"Sergel, come on over, would you?"

"Envoy Whaler, with the other Accord staff gone, matters are somewhat involved . . ."

Nathaniel knew he was lying. The entire Legation staff was grossly underworked.

"I can understand that. This won't take long. I'll be expecting you in fifteen minutes."

Sergel Weintre arrived on time. Nathaniel couldn't miss the dampness on his forehead.

He pointed the younger Information Specialist at one of the deep chairs. Perching on the edge of the desk, the Ecolitan stared down at the man and began in the Old American of Accord.

"First, the situation stinks. I know it stinks. You know it stinks. Second, I don't have time to play games with you. Third, everything we say is being monitored by at least two different groups. Fourth, it doesn't matter. Is all that clear?"

Weintre screwed up his face into a puzzled look.

"No, Envoy Whaler. I'm afraid I don't understand."

Nathaniel ignored him.

"I realize the position you're in, but that's between you and them. I have several questions I expect you to answer."

Weintre shifted his weight, expression blank.

"Who stirred up the question of revision of Accord's trade terms with the Empire?"

"It was the Emperor's decision."

"As I recall, my official presentation of credentials to the Emperor was largely ceremonial. And somehow I doubt that the Emperor could be greatly concerned about the terms of trade with a small third-rate system, even a former colony."

The Ecolitan smiled pleasantly at Weintre.

"So . . . someone had to push. Who?"

"The order was signed by the Emperor."

Nathaniel repressed a sigh. He pulled a compucalendar from the console drawer.

"Weintre, I really don't have time for polite evasions. This is a lie detector, new and improved model. Now . . . why is the Imperial Ministry of Commerce—or is it the military crew—supplementing your already too-generous stipend?"

The Information Specialist swallowed, just once.

"This is totally out of hand, Whaler, totally. You think you can just walk in and threaten? You may have some authority, but you can't do that!"

Nathaniel let the all-wooden dart gun slide into his hand. The weapon would not register on any known detector.

"You know, Weintre, it's too bad you sold us out."

"You wouldn't . . ."

"I not only would, but will. . . . Have you ever studied the Articles of Ecological Warfare of Accord? They've never been suspended, you know. In matters of State, they may be called into force by any Legate or accredited representative of Accord outside the Coordinate . . . and executed by any Ecolitan. Not that they ever expected one to be both."

"I don't believe you."

Nathaniel cocked the dart thrower and fired in one fluid motion. The dart buried itself in the chair less than a centimeter from Sergel's left ear.

"The next one will be closer . . . a lot closer."

"The Empire—"

"Can't do a thing, except declare me persona non grata and deport me to stand trial in Harmony, where I'd be acquitted."

Sergel needed more of a push.

"Weintre, I'm truly sorry . . ."

"No! Reilly-Shiroka contacted me. Aide to Lord Mersen. Helmsworth wants to throw a slide-strip into the talks, hold them up to get better terms for the Empire."

It was the Ecolitan's turn to frown.

"You're making no sense at all, Sergel."

"Look . . . Corwin-Smathers, staff director for Helmsworth, is out to get Commerce. We're just a pawn to force Commerce to deal with Helmsworth's problems."

Nathaniel waved a halt to the flow of words.

"So why involve you? Why pay you off?"

"Helmsworth is supported by the Noram Micronics Association and Corwin-Smathers used to be liaison for External Affairs."

"Look, Weintre," snapped the Ecolitan, leveling the dart gun, "ignorant I may be, but not stupid. Not one word you have said makes any sense. Try again."

"Power struggle between Commerce and External Affairs, but Witherspoon didn't believe me. He's just here for ceremony. Marlaan told me to stay out, do nothing. I've just tried to stay out of trouble."

Nathaniel sighed deeply.

"You still haven't answered anything. Why have you sold out to the Defense crowd? Why do you keep avoiding the military aspects? Which Admiral bought you?"

Sergel looked down, twitched as his ear brushed against the dart.

"The Ministry of Defense . . . uh . . . obviously has some interest . . . and their . . . uh . . . pride . . . their defeat by the Ecologic Coalition . . ."

"Pride?"

"The Ministry of Defense has always felt the responsibility for the loss of Accord and the Outer Rift."

The Ecolitan shook his head. He didn't want to start with a corpse. Not when corpses only led in one direction. Sergel's death would only complicate matters. Besides, the Institute taught that murder out of frustration was clearly futile, and Sergel was definitely frustrating.

"All right, Sergel. You obviously haven't thought this out. I want a written report on the situation, including a listing of all the contacts you're so cleverly avoiding."

"I didn't realize—"

"You didn't think! I want that report in my office here by tomorrow, and it better have those details." He lifted the lethal dart gun.

"Yes, sir."

"Get!" snapped Nathaniel.

Weintre got.

The Ecolitan stood and turned to stare out the expanse of permaglass.

What next?

Should he have Mydra try to reach Lord Rotoller? Or the Special Assistant?

He tapped the console plate. Mydra's face appeared.

"Would you get me Marcella Ku-Smythe? She's the Special Assistant to Lord Rotoller."

"I'll see if she's available, Lord Whaler."

Mydra's image disappeared, and the screen blanked.

From the depths of the swivel, Nathaniel tried to figure out why Mydra's mannerisms bothered him.

"Cling!" chimed the console.

Nathaniel tapped the acknowledgment.

"Lord Whaler, Ms. Ku-Smythe's staff indicates that she is unavailable."

"Fine. Get me the staffer who told you so."

"Lord Whaler?"

"The staff member who said thus. To that person would I speak."

Perhaps inverted syntax would make the point that a simple command hadn't.

Mydra tightened her lips before finally answering, "Yes, Lord Whaler."

The screen returned to its slate gray color.

"Cling!"

The Ecolitan tapped the plate. Another face appeared, that of a tanned and blond young man.

"Nathaniel Whaler, Trade Envoy for Accord, I am. For Ms. Ku-Smythe."

"Lord Whaler, I am so sorry. She is not available, but I know she will be so pleased that you called." The receptionist smiled engagingly, showing even white teeth that seemed to sparkle even through the screen.

"So sorry am I, also. For if she should think to talk trade, available she should be. I had wanted to talk with her first, but since available she is not, perhaps with the honorable Corwin-Smathers I will start."

"I do know she would like to talk with you. Maybe she could break free for just a moment. Please let me check."

The screen went blank for an instant before the image of the blond receptionist was replaced with the visage of Marcella Ku-Smythe.

"Marcella Ku-Smythe."

"Nathaniel Whaler."

"I'm rather flattered, Lord Whaler, that you would call personally. Flattered, and surprised that you would be so insistent."

"Are you alone at the moment?"

"Why, yes, but why do you ask?"

"Because, Ms. Ku-Smythe, I really don't have time for fencing, even if that is the normal mode of negotiating. Now, if you want that, fine; Lord Rotoller, Lord Mersen, and I can mumble polite phrases to everyone's heart's content, and I'll see what I can work out elsewhere."

He could see her stiffen, even on the console screen.

"Aren't you being a bit precipitous?"

"Presumptuous, perhaps, but not precipitous. The Empire is precipitous, which is why I'm presumptuous."

A trace of a smile flitted across the Special Assistant's face.

"This is the Empire, you know, and not exactly a back cluster planet."

"You're deliberately missing the point. I know and you know that the official posturing and positioning may take months. But I'm no smooth-talking diplomat. Nor is Accord a rich system. So it's to everyone's interest to get an early resolution."

He was already in too deeply too quickly, but he had to get things moving before Weintre's military friends sunflared the process.

"Let me think about it." She broke the connection.

For a moment, he stared at the blank screen, puzzled at the abruptness of the sign-off.

Then he chuckled.

He tapped the screen stud to get Mydra.

"Mydra, who is the Special Assistant for Lord Jansen at External Affairs."

"I'll find out, Lord Whaler."

"Do that, and to that person would I speak."

Would any of it do any good? He shrugged and turned

to take another look at the western hills in the morning light.

The screen chimed.

"Lord Whaler, Janis Du-Plessis is the Special Assistant to Lord Jansen. Her assistant says she is unavailable, but I have the assistant waiting."

"Talk with the assistant I will. Thank you."

The assistant to the Special Assistant was a young woman, dark haired and thin faced.

Nathaniel went through his introduction and veiled threat.

"I'm so sorry, Lord Whaler, but she is truly not available, and neither is Lord Jansen. I'll pass along your message, and I am sure Ms. Du-Plessis or Lord Jansen will get back to you as soon as one of them possibly can."

"Most important this is," pressed the Ecolitan.

"It's important to us as well, I'm sure, and I will let her know as soon as I can."

"Thank you."

As the screen blanked, Nathaniel frowned.

External Affairs ought to be far more interested than Commerce, yet they showed little or no concern.

He tapped the comm plate to get Mydra. This time he wanted the top assistant of Senator Helmsworth, one Corwin-Smathers.

"Lord Whaler," Mydra informed him, "Ms. Corwin-Smathers is not available, but the person who is handling the Accord sector is."

Nathaniel swallowed a gulp. He'd assumed that Corwin-Smathers was a man.

"Who is such person?"

"Sylvia Ferro-Maine, I believe, is the name."

"Talk to her I will."

"Lord Whaler?" Sylvia Ferro-Maine was dark haired, fine boned, and extremely competent looking on the fax screen.

"The same. You are Ms. Ferro-Maine?"

"I prefer Sylvia, Lord Whaler. The Senate is quite a bit less formal than the rest of the government."

"About formal matters I had called, such as trade . . . "

"Courtney and the Senator are interested in everything that impacts trade."

"Because of such interest, with them, I had thought to talk . . ."

"Well, Courtney would be the one to see about meeting with the Senator, although he's scheduled for months in advance. As for seeing her, I think, if you didn't mind coming over here, she could see you around 1040 tomorrow."

She waited for Nathaniel to answer.

He didn't like the setup. In essence, he would be packing off as an Envoy to see a mere staff director of one Imperial Senator. On the other hand, it was obvious that the assistants controlled the access.

So . . .

"Appreciate I your accommodation in such haste, and prevail further upon you could I."

"Upon me?"

"So helpful you have been, and so little know I, would you consider lunching today with me? Such short notice it is, but appreciate it I most certainly would."

"Lord Whaler, I don't know what to say."

"Yes, I believe, is the proper word."

"I couldn't possibly get there before 1300."

"That would be fine. At the Legation at 1300, and looking forward to it am I."

Why did she accept? Why had he asked?

He shook his head and tapped the screen plate that stored all the pending messages, waiting for them to flash onto the screen. The wait was short, since he didn't appear to have any messages.

He thought about screening Mydra, decided against it, and walked to the portal, thumbed it, and waited as the heavy door irised open.

Mydra and Hillary, who had been talking, jumped as he approached.

"Lord Whaler, is anything wrong?" asked Mydra.

"Nothing, I think, but a small lunch for two would you please order? For my office at 1300."

"Are you expecting a guest, or is it for a working lunch with someone from the Legation?"

"A lunch for work, but with someone not of the Legation."

Mydra was all business as she entered whatever she thought necessary into her console.

"Do you have any preferences?"

Nathaniel almost laughed. After the years in the Ecolitan action forces, he could eat anything his system would take.

"Something light, I would think."

"Will you notify the front desk, or should I?"

"If you would be so kind . . . the name is Ferro-Maine."

He turned toward Hillary. Her blue eyes met his levelly.

"How long for Accord have you worked?"

"Five standard years."

Nathaniel nodded and turned away.

Back in his office, he tried to take stock. But the answer was simple. He still didn't know enough.

"*Cling.*"

"Nathaniel Whaler."

The caller was Marcella Ku-Smythe.

"Lord Whaler, I've thought it over, and tonight would be fine."

"Tonight also would be fine, but for what is it fine?"

"For dinner and for getting to know you better."

"Would you suggest somewhere?"

"Why not in the Diplomatic Tower?"

"Dear lady, so little I see of your city. Would you have me cooped into an even smaller orbit?"

That created a smile from the sandy-haired Special Assistant.

"Do you know the Plaza D'Artin?"

"I can find it."

"How about 1930 at the Golden Nova?"

"Twenty-thirty."

"Fine."

And that was that.

Except . . . Nathaniel was ready to swallow hard at the aggressiveness of the woman. Not only the aggressiveness, but . . . he couldn't place it, except that he was missing something so obvious he shouldn't be.

He had nearly two hours before Sylvia's presumed arrival, not enough time to go anywhere, had he anywhere to go, and decided the time had come for some faxwork.

"Mydra?"

"If to be effective I am, I must know the people. Would you access the personnel records of all Legation employees to my screen?"

"Now, Lord Whaler?"

"Now is when I need them."

By the time he had reviewed all the records in the personnel files, he was convinced.

Everything was too perfect, and because it was, he hadn't the faintest idea which of the professional staff were planted. The safest assumption was that they all were.

. . . XIV . . .

"Martin," asked the woman behind the desk, "anything new?" She nipped a bite from a thin taper of cernadine, then another. With each chew, the room grew more redolent of the spice drug.

"There's a call from the Trade Envoy from Accord. Whaler, I think his name is. Nathaniel Whaler."

"What's his problem?"

"That's the Rift thing."

"Oh . . . and they didn't like our proposal and actually sent an Envoy. How charming." Janis Du-Plessis swivelled her seat to view the western hills, turning her back on the aide. "Do we have a counterproposal from them yet?"

"I suspect that's why he wants to meet with Lord Jansen. Probably wants to present it."

"You know, Martin, I'm not terribly fond of provincials, especially from places like Accord. They even turned down my visa." She turned back toward the console and tapped the lock panel.

"We're in conference, Martin, and that's far more important than appointment scheduling for Lord Whaler. Far more important."

Her eyes were bright with the effect of the drug, and fixed on the wiry blond man.

"Why don't you demonstrate how important?"

"Now?"

"Why not now? Lord Jansen is skying, and Lord Envoy Whaler can certainly cool his provincial heels a bit longer."

She looked from Martin to the long couch next to her console and back to him. As she tilted her head, he stood to accept her invitation.

The console panels continued to blink, unanswered.

. . . XV . . .

The private screen chimed, twice.

The Special Assistant scanned the office out of habit, although she was alone.

"Ku-Smythe."

"Marcella, is your dinner engagement wise?" The Admiral's voice was level.

"How much of the Accord Legation's fax system do you have controlled? All of it?"

"Why do you think that?"

"Unless my techs are totally incompetent, everything here is blocked. That means it can't be snooped until the reception point. Accord doesn't have first-class equipment, I'll admit, but it's good enough to block anyone but your crew. Besides, you've got most of the plants on the staff. So even good equipment wouldn't keep you from finding out . . . but not this quickly."

The Admiral smiled. "It's a pity you wouldn't go the Service route. You're wasted at Commerce."

"Could I have gotten as high at Defense?"

"The man is dangerous, Marcella. Dangerous. Don't forget it."

"You're exaggerating again. No man is that dangerous."

"I wish I could show you how dangerous."

"Why do you care? If you're right, that would give you all the pretexts you need, not that you seem to mind the lack of political concern you've demonstrated so far."

The Admiral frowned. "You continue to believe that politics is more important than military capability?"

"No. Your kind of military capabilities are irrelevant, I suspect. That's more the kind of judgment the I.I.S. should make. But you don't trust them either."

"Marcella . . ."

"Why don't you ask yourself why Accord wants to negotiate?"

"I have. They don't want to fight. Neither do we, but we need the trade routes to the Outer Rift."

"Nonsense. You're still trying to prove that you can undo the Secession with pure military applications. Besides, Accord has never blocked the trade routes. It just happens that we can't compete, not unless Accord is no longer a factor."

"As I said, Marcella, it's a pity you're wasted at Commerce."

The Special Assistant just looked through the screen at the Defense Chief.

Finally, the Admiral looked away, and the screen blanked.

. . . XVI . . .

"Cling!"

"Whaler."

"A Sylvia Ferro-Maine for lunch, Lord Whaler."

"Yes. Please send her in." He paused. "And how soon will the food be ready?"

"Shortly, Lord Whaler. I just checked on it."

He stood and moved toward the entry portal, which was opening as he approached.

The woman, who at first glance might have passed for a girl, was dark haired, a brown nearly black, almost as tall as he was, well muscled, but fine boned, with the look of a dancer. Her fair complexion added to the chinalike impression.

"Lord Whaler?"

"One and the very same, Lady dear," he replied with a broad accent. "And you are fine?"

"A little rushed, Lord Whaler, but fine."

He gestured toward the deep office couch.

"You have very spacious quarters here."

"Spacious? I had not thought about the matter, but would such as this be considered spacious here? In New Augusta?"

"Quite comfortable." Sylvia looked around the office, her eyes lingering at the vista of the western hills. "Quite comfortable."

As she sat down, he plopped himself into the chair across from her.

"Know you much about Accord?"

"Only the standard. What should I know?"

Nathaniel shrugged. "So much there is to say. Where would one start? Not at the beginning, for too long that would take. Not in the middle, for too confusing that would be. And at the end, nothing would I be saying. So . . ." he dragged it out, "at the beginning will I start, but more quickly."

"Before start I, hospitality should I offer. Alas, however, my resources here limited are. I have ordered lunch, and arriving in a while it will be. Now I offer you liftea, cafe, or the wine white. You would like which?"

"If you don't mind," the woman responded, carefully crossing her trousered legs, "I think I'll wait until lunch arrives. But do go on with your story . . . I mean, your history."

The Ecolitan cleared his throat.

"In the start, Accord settled was by those fleeing after the fall of the first Federation, and with special skills. The Ecolitan Institute founded shortly thereafter to further and to hand down those skills. All citizens must take Institute training to some degree. Fortunate enough was I to be selected for full training and later to teach there."

He paused to clear his throat again and study Sylvia Ferro-Maine. Odd combination, with the slate gray eyes, dark hair swept up like a dancer's, and the light complexion. She conveyed an impression of fragility.

"Institute does not play now so large a part in our history as once it did, though this time, at crossroads in trade talks, the Institute was indeed consulted. For that I should be most grateful, for that has allowed me the opportunity to see New Augusta."

"Was the Institute the same as the 'Black College' that trained the ecological terrorists of the Ecologic Rebellion?" Her tone was casual, curious, almost uninterested.

"All citizens of Accord did rally together at that time, but the question you have asked, dear Lady, presupposes the Empire was right and Accord wrong. If I answer at all, then I justify your assessment of us all." He shrugged as if puzzled.

She laughed, and the short, sharp sound was nearly musical. "I surrender. Let me put it in another way. Did the Institute play the key role in the Ecologic Secession, as I believe you call it?"

"Most key role, since only the Institute at that time had all the necessary skills gathered under one roof. Times have changed, now, with the five colleges, and the outworld learning centers, and there is less reliance upon the Institute."

He leaned back in the low chair, almost losing his balance as he discovered that the chair reclined and swivelled simultaneously.

"What changes do you see as the most important?"

"Already lengthening what I promised would be short, dear Lady. After Accord was settled and the Institute founded, the government created emphasized self-sufficiency, balanced use of resources, and independent means of interstellar travel. All with good results, until the Empire became most insistent on taking a control over us and over our uninhabited systems. We resisted. Others understood our plight and joined us."

He shrugged. "Now, once again, the Empire has questions about trade and commerce and what systems belong to whom, and here I am to mediate if possible what can be done. Accord is older, and wiser, I am told, and would rather talk this out. So we hope the Empire will talk in good faith as well."

He looked away from her and out through the wide

permaglass at the vista of the mountains, sharp and barren, even in the distance.

"Accord like Terra is," he said softly, "with a gravity a touch stronger and a sky that is more green and near the same land masses with oceans as well. Less salty are the seas, and thicker is the air. Accord is younger, and that may be an answer. Our sun is whiter."

The Ecolitan shrugged again.

"Scarcely it seems know I what else to say or what you wish to hear."

"What do you all do? A dumb question, I suppose, but none of your occupations are listed in the socioeconomic breakdowns."

Nathaniel repressed a whistle at the thought of the Empire's collecting socioeconomic data on Accord.

"Like all people everywhere, we work. Some farm, some craft, some heal, some in industry, some in trade. A small microprocessing industry we have, and some small shipyards, but not on large scales, not like New Glasgow or Halston. I had limited scientific talents, and so came into the Institute."

A discreet tapping sounded.

Nathaniel rose.

"Our lunch perhaps arrives."

Standing at the portal was a waiter, trim in solid tan, and guiding a fully set glide table.

"Lord Whaler, your order."

After watching the waiter set up the table in quick and measured movements and ushering him out, Nathaniel gestured toward Sylvia.

"At last . . ."

He sat Sylvia at one side, and pulled the bottle of sparkling white wine from the ice bucket.

The traditional plastic cork would have come out easily, but the Ecolitan struggled with it as if it were difficult, and in the process aimed it almost at Sylvia. The small missile exploded out of the bottle neck and zipped by her face with a centimeter or two to spare. She jumped.

"Ah, dear Lady. I am sorry."

He handed her the glass into which he had dumped the colorless and tasteless powder before filling it.

"Really, I shouldn't."

He poured himself an overflowing glass and sat down across the table from her.

"But you have not explained your presence, your kindness in lunching with an unknown Envoy."

"No kindness, really. Courtney had already asked me to look into the Accord situation. What better way to start?"

Sylvia smiled faintly, faintly enough to chill Nathaniel, and took a deep sip of the wine.

He frowned and pulled at his chin.

After Sylvia had taken a few more sips, the fidelitrol should take hold. The tricky drug left the victim unable to withhold the truth but had its disadvantages. First, the victim remembered everything, and second, any agent could be trained to minimize its effects.

He took another sip of his own wine.

"With a poor diplomat like me? A mere fumbler of figures?"

Sylvia wrinkled her nose . . . then sneezed. Once! Twice! Her glass nearly tipped, and Nathaniel reached out to steady it.

Sylvia leaned forward in reaction to her sneeze until, off-balance, her hand almost hit Nathaniel's wine glass as she groped to steady herself.

"Oh, excuse me, Envoy Whaler. Please excuse me." She dabbed at her face with a tissue.

Nathaniel took another sip of his wine, waiting for Sylvia to recover. At last, she finished dabbing and took another sip, more like a mouthful, of the wine.

"You're fresh from Accord," she observed, "and who else would be a better source here in New Augusta?"

"But you? What role do you play in this?" He hastily

added another sentence to restrict the question. "For the Senator, I mean?"

"I'm the principal investigator for the Committee, dear Envoy, and look into all sorts of things. Now I'm supposed to look into you."

A puzzled look crossed her dancer's face.

"And how did you come to such a distinguished position?"

"Because the Service thought the Senator needed looking after, and because he has a weakness for good-looking women, and you know, dear Envoy, you beat me to it." She smiled, and this time the smile was resigned in nature.

"Beat you to what?" Nathaniel asked. The conversation had taken a decidedly bizarre turn.

"Slipping something into my drink. I've never told anyone that about the Service, nor would I under anything remotely resembling normal circumstances."

Nathaniel realized she was stalling, stalling until whatever had ended up in his own drink took effect.

He laughed.

"Why did you drug my drink?" he asked, jumping to the obvious conclusion.

"Because you aren't quite what you seem, and there doesn't seem to be any other quick way to find out what I need to know."

"Which is?"

"The details of your mission, or missions, including the reasons and rationale : . ."

Nathaniel chilled. He wasn't sure he could fight the fidelitrol as successfully as she was, and he only had a question or two left before her drug, whatever it was, took effect.

"Who sent you? Who is the Service, and what can I do to get a trade agreement?" He snapped out the questions like arrows.

"Courtney Corwin-Smathers sent me because the I.I.S. set her up to have me sent, and the Service is the Imperial

Intelligence Service, and the best way for you to get a trade agreement is to keep everyone off balance, wouldn't you agree?''

Nathaniel tried to frame another question, but instead found himself answering hers.

"That was my initial reaction, but it's difficult to know how to do that when you don't know the real players—''

"What's your real purpose, dear Envoy?''

How was he going to turn the tables on her?

"My real purpose is to get a trade agreement favorable to Accord and to continue to block Imperial expansion back into the Rift and to do both while avoiding any sort of direct armed conflict between the Coordinate and the Empire, which complicates things greatly, don't you think?''

There! He'd thrown his own question on the end.

If it hadn't been so serious, he could have howled. Both were compelled to tell the truth, and both were trying to get the other on the answering side of the questions.

"Greatly, but doesn't that mean that Accord is out for territorial expansion?''

"Only in the commercial sense and not in governmental terms because the Institute doesn't believe in large government, but aren't several factions within the Empire out to crush us anyway? Which ones? Why?''

"Not all the Empire; mainly the Admiral and the Ministry of Defense, probably because they're still smarting over the loss of the Rift, and can't we stop this farce?''

"Yes, if we agree not to ask questions.''

"I agree.''

Nathaniel looked up to see the fine beads of perspiration on Sylvia's forehead, wiped the dampness off his own brow with the back of his sleeve.

He cleared his throat, meeting her slate dark eyes again.

"How . . . I'd like to offer a compromise. I'll tell you what I can, and you can ask me one question afterwards. That question will ask me if what I said is true. Then you say what you can or will, and I ask you the same question.''

She laughed.

"For a man with such a dangerous reputation, you're certainly being straightforward, and I'd even drink to that, but I'd rather not prolong the agony."

Nathaniel coughed, looked down at the linen on the table, and then back at the slender woman.

"My story is simple, as much of it as you probably want to hear. I am an Ecolitan, a professor at the Institute, selected because of my overall qualifications to figure out how to negotiate a trade agreement with the Empire before the Empire can employ the lack of such an agreement as an excuse to justify widespread military action against the Coordinate. The job is complicated because we can't politically accept a degrading agreement. The Institute couldn't accept any agreement whose terms might be difficult to keep because we frankly believe that some segments of the Empire don't want any agreement. At the same time, I should reinforce the idea that armed aggression by the Empire would result in catastrophe for the Empire itself. That will be difficult because no one in the Empire really believes that Accord has that kind of ability. Nor do they want to believe that. It's true, unfortunately."

He spread his hands. "I'd be happy to add any more if it's a suggestion and not a question."

She grinned. "Do you trust me that much? Or do you think you could avoid answering?" She put her hand over her mouth. "Oh . . . I'm sorry."

"No, but I have to trust someone, at least to some degree. It's probably better to trust a professional. I could probably avoid revealing anything I really wanted to."

Sylvia opened her mouth, closed it, then began again. "You seem to have a great deal of confidence, a great deal of faith, in your ability to wreak havoc upon the Empire without taking much in the way of losses." Her expression was calm and composed by the time she finished the statement.

"I did not say that. All-out war would probably destroy

Accord totally. It would not destroy the Institute nor its capability to devastate the Empire. There is a difference.''

"Is all this true, and do you believe it?"

"Yes . . . to both . . . with the qualification that any prediction based on assumptions of human nature has a certain potential for error."

Her laugh was a breeze of freshness. "My . . . you do sound like the professor you are!"

He couldn't help but return her humor with a short laugh of his own.

"I didn't mean to sound so pedantic, but the way you asked the question. . ."

The silence following his words lengthened.

Nathaniel half turned to stare out the wide window toward the foothills and the mountains behind. High white clouds were approaching from the west.

As he brought himself back to meet Sylvia's eyes, he realized he had not even touched the food on the plate before him. Nor had Sylvia.

He gestured.

"Perhaps you'd like a bite or two before you begin . . ."

Looking down, then lifting his fork, he raised his eyebrows, asking an unspoken question.

"No . . . I didn't drop anything in the food, suspicious man. Did you?"

"No, suspicious lady."

Surprisingly, the fish was still warm, and the sweet-sour sauce and a spice he failed to recognize added pungency to the white meat's delicate flavor. The side dish, some sort of vegetable, was soggy, bland, and smelled like overdone seaweed.

It also tasted like seaweed, though Sylvia ate her portion with scarcely a shiver.

He finished nearly all of what was on his plate before realizing she had done the same, and neither had said a word.

"You know . . . Sylvia . . . I wonder if anyone will

really believe what I've said after you walk out and tell
them.''

"Dear Envoy, it's a relief to hear I will walk out." Her
smile was teasing.

"Unlike Imperials," he returned, "we don't tease and
obfuscate issues, which often leaves us at a great disadvan-
tage.''

"The Service already believes you." Her face smoothed
into a professional mask. "For various reasons, no one else
wants to. In that sense, we're allies. But we can't lift a
hand in any direct way to help you make your case.''

"Why not?"

"Since I don't seem compelled to answer that, I won't,
although I will point out that no military bureaucracy has
ever lost the opportunity to destroy rival intelligence
sources.''

"The Institute faces some of the same problems, and I
would guess the same problem occurs in more cultures
than not.'' He cleared his throat. "What else can you, or
will you, reveal?''

"You probably won't get much help from the Ministry
of External Affairs . . . we feel that Commerce will try to
take control.''

"You paint a less than optimistic picture.''

"Should I distort it, Lord Whaler? No one really likes
Accord. Even the Service only supports the idea of a
completed agreement because we like the alternatives even
less.''

Nathaniel shrugged. "What can I say?''

"That you're sorry for the underhanded tactics you use
. . .'' suggested Sylvia with a twinkle in her eye.

"When I am not . . . when the tactics hurt no one, except
the pride . . . ?''

"Touché!''

"After all, Lady, my pride also was damaged.'' Nathaniel managed to keep a straight face despite the outra-
geous statement.

The Ecolitan looked down at his empty plate, wondering why he was regretting that the lunch was nearly over.

"Why the frown?"

"Oh . . . nothing. Things are never quite as they seem, but why that should surprise me I can't quite say."

Sylvia pushed back her chair and stood, catching Nathaniel with the quickness of the movement, although he was standing next to her within instants.

"You recover quickly," she observed, still bantering.

"One tries."

Inclining her head to the right, she gave him a quizzical look, her gray eyes clouding momentarily. "Like you, I find things are not quite what they seem. Nor are you."

"I am what I am."

She was already departing. As the portal irised, she turned back toward him.

"Time is running against you, you know, particularly if you have to react to others." She paused, then continued with a brief smile, "But I did enjoy the lunch."

With that, she was gone.

Nathaniel shook his head as the portal closed behind her.

Only a faint scent, similar to the orange blossoms of his father's orchards, hung in the air to remind him that Sylvia had been there.

. . . XVII . . .

Nathaniel studied his reflection in the mirror. The shimmering tan of the semiformal tunic was not all that flattering, made him look even a bit beefy.

"Can't have everything," he muttered as he tabbed the plate to dim the quarters' lights.

Was it wise to go out the way he was?

Probably not.

Instead of leaving by the private exit, he decided on going through the Legation. The staff offices were deserted except for the duty desk, captained by Hillary West-Coven, the lady whose purpose he had yet to discover.

"Oh, Lord Whaler. You surprised me."

Several emotions flashed across her face, one of which Nathaniel thought might be guilt.

"That I did not mean," he pontificated. "Just departing am I."

With that, he hurried out, checking the area outside the portal.

The corridor was nearly deserted, but the faint shadow along the far side corridor piqued his curiosity. He eased himself against the wall and slipped toward the side branch, the one that would eventually lead to the private entrance to his personal quarters.

After dropping into a crouch, he darted a look around the corner, in time to see three plain-suited figures heading crisply toward the exit portal from his quarters.

Nathaniel straightened, checking behind himself instinctively, and frowned.

The military bearing of two of the three was obvious, despite their civilian attire. But who was the third figure? Somehow the gait had been familiar, almost like an Ecolitan . . .

"Whew!" A soft whistle escaped his lips.

If he'd seen what he thought he'd seen, he was headed for real trouble. The next question was how to defuse the trap without letting onto the deception.

If the three didn't discover one Nathaniel Whaler exiting his quarters shortly, they would go searching, as well as alert their superiors at the Ministry of Defense.

Nathaniel weighed the options, and as he weighed, checked the few items he always carried.

From the inside of his belt he pulled a thin, golden film cloak and a filmy golden privacy mask. While such masks were not normally worn on New Augusta, his real purpose was to confuse his identity for a few individuals for a limited period of time.

Next came the wooden dart pistol with which he had attempted to persuade Sergel. In addition to the lethal darts were those that sent the victims into a delirium and effectively scrambled their memories from several minutes before they were shot until several days later. The Ecolitan opted for the nonlethal variety.

An unseen attack would be best, but if that couldn't be arranged, surprise would substitute nearly as well.

The corridors narrowed as they approached his private quarters, but Nathaniel trailed the three until it was certain they were staking out his quarters' exit.

From the corner behind which he waited, the range to the nearest "sentry," a blond man perhaps six centimeters shorter than the Ecolitan, was roughly eight meters. The other military operative was stationed to guard the cross corridor, and the third, the one who also wore a privacy cloak, the one whose face and bearing resembled the Ecolitan himself, stood by the exit portal with a drawn stunner.

Nathaniel eased the dart pistol around the corner and fired.

"Thwick!"

"Thwick!"

The nearer sentry pulled at his neck, twice, before dropping his hand to look at the dissolving residue of the dart.

His left arm twitched, followed by his right leg.

The further sentry, the dark-haired and taller woman, had already snapped her head around.

"Thwick!"

"Thwick!"

The first victim began to thrash on the corridor tiles, dull thuds echoing down the long and otherwise empty passageways.

Nathaniel wondered at the man's self-control. By now, most would have been raving wildly.

The woman looked at the disintegrating splinters of the dart which rested in her hand, her eyes widening. Before she could analyze the pattern, in turn, she shuddered as the neural disruptor began to take effect.

Four shots to hit two sentries. Lousy shooting, Nathaniel thought as he reloaded the dart thrower.

The remaining Imperial, the bogus Ecolitan, turned his head from one side to the other as if to determine from which of the two intersecting corridors the shots had come.

Finally, the man made the right decision and dashed for the corridor where the woman lay thrashing, the one farthest from Nathaniel.

The Ecolitan snapped the dart gun together, waited until the other had cleared the corner, and sprinted nearly noiselessly after the man.

As he came around the corner, he saw the fleeing Imperial collide with a passerby, a mid-aged man, and knock him to the tiles. Nathaniel didn't hesitate but used a single dart on the bystander as he passed at full sprint.

The Imperial stopped at the next intersection, the one perhaps thirty meters from the main corridor leading to the lift/drop shaft, and turned to level his stunner at the oncoming Ecolitan.

"*Thwick!*" Nathaniel triggered the dart pistol, knowing the distance was too great but anticipating the other would flinch. He did.

"*Thrummm!*"

The stunner bolt passed over the Ecolitan's left shoulder.

Nathaniel dove to the right and into a roll. He came out still running.

His right hand went dead, but that didn't stop him from firing the dart thrower.

Another advantage to being left-handed, he noted absently as he closed on the Imperial.

"*Thwick!*"

The dart caught the Imperial agent full in the throat, the only area unshielded by clothing. The man staggered momentarily, just long enough for Nathaniel to slash away the stunner and follow through with a quick elbow across the man's jaw.

Without hesitating, Nathaniel pocketed the dart pistol, retrieved the stunner, and hoisted the unconscious but twitching form of the other over his shoulder. In less than a minute he had stowed the man in the public call booth near the lift shaft.

Only one passing couple caught his transit, the woman quickly turning her head, the man still peering back as the two descended the drop shaft.

As he tapped out the codes he wanted, Nathaniel stood to shield the body from full public view.

"Senator Helmsworth's Office."

The respondent was not the urbane male receptionist,

but a woman, dark haired and slightly disheveled, in a pale
blue tunic.

"Nathaniel Whaler for Sylvia Ferro-Maine."

"Let me check."

The screen blanked, only to be replaced with Sylvia's
slate gray eyes and dark hair. She still wore the green and
gray she had worn to lunch.

"Lord Whaler . . . what a surprise."

"Not so much as what I have for you." He stepped aside
and dragged the unconscious Imperial agent into the focus
of the screen.

"Oh . . . and why are you faxing me?"

"I had thought that some of your friends might want to
have a chat with this gentleman before he wakes up.
You'll note his remarkable similarity to me. That is, your
friends might enjoy the conversation if they could pick him
up before his dispatcher does."

"Where on earth are you?"

"In the main corridor pubcomm station, right beyond
the lift shaft, where you had lunch."

"In that case, something might be arranged. Will you
be there?"

"Not for long. I'll call you later. I've probably been
available all too long in any case."

"I understand."

The screen blanked.

Nathaniel shook his head. As quick as he thought he
was, she was even quicker.

He let the agent slump into a heap in the back corner of
the booth, hardly noticeable from outside, and strolled out
and toward the drop shaft and his dinner engagement with
Marcella, hoping the I.I.S. could retrieve the imitation
"Nathaniel" before the military could.

. . . XVIII . . .

After the quick drop down the public shaft to the tunnel concourse, Nathaniel summoned a public tunnel cab to take him to the Plaza D'Artin, the Golden Nova, and Marcella.

As he sat in the back of the cab, he flexed his right hand, squeezing it with his left. Some of the feeling was beginning to return.

Was the lady responsible for his recent reception committee? If not, why the coincidence?

He shrugged and took a deep breath, shaking himself slightly to relax muscles that were too tight.

Despite its name, the Golden Nova occupied a quiet corner of the multileveled plaza. Nathaniel was amused to note that his choice of dinner wear, while commonplace among the younger men, was definitely in style.

"I see you found it without trouble." Marcella Ku-Smythe was waiting for him in the restaurant's anteroom.

She wore an amber outfit with a high neck, narrow waist, and slightly flared pants. Much more becoming to her light skin than the maroon of the Imperial Commerce Ministry, he reflected. He didn't miss the bulge of the stunner tucked into the waist folds of her jacket.

A waiter materialized and led them to a corner table. The dining area was filled, obviously with wealthy souls. The use of waiters alone attested to the price levels. So Marcella was well-off in her own right. Or the government was picking up the tab. Or both.

After they were seated, he asked that question.

"You're too forthright even for me. Let us poor Imperials have a few secrets."

"You're more of a mystery to us," he protested. "So many things puzzle me. Terra is the center of the Empire but few live here. You build towers into the sky, but seal them off and travel underground."

"You should know." It was the first trace of hostility he'd heard in her voice. "Or have they forgotten to teach *all* the history on Accord? Or don't you recall why the war was called the Ecologic Rebellion . . . pardon me, the Ecologic Secession?"

"Forest Lord! Still?" he asked apologetically. The history tapes mentioned the use of ecological weapons against Terra itself by the Institute, and the techniques were still taught. But Accord had long since recovered from the war's effects.

She waved his apology aside.

"I suppose you wouldn't have any reason to understand the lasting impact. Terran ecology was so fragile at the time. We never really recovered from the Age of Waste and the first planetary wars. Yes, we could go outside, and some are allowed, but we're erring on the side of caution. If you notice, all the towers—a necessary requirement of Empire—are within New Augusta. Elsewhere we try to minimize any adverse impact on the environment."

After that exchange, he was more on edge.

"For a man so intelligent, so ostensibly open, you reveal little of what you are."

He spread his hands. "My life is an open book."

"Of blank pages," she added with a wry laugh, "or pages written in an ancient and unknown language."

He looked around the dining area from his position against the wall. Something about the seating arrangements bothered him, but he couldn't pin it down.

"Marcella, you are a witty and brilliant lady, and you entertain me marvelously. Can you entertain me further and tell me how and what I need to do to follow through on the trade agreement talks?"

The smile disappeared from her face.

"Not here. Come see me tomorrow. Say around 1400."

Question asked; question answered.

"I bow to your superior wisdom, and speaking of wisdom, can you enlighten me on what should be ordered."

When he had seen her earlier on the vidfax screen and in person at the Commerce Ministry, she had worn her hair up and more severely. Now, with the swirl of sandy hair across her shoulder, with the light tan of her skin and the dark amber of her outfit, he tabbed her more as a golden girl, mature woman or not. Her green eyes were a shade less intense than in full daylight, but she still missed nothing.

"Their specials are always good, but I'm fond of the flaming spicetails."

"Then I'll have the flaming spicetails."

"You'll actually take the word of a hard, hard, Imperial bureaucrat?"

"On this small matter, at least."

A brief shadow flickered across her face, so fleeting the Ecolitan wondered if she were aware of it, but it brought him back from the edge of relaxation. Marcella Ku-Smythe was not used to having her word doubted—on anything.

"How did you find your way into the bureaucracy?" Nathaniel figured it for a safe question.

"In the same way as any other bright student of applied political theory from a nonnoble family. Took the Emperor's exams, passed with distinction, and was placed in the Commerce Ministry." Marcella furrowed her brows briefly, as if the beginning of a career which had led her to becoming one of the top assistants in the Imperial bureaucracy was nothing unusual.

"Your family?"

"My mother was pleased, although she's from the Eagles and would have preferred me to take a commission. My father, well, he just wanted me to do what I wanted. Nothing any different about me from any other aspiring assistant.

"You, on the other hand, embody romance, mystery, and a hint or so of danger."

"Why? Because I'm from the nasty planet of Accord?"

Marcella was spared an answer by the arrival of a purple clad waiter.

Nathaniel nodded at Marcella.

"Two of the flaming spicetails, Imperial salads with Maccean nuts, and a carafe of Kremmling." She looked at the Ecolitan. "Do you want anything else?"

"I'll leave that up to you."

"The cheeses as a mid-course," she added to the waiter.

"Honored guest . . ." she started, with an appealing lilt in her mocking tone.

"Damn it! I'm Nathaniel. Always was. Always will be. None of this 'honored' this or 'honored' that. Honors never did the work."

"Nathaniel, then. You still haven't answered the question you haven't let me ask."

"Which was?"

"Why you seem to personify the whole concept of mystery."

"There's nothing mysterious about me."

"Oh?"

"I'm thirty-eight standard years old, sandy haired, and I've been employed in some capacity by the benevolent Institute for the past fifteen years."

"Ah, yes. Combat arm of the Institute, but a renowned economist. Highly rated scout pilot, but a teacher. You're pulled out of the Institute and thrown to head a trade delegation at the last minute. That's not mysterious?''

Nathaniel was impressed with Marcella's ability to tap into the pipeline, particularly since the information existed in written form only on Accord.

He shrugged.

"What can I say?" He forced a grin. "I thought you weren't going to mix business with socializing."

She had the grace to smile back, and the coldness left her eyes for a moment.

"You win."

Nathaniel opted for generosity.

"Not that it's not a good observation, Marcella. But I could say the same about you. All I know is that you are extraordinarily talented and that you work for Lord Rotoller, and that . . ."

"And what else?"

"That I'm perilously close to mixing business and socializing. No sense in drawing a second reprimand."

He took a sip of the Kremmling, a light white wine with a hint of a sparkle, and waited for Marcella to taste the salad which had just appeared.

Was she waiting for him to take the first bite? Style be damned. He picked up the fork.

After the first three bites, Nathaniel decided there was a solid reason why the salad was termed "Imperial." It was too rich for anyone but an Imperial.

"What do you really think of New Augusta?"

An innocently loaded question, but Nathaniel decided to be as truthful as possible under the circumstances.

"I haven't had a chance to see a great deal, but already I feel cramped by not being able to get outside. I suppose that's one reason why you've made the effort toward high-ceilinged architecture."

"You'd have to confirm that with the Imperial architect, but it's as good a reason as any. We just accept it because that's the way it is."

"What happens if someone doesn't accept things?"

Marcella shrugged. "Every society has some who don't fit in."

"I can't say that I've noticed an overt police system, but I have the impression that things are definitely under control."

"As well as could be expected."

"Do the unhappy ones get mental treatment or what?"

"Not necessarily. That's the beauty of having an Empire. If they don't like it on New Augusta or elsewhere on Earth, they can outship to a good hundred planets."

"And you encourage that migration?"

"Yes . . . since we're being frank. The fewer bodies here, the less strain on the ecology and the lower the population dissatisfaction critical point."

"Isn't that merely a mythical assumption, that population densities and comfort levels really have a bearing on civic harmony?"

"The original Living Space Riots, the work of your own scholar Vonderjogt, and the experiments of Kliemersol all would indicate otherwise. Practically speaking, no government could ever let the situation deteriorate that far, not and retain any pretense of civil liberty."

"Isn't dealing with such theoretical matters ranging a bit out of your field?"

"Not really."

He dropped the questioning to concentrate on the flamed spicetails.

"Very good."

"You haven't tasted them before?"

"No. Our fare is much simpler."

"What's Accord really like? I don't mean to ask for a travelogue. We've seen the standard reference works, the tapes, and the footage from back to the Secession, but what is Accord today? What are your candid impressions of the differences between the Empire and Accord?"

"I'm not sure I can answer with any great accuracy."

"I'll take an inaccurate impression." She laughed and her voice relaxed. "You know, you're very careful. I can't blame you, but let go a little."

"First, then, I'll say that you can see the sky. It's a shade greener than yours and our sun is whiter . . ." Nathaniel turned up his hands. ". . . but all the comparisons are conjectures. I see your sun through permaglass, and I see mine in my gardens and in the woods. I know everyone in the town where I grew up, and here I don't see how anyone knows anyone. On Accord, everyone produces something. Even our bureaucrats grow their own vegetables, or write, or compose, or sing . . ."

"You make it sound like utopia."

"Far from it. We're a young society. People have to work hard at two or three jobs. It's only been in the last generation or so that we've been able to afford career politicians and bureaucrats. I'm not convinced that change has been good."

Marcella frowned.

"You picture Accord as a young society. Nearly four hundred years ago, which is a long time for a small political and social system like Accord, Accord was advanced enough to foment, direct, and successfully coordinate a multisystem revolution which cost the Empire all chance of immediate expansion into the Rift area. In addition," she added drily, "roughly fifty systems discovered they would rather not pay levies to the Empire. I'm not sure how you can describe any society that effective as young."

Nathaniel shrugged. "What can I say? You asked for my impressions. Compared to the Empire, we're mere babes."

"You still haven't written much on those blank pages, Nathaniel."

"What blank pages?"

"The ones that compose the open book of your life."

The Ecolitan finished off the last spicetail rather than attempt an answer. The lady knew far more than any mere assistant to the Deputy Minister should. The question was why.

"Is everyone from Accord so reserved?"

"No."

"What's an Ecolitan?"

That was one question he definitely didn't want to answer. It sounded so simple, but trying to give any real answer would create more problems.

"I really don't know how to answer that one."

"You can't be serious." A touch of sharpness crept into her voice.

"We Ecolitans keep pretty much to ourselves. So it's hard to make comparisons. Originally, we were a totally separate and unified force which represented the bulk of Accord's military capability. That is no longer true, although we do keep a number of ships. We are still totally independent of the Coordinate government and don't have all that much to do with them. Call us scholars with the power to remain independent of any government."

"Scholars are usually considered peaceful, and somehow I don't see the Institute as a peaceful force or the selection of an Ecolitan as a peaceful move."

"Scholars shouldn't necessarily be regarded as pacifists. You also have to remember that I was a compromise selection, since neither the Normists nor the Orthodox opposition could agree on one of their own candidates for the position. Besides, any compromise reached by an Ecolitan could not possibly be questioned by even the most fanatical Orthodoxist."

Marcella nodded slightly.

"Put in that light, your position becomes clearer. Only slightly clearer, I might add."

"Whereas yours is still totally unclear."

"What kind of art is most popular on Accord?"

Nathaniel accepted the abrupt changes in subject matter as an indication that Marcella had found out what she wanted to know . . . at least for the moment.

The only other awkward moment came after dinner.

"Excellent dinner, Marcella. May I see you to your quarters?"

"Perhaps it would be better if I did the escorting."

"Is that the Terran custom?"

"Usually," she noted, "but with diplomats, one can adjust to almost anything."

"How about a compromise?"

"Leave as we came?"

"Just this time."

"All right. But I promise I'll hold you to your word."

"In the meantime," Nathaniel concluded, as he turned to go, "I'll see you tomorrow."

. . . XIX . . .

Nathaniel took another tunnel cab back to the Diplomatic Tower, alert for another possible attack. Both the trip and the walk back to his private entrance were uneventful.

The stunner he had taken from the Imperial ready, he touched the lockplate and let the door dilate.

The silence was an alarm in itself. He had left the music on. Instinctively, he dropped to his knees and fired the stunner around the edge of the door into the blind space he couldn't see, following the shot with a quick dash from the corridor into the quarters.

The anteway was empty, as was the living area. So were the cramped kitchen area, the dining area, and the second sleeping quarters. But someone was still in the quarters. An almost imperceptible rustle from beyond the bedroom confirmed his unease.

He surveyed the dimly lit main sleeping quarters again. If anyone were still in the quarters, he or she was probably in the hygienarium or behind the bed.

No sense in being any more of a damned fool.

The Ecolitan sat down noiselessly on the plush flooring, shielded completely by the bedroom door edge, stunner resting on his knee and leveled at the half-open door to the hygienarium. He set it at half charge and went through the drill to sharpen his vision.

After ten minutes, he heard a shuffle. He didn't move.

Close to an hour later, a face peered around the doorway across the room.

Nathaniel got him with a single shot.

Something about the falling figure struck him as familiar, but he couldn't place it. Another stifled gasp announced a second intruder.

The waiting trick wouldn't work a second time, and, besides, who knew what the other snooper might try?

Slowly, he eased the flat pressure foil tube from his belt, nicked the seal, and tossed it gently onto the far side of the bed.

"Hssssss . . ."

A stunner pointed over the top of the bed. The Ecolitan stayed behind the wall as the useless charges struck.

A few minutes later, he stood and slowly edged around the wall.

Now two figures were sprawled on the bedroom floor.

The closer, the one he'd gotten with the stunner, was Sergel Weintre.

The second was a younger man, black haired, olive skinned and clean shaven, perhaps 160 centimeters from head to toe.

A quick but thorough search of both revealed nothing. Sergel had carried only the stunner and a few personal items. The stranger had no identification whatsoever, but the standardized singlesuit and new stunner announced all too clearly his military connections.

In turn, the Ecolitan dragged each to the private exit and dumped them outside.

He returned to his quarters and faxed the tower's emergency number.

"Envoy Nathaniel Whaler am I, and a disturbance has occurred. Outside my door. My composure has gone."

"Lord Whaler, I'll send the Domestic Protective Service up immediately. You say, outside your private suite?"

"Outside. That is correct. A fight, I think. Or several."

"Is it still going on?"

"No. But loudly it ended. A large noise. Someone falls, but check I wish not to do in person."

"Don't worry, Lord Whaler. We'll take care of it."

"I thank you."

So much for that. He made sure both doors were locked with the handbolts and stretched out on the rumpled bed, slipping the stunner under the pillows.

Going back to the disciplines of the Institute, he concentrated on the sleep-time exercises, telling himself to wake at the slightest sound or in five hours.

Five hours and ten minutes later, he woke abruptly. Instantly alert, he listened. No sounds. Apparently, the Diplomatic Police had come and carted Sergel off without much noise, although he wouldn't have heard if they'd brought an entire blasthorn section. The soundproof nature of the walls and doors was a flaw in his story, but he doubted anyone would call an Envoy on such a minor discrepancy.

Nathaniel took his time about freshening up, showering, and dressing for the day ahead.

The last item before entering his official office was a quick fax to one Sylvia Ferro-Maine.

"Lord Whaler . . . and what can I do for you this early in the morning?"

"I had wondered if perhaps your friends had received the package I had left . . . or if you knew."

"My understanding is that the pickup went smoothly, but that they have not had the chance to evaluate the value of the shipment." Sylvia's face was without emotion. "Is that all?"

"I would hope that we could get together again before too long . . ."

"You honor me, Lord Whaler, and I will certainly await your call. And I must be going, but thank you."

Nathaniel was left staring at the blank gray of the faxscreen.

He shook his head. Now what had he done wrong?

Why did he imagine the scent of orange trees?

"Ridiculous . . ." he muttered. "Absolutely ridiculous."

Maybe Sylvia was worried about the leaky nature of the communications at the Accord Legation. He'd have to check back later . . . from somewhere else.

In the meantime, he had the rest of his job to do.

He marched from his quarters into the official office, sat down behind the console, and tried to review the incoming messages that awaited him.

Within ten minutes the intercom chimed, and Mydra's face appeared on the faxscreen. He punched the Accept stud.

"A call from the Diplomatic Police."

"I'll take it."

The young officer who waited on the screen was stern faced and female.

"Envoy Whaler? You complained about a disturbance last night?"

"Yes. There was a fight in the corridor, I believed."

"Lord Whaler, as you mentioned, there was a disturbance. Some of our normal public monitors were apparently damaged. We also found one man lying in front of your private entrance, stunned out. He claims he works for the Legation. His name is Sergel Weintre. The documentation matches, but we thought you as the Envoy should know."

Interesting, thought Nathaniel. I dump two men, and they only find one. Or find two and only let me know about one.

He frowned at the officer.

"Well . . . we do have a Sergel Weintre who works here

as an Information Specialist. Let me see if he has shown up."

He put the black-haired and square-jawed officer on hold and rang Mydra.

"Has Sergel Weintre come in this morning?"

"No, and that's very unusual. He's usually the first one here. If he's ever late, we all are notified. The main desk says he doesn't answer his quarters' number either."

How interesting, reflected the Ecolitan. Everyone knows everything about everyone.

He went back to the Diplomatic Police officer.

"Mr. Weintre has not shown up this morning and cannot be reached at his quarters. So quite possible it is that Sergel Weintre you do have. Do you have a visual?"

She split the screen, and Weintre's image filled the right half. He was scowling, and his right eyelid twitched above a clinched and unshaven jaw.

"I would say that is Mr. Weintre. Is any way there that he could be released to the Legation?"

"That would not be proper procedure."

"I understand. On the other hand, the Legation is most short staffed at the moment, and I would certainly appreciate any suggestions you might have about how to accomplish Mr. Weintre's speedy return."

"Once a complaint is made, sir . . ."

"Since the complaint was made by the Legation, so to speak, could not I have that complaint withdrawn?"

"That would be most unusual."

"But not impossible?"

"I'll have to check on that, Lord Whaler."

"I'll be happy to wait."

Nathaniel flipped through one of the trade folders while the faxscreen displayed the emblem of the Diplomatic Police.

"Lord Whaler?"

"Yes."

"I understand you made a complaint about Mr. Weintre's creating a disturbance?"

"Concerned was I about the noise and merely reported it and did not charge anyone with anything."

"Under those circumstances, I believe we can release your employee directly to you, but we will still have to continue our investigation into the broken monitors."

"I understand, but I appreciate your consideration of our shorthanded state."

After signing off with the Diplomatic Police, Nathaniel caught Mydra on the faxscreen.

"As soon as Sergel gets back, I would like to see him."

"Yes, Lord Whaler, I'll tell him."

Two to one, thought the Ecolitan, Sergel isn't going to get that message.

In the interim, he decided to check the trade figures and review the presentation materials he had brought with him. Not that he expected anything to be overlooked, but the way things were going, who could tell?

After spending close to an hour rechecking the quota figures he worked out before leaving Accord, he took out the "confidential" briefing folders and placed them on the top of the pile inside the datacase he was going to leave by the console. He set the internal counters, and locked the case.

Then he took the "official" briefing folders, three sets worth, and placed them inside the case he planned to take with him.

The "confidential" figures showed the same basic statistics on trade flows between the Coordinate and the Empire, but the projections showed a far more adverse effect on the economy of Accord than the set he was going to present to both Corwin-Smathers and later to Marcella.

He wondered who would get the confidential figures first. If he had to bet, his choice would be on the military types who were slinking around.

That brought back the question of Sergel. Sergel didn't seem to understand that the third-ranking officer of the

Legation of a third-rate power didn't rate the kind of attention he was getting merely for his irresistible charm.

He shook his head and looked at the western hills.

With all the angles subdivided by angles, he had the feeling he'd be fortunate to find out all the real questions in six years, let alone in the few weeks he probably had.

Could it be done before Witherspoon wandered back, before the political compromise on Accord eroded, before the Empire figured out a way to militarily moot the whole question?

The second time around, after the experience of the Secession, the Empire just *might* be willing to sacrifice a fleet or two and several dozen planets for a millennium or two to eliminate permanently a thorn in its side.

He brought himself up short and checked the time. 0940—almost time to depart on another trip through the tunnels for his appointment with Corwin-Smathers.

Sergel still hadn't called in.

He flicked the code for the Information Specialist's quarters.

"Weintre," a sullen voice responded. The faxscreen remained blank.

"Whaler here. Let's have the screen, Sergel."

The picture came on. Sergel stood there, stripped to the waist, showing a small paunch over the black waistband of his too-tight rust trousers.

"Why didn't you answer my message?"

Sergel's mouth opened, moving back and forth soundlessly. Finally, he sputtered. "No message . . . I mean . . . no one left a message for me."

"The way everything else works around here, I can't say I'm surprised. Not that important, but what I have to say now is. I don't know what you were doing prowling around my quarters last night, but you'd better have a damned good explanation. I don't want any more phony answers. Face it, Sergel. You can't lie to me and make it stick."

He glared through the faxscreen at the younger man to reinforce the growling tone of his lecture.

"Well . . . umm . . . I hate to say it, Lord Whaler, but I got pretty stung. Thought I was somewhere else. I really did."

"Sergel, you're lying. Don't try to bluff through it again. If an explanation of what you were up to and the report I asked for aren't both on my console by the time I get back this afternoon, you're leaving on the next ship for Accord. Even if it's via the Alparta and takes two years objective. Is that clear?"

"Yes, sir. Perfectly clear."

Nathaniel could almost see the thoughts in his head. Sergel was wondering who had caught him out. He *knew* Nathaniel would have dispatched him, possibly without a trace.

Let him stew, thought the Ecolitan. He deserves it, and then some. In the game of mass confusion, perhaps some by Nathaniel might give Sergel, and his underground pay-masters, some second thoughts.

"Remember, Sergel, those reports or you're on your way."

"Yes, sir."

The look on the Information Specialist's face told Nathaniel one more thing. Sergel was more afraid of someone else, much more afraid.

He broke the connection and looked at the blank screen a moment before returning his attention to the datacase he intended to take with him. The locked case was still beside the desk console.

He finally marched out into the general staff office.

"Mydra, sometime this afternoon will I be back."

"Is there anything else, Lord Whaler?"

"Not at this moment."

Nathaniel waved pleasantly to Heather Tew-Hawkes as he left the Legation and strode down the main corridor to the drop shaft.

He wondered if he were being tailed. It didn't matter at the moment. He slid into the high speed section and savored the fall. Almost like using a jump belt, except there was no risk in the drop shaft, no worry about enemy fire.

Out in the underground concourse, he caught a public tunnel cab, driven by a man with long and silver-glittered hair.

. . . XX . . .

"What were the results of the interrogation?"

"He'd been totally blocked. If we'd gone any deeper, it would have turned his mind to mush. Didn't want to risk that, particularly since it's obviously a Defense conditioning job. So we released him, ostensibly after treating and detoxifying him. And we sent a confidential report on the detox results to the Ministry of Defense."

"Detoxifying?" asked the Director.

"Whatever Whaler used, we couldn't analyze. Even with a blood sample as soon as we got him, all we had left was molecular soup. Could have been a dozen things, but we think it was a short-term synthetic virus that acts as a temporary neural disruptor."

"How can you have a temporary and synthetic virus? And how could you develop one that wasn't fatal?"

"Damned if we know, but that's what it looks like." The Research Chief shook his head slowly.

The Director turned in her swivel. "That's the sort of weapon we'd give a dozen agents for, and Whaler doesn't mind using it right off. That says a couple of things. First, that it's something that they don't mind revealing. Second, that the trade talks or whatever Whaler is really doing is more than just important to Accord. And third, that Defense doesn't understand what we're up against." She snorted. "And Admiral Ku-Smythe thinks that we could win a war with Accord."

The Research Chief nodded, then added, "There's one other item. Their agent—and his profile matches Idel's, but who can tell—says he hit Whaler with the stunner. Not full, but enough to deaden one hand, maybe part of the arm."

"So?"

"Idel used a military stunner, set close to a lethal jolt, and Whaler still ran him down, apparently slugged him unconscious, and called Sylvia without betraying any discomfort."

"He can override pain to a fantastic degree . . . or our stunners just don't affect him . . . is that it?"

"Those are the only two explanations I can think of. Do you have a better one?"

"Idel missed."

"When was the last time a military Defense agent totally missed a target running straight at him?"

The Director shook her head. If only the Defense Ministry would understand, but that was like asking a tunnel roach not to scavenge.

. . . XXI . . .

The offices of the Imperial Senate occupied an entire tower of their own, Senator Helmsworth was listed as having half the two hundred and third level to himself.

Nathaniel swung out of·the lift shaft with fifteen minutes to spare and studied the directory before realizing that Corwin-Smathers' office was only fifty meters from the·drop shaft.

The young man sitting at the front console.of the staff office labelled External Relations Committee Staff greeted him eagerly.

"Lord Whaler! What a pleasure! Ms. Corwin-Smathers is tied up, but she'll be right with you. You know, it's a pleasure to meet someone like you. It really must be different outside the Empire, to be from a faraway system like Accord, and to be a Trade Envoy." He smiled brightly.

"Now, Charles," interrupted the dark-haired woman as she appeared from the side office, "you'll have Lord Whaler teaching you all the secrets of his success, and then what will I do to replace you?"

The Ecolitan offered the finger touch gesture he'd seen used. He thought it was between equals, and that wouldn't hurt.

"I'm the one who should be honored," she replied, "but I do appreciate the flattery."

"Only according you your due," he replied, suppressing a wince at his unintended pun.

She motioned toward a portal at one side of the reception office—not the one from which she had emerged a moment earlier—and paused, waiting for him.

From what he had seen thus far in the Imperial bureaucracy, her office was modest, although not a great deal smaller than his.

Restrained browns, contrasted with touches of brighter colors, set the tone. The console, chairs, and receiving table were modeled along the clean lines of fortieth century functionalism, but the dark shade, similar to stained lorkin, indicated it was from a later period.

Nathaniel selected the nonreclining pilot chair, rather than one of the deeper, ostensibly more comfortable sink chairs, but stood beside it for a minute, studying Courtney. By her posture, he could tell she was waiting for him. After standing for a few seconds longer, he settled into the pilot's chair.

"I appreciate your courtesy in seeing me on such short notice and for understanding the peculiar situation."

"Peculiar?"

"Peculiar to us. First trade talks with the Empire in seventy years, and only the second in over four centuries. I forget this sort of thing goes on day in and day out here in the Empire."

"Scarcely that often, and certainly not with an out-system with the, shall we say, prestige of Accord."

"Now you're overdoing the honor business," protested the Ecolitan.

"I don't think so. For a system which has but three nationals here normally to send such a highly qualified individual for trade negotiations honors us greatly. The fact that you have also contacted one of the most interested Senators shows how close you are to the pulse of things."

"We're just trying to chart all the orbits."

Courtney did not reply. She smiled.

A hush, almost absolute silence, settled on the office.

"I assume you do have a reason for asking to see me."

"Alas," began Nathaniel, "a glib charmer like most Envoys, I am not. Someone who can say nothing while saying everything, that I am not."

"That's a pretty good start."

He shrugged. "I have come to talk about trade. And what Accord would like is clear. Clear it has been from the beginning. So why no one will talk is difficult to understand. All tariffs? Are they the question? Or trade policy? Perhaps the overall trade balance? I know not."

"Are we talking appearances or realities? Politics or economics?"

"I don't know your politics. From outside New Augusta how could anyone really know? And why on poor Accord does the Empire center? After seventy years of quiet, we are protested, instead of I Found It!, the Fuardian Conglomerate, Halston, or other independents.

"As for economics—we do produce a few micro-components for export, but by themselves why such a fuss they would create I cannot see."

"Really, Lord Whaler, dealing with the Empire is not that difficult."

"About that, you might ask the former Envoy from Haversol. His negotiations, they did not go well, and that precedent worries Accord."

"If you are that worried, why doesn't Accord merely accept whatever proposal the Empire has offered?"

"As I recall, dear Lady, the Empire has offered nothing. Nothing except the declaration that the present terms of trade most unsatisfactory are. So here we are, and I am here also."

"That puzzles me. You are a full Envoy. You have had lunch with a staffer of mine, then requested an appointment with me, prior to any substantive talks being started. Why not the Senator? Why not the government?''

"When requesting an appointment of the Senator, I was told it might be some time before he was free. Some time no one has, whether they know it or not. Also I have had some talks with the government, so far going to no destination.''

"Why are you here? Really here?"

"To see you." She was so intent he couldn't resist the jab.

"Lord Whaler, while I appreciate the flattery, you have not told me what you want, why you want it, and why I should help you, if indeed that help is what you want.''

Her sharpness brought Nathaniel up short. He looked at Courtney, evaluating what he saw.

The dark eyes, deep set under heavy black eyebrows and lashes, dominated a smooth white face and pale lips. The tightness of her skin and the fine lines radiating from the corners of her eyes emphasized the energy she contained. Her black hair, cut short well above the standard Imperial collar, showed silver streaks. Since standard cosmetology treatments allowed anyone to retain their natural hair color for life, either Courtney didn't care or hadn't had time for recent treatments.

"As you know," he went on, "Haversol refused to negotiate, and the result we all know. We would be willing to negotiate, within reason. Profession of willingness appears with the government, but no negotiation, only buildups of the Imperial fleets. While diplomacy has not been a strength of Accord, try it we would hope, even though some members of the House of Delegates are opposed. We judge that Senator Helmsworth might play a critical role, perhaps in creating momentum. You are the critical assistant to the Senator.''

The Ecolitan waited.

"Lord Whaler, one thing comes through clearly. You are racing against time. Why?"

"Dear Lady, perhaps I continue to underestimate you. You have said nothing, committed nothing, and demanded everything. For that, I must have underestimated your power."

"You do me far too much credit."

"Only that which you are due."

"Perhaps, also," she returned, "I have not been as courteous as I should have been, but on the surface there seemed to be no problem, and I hope you understand that right now, particularly with all the Parthanian Cloud questions, the ad valorem tax changes, and the Force Command tax proposal, things have been a bit hectic."

"I understand, but much lies beneath the surface. And everyone avoids what lies there."

"And just what do you mean by that?"

A frown creased Courtney's forehead.

"I doubt that the Empire wants another ecological war. While it would mean the end of Accord, history shows that the Empire as you know it could not survive another such conflict. Now, I'm not advocating anything, just pointing out that failure to reach an agreement could lead in that direction."

"What do you suggest?"

Rather than answer directly, he handed her one of the folders.

She looked it over, then laid it down.

"It appears rather generous on the surface. That means there's more to it than meets the eye."

"We can make concessions now that would be somewhat more difficult two years from now when the one-year Delegate selections take place. Economically, it doesn't make that much difference, but . . ." he dangled out the implication.

"You're implying the present political conditions on Accord will turn for the worse, from the Empire's point of view, after the next elections. Is that a fair assumption?"

"Obviously, any prediction of any election result more

than a year in the future is little more than a guess, but recently the Orthodoxist extremists have been making a comeback. The failure of the more moderate Normist majority to obtain a trade settlement might well increase the appeal of the Orthodoxist party."

"Isn't that blatant pressure?"

Nathaniel cleared his throat.

"Ms. Corwin-Smathers, it is obvious that talks we are approaching from totally different backgrounds. For you, trade with small systems can be pushed into the background. You view Accord as a fifth-rate out-system with no real right to question the almighty Empire, and with no real military options."

For the first time, Courtney leaned forward, as if she were interested.

"Let me assure you, madam, that while Accord would be the first to wish to avoid the use of military means, ecological or not, ethical or not, we have the means to prevent the Empire from making us another dependency. We will not be bullied, and we will not hesitate if pushed to the brink.

"The Empire has made such a mistake once. I sincerely hope, for all our sakes, you do not try again. We would prefer to negotiate, and we will, if anyone is willing."

He pointed to the folder she had laid carelessly across her console.

"Those are the facts as Accord sees them. If you feel otherwise, then I am certain you and the Senator will indeed let us know."

Nathaniel ended with nearly a military snap.

"Accord is fortunate to have you, Lord Whaler." She smiled coldly. "I wish you luck in all your contacts. I trust you will be as forthright with them as you have been with me. Who do you plan to see next?"

"The Ministry of Commerce. Then the Ministry of External Affairs."

"I assume you're seeing Marcella Ku-Smythe."

Courtney's statement was not a question but a declaration.

"Before I leave," Nathaniel added in a softer tone, "do you or your staff have any changes you would like Accord to consider?"

She shifted her weight. "It's not really up to us, you know. Ms. Ku-Smythe could endorse your terms, and the Commerce Ministry would approve her recommendations, if that's what you wanted."

"I would prefer your candid appraisal," responded the Ecolitan, backing away from the implications of Courtney's comments. "At the moment, we do not feel anyone should be excluded, since a consensus agreement would raise fewer objections. For example, if we had chosen to exclude you and the Senator, you could easily have suggested a long and drawn-out investigation and hearings that could block any agreement. Drawing things out would not help anyone, except the Federated Hegemony, Halston, the Fuards, or anyone else who was left to pick up the pieces.

"Your candid recommendations could ease the way for a more easily accepted settlement."

"Wait a moment," she commanded as she picked up the folder and rose from behind the console.

Nathaniel nodded, but as she left, let the stunner slip down from inside his wide cuffs to a point above his left wrist.

Courtney was on her way to contact Imperial Intelligence, the Noram microprocessors, or both.

While she was gone, with one eye on the portal, he studied the office in detail, from the Cereberium eternal clock to the real leather desk pad to the all-wooden desk and matched credenza. He also took the liberty of leaning forward slightly and memorizing the two private line numbers on the console.

Again, the nagging questions were piling up, but behind them was an obvious fundamental assumption, something so glaring he was overlooking it, something so common he couldn't see the swamp for the water. He knew it was there. He just couldn't put his finger on it.

It wasn't the arrangement of the office or Courtney Corwin-Smathers herself, as arrogant as she seemed to be.

Courtney was absent fifteen standard minutes. By the end of the fifteenth minute, Nathaniel was ready to leave.

She returned with a smile.

"I was able to reach the Senator, and the general terms of your proposal, provided the facts are as we think they are, will probably be acceptable to the Senator and the External Relations Committee as a sound beginning point. The staff will have to work out more specifics, but by tomorrow I should have a better idea. Can you give me a fax then?"

"That should be no problem. Do you have any objections to my giving the same information to Commerce?"

"Why should I? We're poor innocent bystanders as far as Commerce is concerned."

Nathaniel rose to his feet and gave Courtney a half bow.

"I appreciate your candor and your willingness to work toward a mutually acceptable agreement."

"Lord Whaler, you have been most forthright and very gallant under what I know must be very trying circumstances. Appearances in and among the various bureaus and Ministries can indeed be complicated and deceiving."

That was the second double message.

"I'm learning that." He laughed as he turned toward the portal, keeping an eye on Courtney.

"I hope we'll have a chance to talk again before long."

"Sure hope you'll come to see us again, Lord Whaler," chimed in Charles, the receptionist, who brushed against Nathaniel as he returned to his console just as Nathaniel was trying to get past.

For some reason, the Ecolitan felt on edge, the same way he had during jump training or when he'd been in the Trezenian Police Action, the time he'd avoided leading his patrol into ambush.

This is the Empire, he told himself, not the outback of Trezenia. Out of habit, he checked the people in the corridor as he left the Senator's office.

Only a handful were in the throughway to the drop shaft.

Dropping quickly into the high speed section, he plummeted toward the concourse level where the tunnels cross connected.

The drop shafts were one of the few things he enjoyed about New Augusta.

Swinging out onto the permatile of the bottom level, he looked for the flashing indicators of the tunnel cabs, rather than heading for the tube system. The tunnel trains reminded him too much of the Institute's fast troop carriers.

As he walked toward the tunnel cab dispatching point, which superficially resembled organized chaos with the cabs flicking in and out of wall tunnels in some sort of nearly random order as the passengers inserted their universal credit cards into the dispatch gate, he wondered how the system really worked.

The tunnel cabs worked—no doubt about it—but the intricate traffic patterns leading up to the dispatch stations seemed decorative rather than functional.

Nathaniel inserted the Legation credit card into the slot, punched in his proposed destination, the Ministry of Commerce, and waited.

A silver electrocougar glided out of the third portal and whispered to a stop directly in front of him.

The driver was a woman, dark hair severely cut, the Ecolitan noted as he bent and eased into the rear seat.

"Ministry of Commerce?"

"Right. Main Tower."

The electrocougar pulled away from the silver walls of the Senate Tower concourse and dropped into the cab tunnel.

Nathaniel looked at the back of the driver's head. From the back seat, he could see the high, dark brown collar of her tunic, so plain it almost resembled a uniform, and the squarish cut of her hair. She was nearly as big as he was, far bigger than any of the cab drivers he had seen so far.

Something was wrong. Of that he was convinced, and it was linked to the growing feeling he had overlooked something so incredibly basic that he and everyone else in New Augusta took it for granted, whatever "it" happened to be.

As the tunnel cab hummed through the frescoed tunnel toward the Ministry of Commerce, he tried to take stock, mentally ticking off the possibilities.

Both Marcella Ku-Smythe and Courtney Corwin-Smathers were more powerful than their titles would indicate. Everyone deferred to a limited degree to him as an Envoy, but no one seemed to expect much from him.

A small flashing light interrupted his reflections.

"Destination approaching. Please insert credit card."

He complied, and the dispenser promptly burped the card back into his hand. He slipped the square plasticard into his belt pouch.

Abruptly, the cab halted.

Already tense, Nathaniel flipped open the door and stepped out before realizing he was not in the concourse area of the Ministry of Commerce, but in the flat area outside the tunnel, a good hundred meters away from the brightly lit portal where other tunnel cabs were entering.

As quickly as he turned, the driver had been quicker and was pulling away before the cab door was fully closed.

The spot where he stood, datacase in hand, was lit sporadically, patches of light and shadow alternating.

A low scrape registered. He ducked and whirled, dropping the case and letting the combat training assert itself automatically. Without thinking, he kicked aside the force-blade, grabbed the other's arm, momentarily paralyzed the hand nerves with a grip above the elbow, snapped his left hand across the opponent's opposite wrist in time to send a small hand weapon skittering across the plastistone pavement.

He finished by sweeping the other's feet and leaving the would-be mugger in a heap. Only after the fact did he realize his assailant was a woman almost as tall and heavily muscled as he was.

He reached down and ripped the belt pouch from her jumpsuit, kicked her feet out from under her again, and flipped through the contents.

Miniature knife, tube stunner, Caesar notes, change . . . nothing.

"Any reason why I shouldn't break your leg on the spot?"

"Just like all men. If you're going to do it, do it. Otherwise don't talk about it."

Why hadn't he seen it? In this crazy Imperial society, the women held all the real power. Why hadn't he noticed?

He gritted his teeth, pulled the woman to her feet with his right hand, keeping his weight balanced and ready for any trickery. As soon as she had full weight on both feet, he let go of her hand and with a fluid kick-through shattered her left knee.

She collapsed without a sound.

Deciding that retreat was the better part of valor, he pulled the tube stunner from the attacker's pouch and turned it on the woman, who slumped back into a heap. He then wiped off all the items he had touched, replaced them in the belt pouch, and dropped it by her feet.

Shrugging and taking a deep breath, he picked up his discarded datacase and moved quickly toward the tunnel portal.

Was Courtney out to get him? Or had she been trying to warn him that the situation was beyond her control?

As he edged through the cab portal, narrowly avoiding a speeding tunnel cab whose small driver gaped at him open-mouthed, he wondered just how many people wanted him out of the way.

Several cab passengers stared at him as he vaulted over the barrier where they waited by the dispatch stations. Someone would doubtless report the incident, but, one way or another, his mission would be over before any investigation could be concluded.

. . . XXII . . .

The last thing Nathaniel wanted was to stay around long enough for some public-spirited citizen to link the unconscious woman in the tunnel with the character in black who vaulted the public barrier in the concourse. Not that the linkage wouldn't occur, but the later, the better.

Cowardice was the better part of valor, and he walked quickly toward the lift shaft.

With the time only 1200 local Imperial, he needed to kill some time before appearing on Marcella's doorstep. And he was hungry.

His stomach rumbled as he strode into the circular take-off area for the Commerce Tower lift shaft. He paused, turning his head to search for the directory. Surely, there had to be a directory for services in the tower.

He found it on the far side, flashing in muted maroon, the ever-present color of the Commerce Ministry.

Advertised on the directory were both a public foodomat and an official servarium. The public foodomat had the advantage of speed and relative anonymity. At the servarium, if he could use his official Accord credentials to get in, he'd have more time to think things over and a somewhat quieter atmosphere.

Acutely conscious that he was beginning to react to situations rather than controlling them, he decided on the servarium, listed as being on the forty-first level.

As he eased into the upward lift, he felt watched.

"Come on, Nathaniel," he muttered to himself, "you're getting paranoid."

He shifted his weight enough to turn his body.

Three quarters of a turn and ten levels later, he spotted the woman, rising in the slower outer lane. She was now wearing a light blue cloak, but the squarish face and dark severe haircut were the same. She had been the driver of the tunnel cab that had dropped him off outside the concourse.

"Don't they ever give up?"

Before he finished mumbling the question, he realized the stupidity of it. And the irony. Here he was, trying to get the Empire on edge, and already they were harassing him, trying to get him on edge.

One thing was becoming clearer and clearer. There were more players and higher stakes than Accord had anticipated. When he had a moment, if he ever had one again, that should be conveyed to the Prime.

For the time being, he had another problem. First, was whatever faction of the Empire trailing him going to be content with merely keeping tabs on him, or would they attempt another put-away action? Second, was the driver an attempt to divert his attention from a more immediate and closer danger?

He shifted his weight again, leaning to let himself slide into the highest speed central lane. Shifting lanes in mid-level was frowned upon but not forbidden.

With half an eye on the well-built woman driver, he began to study the others in the shaft both above and below him. A front tail was certainly possible.

Only a thin young man who was squirming into the high speed lane had showed any possible reaction to Nathaniel's shift.

As the Ecolitan passed the fiftieth level, he jumped onto

the high speed exit stage and trotted straight down the walkway toward the drop shaft on the other side.

Coming up on the drop side, he studied the drop lane, then jumped to the top of the side barrier, rather than walking all the way around to the entry point, and took a running dive down through the traffic.

"*Clang! Clang!* Danger! Danger! Unauthorized entry!" screeched the automatic warning devices, slowing the drop shaft speed momentarily.

Nathaniel let his momentum carry him to the far side of the shaft, reaching the exit stage and an upright position and the forty-first level all at the same time.

He saw neither the woman nor the nervous man.

The public fresher on the corridor to the official servarium served several purposes—letting him relieve himself, allowing him to catch his breath, and affording him some privacy while donning a thin gold film cloak to reduce the impact of his diplomatic blacks.

Before leaving the fresher stall, he took from his inside thigh pouch a small wooden tube, a smaller version of the dart gun he had used earlier but with the same type of dissolving needle darts that rendered the victim delirious within seconds and which dissolved within minutes.

The drug wore off within two or three hours but left the victims with scrambled memories and intermittent headaches for days.

If those tailing him were as persistent as he suspected, at least one would be waiting somewhere.

Both were—right outside the servarium and seemingly oblivious to each other.

The woman stood by the main entrance, visibly consulting her timestrap and pocket calendar as if to call attention to the fact that her friend, contact, or lover had been delayed.

The thin and nervous man, now wearing a rust cloak, sat on a public bench several meters away reading a faxtab. Neither had noticed him.

Since the servarium was close to the lift shaft, the
corridor was wide and foot traffic frequent—perhaps several people moving past the entrance every few seconds—but
the spaciousness of the ten-meter width and the high ceil-
ings reduced the visual impact of the numbers.

Nathaniel didn't hesitate. If the Empire wanted to play
hardblast, he'd oblige them. Placing his locked datacase
against the corridor wall, he slipped the tranquilizer tube,
good for two shots, one from each end, just so he could
trigger it without the action being obvious to others.

The way the woman was positioned, the Ecolitan should
be able to get within a meter or so before she would be
aware of him.

She saw him in the wide-angled mirror attached to the
calendar and twisted it in an effort to line up the long axis
of the calendar toward him.

Nathaniel dropped, triggering the tube with the facility
of long practice.

The needle caught her in the neck and began to dissolve.
At the same time, he was inside her guard and knocked
aside the pocket calendar and whatever weapon it concealed.

"You . . ." she muttered, as she began to shudder.
"Told me you were slick . . . devils! Get the devils!" Her
voice mounted to a shriek.

She began to convulse. Nathaniel knew the muscular
contractions were not exactly convulsions, but anyone not
versed in the depths of Coordinate military medicine would
not catch the differences soon.

Three or four passersby immediately gathered. A chime
in the corridor began ringing.

Nathaniel had already left the woman and had covered
half the distance to the bench and to the thin man.

The nervous Imperial agent was better than the woman
or took advantage of the slight warning he had. The glint
of metal as the angle of the faxtab held by the sitting man
shifted indicated he held something ready.

Nathaniel stretched his arm toward the man, triggering

the tube from three meters. On the range his accuracy was only about eighty percent. Here he needed one hundred percent.

The Imperial twitched as the needle whistled by his ear, losing his concentration momentarily. Long enough for Nathaniel to cover the last meter at full dash and knock aside the short barreled weapon with his right hand as it discharged. The Ecolitan felt the surge of nerve pain in his right shoulder but clamped down on his reactions.

Jabbing his left hand with force just short of crushing the larnyx, he silenced the bench sitter, who was trying to get to his feet. Despite the waves of pain radiating from his shoulder, he snapped three fingers of the man's right hand in forcing him to drop the nerve tangler.

A knee to the groin left the Imperial agent retching on the ground. After taking only seconds to snap another needle into the tube, Nathaniel fired it into the man's neck while bending down as if to help the poor unfortunate.

As the emergency medical unit, a low-slung silent cart, pulled up, he kicked the tangler under the bench and slid the faxtab over it.

"Here! Here!" he called.

A health officer and a medtech appeared.

"What happened?"

"I was walking up to get something to eat. This man started yelling. He threw down what he was reading, got sick, and went into convulsions."

"May I have your name, citizen?"

The new voice belonged to an Imperial Monitor, otherwise known as the Emperor's Police, who was dressed in a silver tunic with gold piping and brandished a computab, all with the bored look of all police in all eras.

"Not a citizen am I, but a visitor, and quite surprised, officer. I have an appointment up-level later, but I wanted to eat. This man goes crazy. Then somebody behind me yells and screams. I just don't understand. Now you want to know who I am. He's the one who started this business."

"I understand that, sir. But could I please have your name for the record? In case we need witnesses."

"Of course. Nathaniel Whaler."

"Whaler?"

"W-H-A-L-E R."

"I.D. number?"

"Don't have one. Diplomatic number." Nathaniel pulled out the diplomatic I.D. "A-C-O-3."

"Very sorry to bother you, Lord Whaler. Can we call you if we have further questions?"

"Certainly. I'll be back at the Legation after 1500."

By the time the few questions had been answered, the two Imperial agents, if that had indeed been their calling, had been carted off in small and silent corridor buggies.

Luckily, his datacase was where he had left it, apparently untouched.

Getting into the servarium wasn't nearly so hard as getting there had been.

"Do you allow diplomatic credentials?"

"Of course, sir. Of course."

Most of the clientele seemed to be mid-level junior bureaucrats. Two women to every man. Servarium was a fancy name for self-service off a compuchef, but the odds were that his food at least wouldn't ambush him.

Settling on an elaborate omelet and liftea, he gave the machine his credit card, took it back, and made a hornetline for a small corner table where he couldn't be approached from behind.

"You're getting paranoid again," he said to himself.

After a minute, he decided he needed to answer himself. "Just because you're paranoid doesn't mean that they aren't all out to get you."

He wasn't sure he believed himself, but he dug into the omelet anyway, which seemed half real, half synthetic, but filling all the same, and polished it off.

The lemony taste of the liftea relaxed him fractionally, just enough to lower his pain threshold and bring the throbbing in his shoulder back to his attention. He let his fingers run over the shoulder, but there was no exterior soreness, and the nerve twinges would probably pass within a few hours. So he hoped. Two shots to his right arm and shoulder area in a matter of days wasn't helpful.

If the nerve tangler had hit him full in the chest at that power, he'd have been the one carted off, with an emergency sheet over his face and the diagnosis of coronary arrest.

Checking his other shoulder and the rest of his blacks, he'd noticed a black bump on the fabric behind his upper arm almost impossible to see. He recognized the snooper instantly.

When had anyone touched him? Not Courtney. She'd kept her distance. The Imperial crowds were sparse and avoided each other. No one had come within body lengths.

Charles! The friendly receptionist had brushed him when he had left Courtney's office.

That was how he'd been tracked. The only question was for whom Charles worked.

He resisted the impulse to crush the bug on the spot. Instead, pretending to adjust his cloak, he worked it free and slipped it onto a scrap of plastic.

He studied the others eating in the servarium, listening while he looked, finally zeroing in on an obnoxious-sounding man who was complaining to his tablemate, another man, about the unvarnished ambition of his boss, a woman.

Nathaniel headed from his table toward the exit. Stumbling slightly as he passed the complainer and banging the datacase against the table, he brushed against the man and left the snoop affixed on his shoulder.

The stumble had gained him a momentary dirty look, but so intent was the man that he scarcely let up on his tirade. The switch would only deflect things for a few minutes, and he'd have to be even more on guard from now on.

Outside the servarium, in the same relative positions as

the previous team, were another man and woman, both consulting pocket "calendars" which presumably indicated that Nathaniel was still inside. Neither reacted as he passed.

Checking as he went, he could find no one tailing him as he took the lift shaft to the one hundred fourth level and to the office of Special Assistant Ku-Smythe.

The exit stage time readout indicated 1410 when he walked off and toward the directory. Marcella's office was down the branch corridor to the right.

Before he got close to her office, he ran into a security gate and a console with maroon clad guards sporting both blasters and stunners.

"Your business, citizen?"

"I'm not a citizen." He drew back the cloak to reveal his diplomatic blacks.

"Your business?" repeated the woman, not knowing or caring what the uniform meant.

"Nathaniel Whaler, Envoy of Accord. Fourteen-thirty appointment with Ms. Ku-Smythe."

"Your I.D."

The Ecolitan handed it over.

"One moment, Lord Whaler."

The guard tapped several keys on the console screen.

She seemed startled at the result.

"You're expected!"

"I knew that before you asked," he said flatly, knowing he was being snide, petty, and nasty, but tired of all the potshots, literal and verbal. "Room, 104 A-6?"

"Yes, sir."

"Thank you."

The gate opened. Hoisting his datacase, he went through. The gate buzzed loudly.

"Weapons, sir?"

"Just a stunner." He fished it out of his pouch and handed it to the guard.

"You can pick it up on the way out."

Ten to one, by the time he left it would have been

rebuilt with a complete snoop and trace system inside. He decided to "forget" to pick up the stunner. He also wished he could get rid of the datacase—the damned thing was always getting in the way. He was used to having both hands free. Room 104 A-6 was a small, functional reception area with two maroon pilot chairs, a table, indirect lighting, and a receptionist.

For the first time, it seemed, the receptionist was a woman, small, coming to his shoulder, with long black hair and brown eyes, olive skin, dressed in a maroon and cream tunic with matching maroon trousers.

"Lord Whaler?"

"The same."

"You are early, but Ms. Ku-Smythe will be with you shortly. Please have a seat. Would you like anything to drink?"

"No . . . but do you have the latest faxtab?"

"Standard, Ministry, or Court?"

"What's the difference between Ministry and Court?"

"Not much. They have the same columns and gossip."

"What do you recommend?"

"The Privy Council reads the Ministry edition."

"And the Court edition is mainly for socialites and appearances?"

The receptionist smiled, one of the first genuine smiles the Ecolitan had seen since he'd arrived in New Augusta . . . except perhaps for Sylvia.

"I'll take the Ministry edition."

She tapped several studs on her console, and with a series of buzzes, three pages burped forth, which she delivered to Nathaniel.

"There you are, Lord Whaler."

About half the faxtab consisted of factual briefs a paragraph or two long in relatively simple Panglais. Fifth Fleet dispatched to Sector Eight in support of the Sector Governor on Byron. Would Senator Rysler retire and turn over his Agriculture Committee to Ngnoma?

Failure of the synde bean crop on Ferne II and the need for Imperial aid. Possible breakdown of the Parthanian Cloud talks. Need for tax reform more urgent and might appear on the Emperor's Legislative Calendar for the new Senate. Repeal of the sex determination ban to be brought up again by the pro-choice faction.

Nathaniel skipped to the "personality" section or "Scandalous Sam."

Nothing mentioned about Accord or one Envoy Whaler. That was a relief after such bits as: ". . . should we tell you which Assistant Deputy Minister, after being seduced by his luscious receptionist (what a man!), asked his contract-mate for a dissolution?" Or ". . . it's rumored that the coronary arrest suffered by the Delegate from Greater Srik Nord wasn't."

"Lord Whaler?"

"Yes?"

"Ms. Ku-Smythe will see you now. Through the portal on the left."

He folded the faxtab, laid it on the table, slipped to his feet, picked up his datacase, and strode through the left portal.

The office, with cream wall hangings and a sweeping panoramic window, was three times the size of either his own office as Envoy or that of Courtney Corwin-Smathers.

Marcella was attired in a formal cream tunic and matching trousers, with a set of gold Commerce pins on her collars. A single maroon ring circled each tunic cuff. Her hair was upswept, severe, and she stood behind her wraparound console, formally, not advancing to meet him.

The console, at the far end of the office, allowed Marcella to survey both entry portals and the window.

He bowed and could feel the portal shut behind him.

"Greetings again, Nathaniel."

"Greetings to you, Marcella."

She gestured to the padded antique leather wing chair across from her console. He wondered at the real age of the chair with the new maroon leather, but sat down with the datacase at his feet.

"How's the business of Commerce with the Special Assistant?"

"As well as can be expected. What about you?"

He hesitated. Should he tell Marcella anything?

He let his face show some indecision.

"Not terribly well received somewhere, is that it?"

"More complicated than that. I'm not sure where to begin, and beginning at the beginning would take much time."

He pulled at his chin. "This business is getting more involved than I'd anticipated, and did I not think I would have any illusions about the degree of difficulty."

Marcella sat back in the swivel, waiting, seemingly ready to let him take his time to get to the point. He doubted she had that much patience. But she was capable and a good actress to boot.

"Yesterday, Courtney Corwin-Smathers suggested I come by today to discuss Senator Helmsworth's interests in trade negotiations. I arrived at the appointed time, was warmly greeted, explained our interests in arriving at a favorable settlement without antagonizing any of the parties involved, and left her a copy of our preliminary proposal."

He thought Marcella's eyes narrowed slightly, but went on.

"Rather politely, and oh-so-pointedly, Ms. Corwin-Smathers suggested that while I certainly could let the Ministry of Commerce see such a proposal, I would be well advised to put my faith in the Senator."

"Did she put it exactly that way?"

Marcella leaned forward in her swivel, brushing a strand of sandy hair back over her ear.

Nathaniel chuckled. "Are you serious? Let me see if I can recapture the essence of the conversation. I am not much on innuendos, you know, but try I will."

He composed his face into a stern mask.

"I do wish you luck with your contacts . . . we're

regarded as poor innocent bystanders . . . and Commerce could certainly ratify your agreement if that is *really* what you want . . . Ms. Ku-Smythe would surely be pleased not to deal with other influences . . ."

"She mentioned my name?"

"As I recall."

"Did you say you were coming to see me?"

"No. I made a point of being vague about my appointments, but she seemed to know I had an appointment with you. And that leads on to the next thing, which was even stranger."

"Stranger?"

"I took a tunnel cab over here from the Senate Office Tower and was dumped out in the tunnel outside the concourse—"

"Outside the concourse?"

"Outside the concourse. With a stunner, a woman strange to me tried to attack me. The tunnel cab took flight."

"Obviously, you survived."

Nathaniel shrugged and spread his hands. "Some luck, I think. But left I in a hurry. So why should someone be after me? If Senator Helmsworth wanted one set of terms . . . if you another . . . and External Affairs another . . . but before anyone has said anything? This it would seem would mean that someone wants no talks."

Marcella frowned. "I'm not sure I understand."

"Why would you have me assaulted? I would think you would want to see what Accord had to offer. Is that not so?"

"That's true. It wouldn't make sense, not from my point of view."

"That implies that more than one point of view there is within the Commerce Ministry."

Marcella looked straight at him.

"I have this feeling you've been underestimated, Lord Whaler. I'll try not to make the same mistake."

"Lucky I have been, so far." He leaned back in the

leather chair. "Secondary to something else are questions of trade, and to some facet of Imperial politics not immediately obvious to outsiders." The Ecolitan bent down and lifted the datacase into his lap.

"Imperial politics do become somewhat involuted," added Marcella, "and could be rather confusing to an outsider."

Nathaniel didn't like Marcella being patronizing any more than he had Courtney Corwin-Smathers, but he only opened the datacase and pulled out a trade folder before closing the case and returning it to the floor. He stood abruptly and leaned toward her, watching her hands flick down toward the edge of the console. Ignoring the danger, he read the private line numbers and memorized them.

So . . . the console had a full protective system, and dear Marcella didn't trust him all that much.

"Here's the folder with our proposal," he said as he extended it slowly. "I'm sure you can handle far better than I the intricacies of Imperial politics. After you study it, I would be most interested in your thoughts."

"After we study it, I'll be happy to talk with you."

"You know, Marcella, you can trust me or not. But if you really need a console protective system, the controls ought to be in the arms of the swivel."

He bowed to her. "Your leave, Marcella?"

He could see the play of emotions under her tightly controlled face. No secrets there at the moment. He'd gotten to her, and she wasn't pleased about it.

"You do me honor, Lord Whaler."

"The honor is mine, and outside the questions of diplomacy."

She flushed ever so slightly at the compliment, but so quickly he almost missed her reaction.

He gave a mental shrug as he walked out through the portal, case in hand, to the reception area.

"Lord Whaler?"

He looked at the receptionist.

"Did you leave anything at the security gate?"

"I do not believe so."

"Ms. Ku-Smythe arranged for your return transportation in one of our tunnel vehicles to spare you the rush period congestion. I am to escort you."

"Indebted I am."

The small woman led him through a corridor vaguely familiar. He caught a glance of a receiving hall, and the memory jibed. This was the hall he'd come up to meet Rotoller and Marcella.

They stopped in front of the small lift/drop shaft.

"Now where?" he asked.

"We'll go down to the Commerce official concourse."

"Indeed a step up over the public transport," he commented inanely.

While several guards patrolled the corridor, none seemed to take notice of either Nathaniel or the receptionist.

She stepped into the shaft, assuming that he would follow.

He did.

As he exited, the receptionist handed him a small flat envelope.

"I think you dropped this in the shaft. It floated past me."

Nathaniel hadn't.

"Thank you. I was careless."

He surveyed the guards around the concourse, both men and women, as they walked to the embarking platform.

An electrocougar was waiting.

The receptionist stayed until he was inside with the door closed.

The car was upholstered in maroon, but the fabric was less yielding than that in the official car that had brought him to his meeting with Rotoller.

The male driver was in a plain maroon tunic.

As the car pulled away, the receptionist waved before she turned. No one had done that before, not on Terra. He turned the envelope over.

The heavy cream paper was without name or address, except for three intertwined initials on the reverse flap, and was barely sealed . . . just at the tip of the flap. The three initials were MKS.

Before opening the envelope, Nathaniel looked up at the back of the driver's head as the limousine dropped down into the tunnel. Nothing he could tell.

Holding the envelope gingerly, feeling stupid about his qualms, he used his belt knife to flick it open. He turned the envelope, and a small card fluttered out onto the seat cushion.

A single word appeared on the blank card, handwritten: *CAREFULLY*.

He resealed the envelope and card and put them in his belt pouch.

The writing might be Marcella's, but since he'd never seen it, how would he know?

And for Cloud's sake, what specifically was he supposed to be careful about? He was already too cautious.

The more he found out, the more he didn't know.

. . . XXIII . . .

Alert to the possibility of another tunnel cab incident, Nathaniel spent the ride back to the Diplomatic Tower fully ready for anything. The Commerce Ministry electro-cougar delivered him to the Diplomatic Tower without mishap.

"Your destination, sir."

"My thanks."

Despite all his suspicions, he made it up the lift shaft and to the Legation's front entrance without an obvious tail, and without anyone else attempting to take any pot-shots at him.

"Good afternoon, Lord Whaler. Were your meetings successful?" asked Heather as he walked past.

"Everything went as expected."

He didn't recall telling anyone he had a single meeting, let alone two. He sighed audibly. In New Augusta, if more than one person knew a secret, it wasn't a secret.

"Greetings, Lord Whaler," added Mydra, as he paused outside his office.

"Any calls for me?"

"No. Things are relatively quiet here. Have you seen the faxnews?"

"Too busy have I been. Why?"

"I wondered if anyone else from Accord was in New Augusta. The afternoon casts reported a strange man in black assaulted an Imperial Intelligence agent in a tunnel, broke her leg, stunned her, and escaped. The Imperial Intelligence Service is denying the report. No one has seen anyone in black in the area."

Mydra was giving him a calculated look.

"You know, Mydra, after days like today, sometimes one would wish to be more violent. But professors, we are not known as such. Today I have talked to too many who say, 'Maybe yes. Maybe no. Let us think about it.' "

He went on. "I do not think I should like to meet such an Imperial Intelligence agent. I hear most competent they are."

"I'm glad to hear that, Lord Whaler. After the report hit the fax, I called a friend of mine. She's an office manager at I.I.S. I asked her about it. She couldn't say much, but the agent who was allegedly attacked was one of the best. The next time they go after that fellow, they'll go with lethal weapons, I understand."

"Most interesting. Does this happen often here?"

"I don't believe I've ever heard of another case."

The Ecolitan shrugged and entered his office.

The room had been searched, thoroughly, and more than once. Items were fractionally out of place, and the datacase on the table had been moved. He scanned the case with the belt multitector. A rather large mass was inside, doubtless something unpleasant and explosive.

Sergel had left his report in the in-tray, and Nathaniel swept it up as he walked back to the portal and began to scan the office.

Two new full-scale snoops showed, one right above the console and the other almost over his head, plus a fluctuating energy concentration right between the two.

He'd seen the pattern before.

Not waiting to see the needle peg off the scale, he dove out the doorway and into the main office.

"Down! Hit the floor!"

The first explosion cut off his words, and then the gimmicked datacase followed with a roar, the second explosion bulging the wall outward.

As Nathaniel picked himself up, he ran a quick sweep of the staff office. Three standard snoops, period.

He hadn't been back in the Legation for more than ten minutes, and he'd been delivered three messages—two explosive ones and a veiled threat through Mydra.

Was Mydra working for the Imperial Intelligence Service or someone else? Was the I.I.S. telling him they didn't care what he knew? Was the military behind Sergel . . . and the bomb he'd planted?

Mere trade negotiations couldn't be that explosive, could they?

"Lord Whaler! What happened?" demanded Hillary West-Coven, her left arm bleeding from a long scratch.

"Fortunes of trade, Hillary. Fortunes of trade."

Mydra was standing at the door from the hallway to the staff office. How much coincidence had her temporary absence been?

Nathaniel almost shook his head.

"Mydra, my office has been somewhat damaged, and to my quarters I will repair. Would you arrange for the necessary repairs?"

He marched out, going straight through his shattered office and into his private quarters.

Once inside, he swept the rooms for snoops, but found only a single additional visual. He used his tool kit to disable it.

After that, he turned up the background music and used the private comm.

"Ms. Du-Plessis' office."

"Lord Whaler, Accord Legation. Is she in?"

"I don't know, sir. I believe she is in conference."

"Find her. That is, if she expects either to retain her position or to have some trade talks with Accord."

An ivory-skinned, black-haired woman of the indeterminate age range that had characterized Courtney Corwin-Smathers appeared on the screen.

"Lord Whaler, aren't you overly free with the positions of the Ministry and their disposition?"

"Ms. Du-Plessis, the situation is deteriorating and called for drastic measures."

"Oh?"

"Madam, Accord, you, and I are running out of time for reasons unclear to me. I do not have time to fence with words, nor words to fence with. How many times have you tried to reach me, and what were you told?"

"Five or six, at least, and I was told you were behind in returning your calls. I told . . . I mean . . . Lord Jansen also called and received the same response, which was most puzzling."

"I can see that it would be, considering I'm here to talk with you and Lord Jansen. Where is your office? External Affairs Tower?"

Janis Du-Plessis nodded.

"What room?" snapped the Ecolitan.

"Uh . . . room 203, C-4."

"I'll meet you there as soon as I can get there."

"But—"

"Madam, you will be there."

"I don't understand, and I don't like orders from outsiders."

"Ms. Du-Plessis, I do not think you want to understand. Or you are putting me on. I have been on this Imperial planet less than one standard month. During the past two days, there have been two attempts on my life. Before that, an assassin almost needled me on the day I arrived. A bomb just destroyed my office with me almost inside it. And you don't understand.

"All my calls to you have been rerouted, and you

indicate that yours to me have been blocked. Now . . . do you understand my urgency?''

"I find this rather difficult to believe."

"Then let me explain it again . . . in person."

Nathaniel broke the connection and checked his belongings. So far as he could tell, nothing had been tampered with.

He picked up Sergel's report again and folded it inside his tunic. Still he hadn't had time to read it.

He left the datacase in the study, only pulling out the remaining trade terms file. No more lugging around unnecessary baggage when all the warnings had been laid out.

The private comm line buzzed. He debated answering, finally jabbed the Accept stud.

"Whaler."

The face on the other end, filling his screen, was that of Sylvia Ferro-Maine, slate gray eyes, dark hair and all. She was not smiling.

"Lord Whaler, since your office line is strangely out of order, I thought I might be able to reach you here."

"Yes. My office line is out of order. As a matter of fact, Sylvia, my entire office is out of order. An explosion of rather large dimensions has rendered it nonfunctional."

"You're all right?" Her tone was perfectly even, as if she were asking about the weather.

"Fortunately, I seem to be together." He paused. "And to what do I owe this call?"

"I had only wanted to let you know that you made quite an impression on Ms. Corwin-Smathers, and that she will be taking up the matter with the Senator shortly."

He repressed a sigh.

"Glad am I that such an impression was created. Unfortunately, such impressions seem to be spreading, since the explosion within my office was not of an unplanned nature."

"Given those circumstances, Lord Whaler, you are indeed fortunate."

The Ecolitan did not respond immediately, just looked

back at the woman. She could be anything—the staff aide she said she was, an intelligence agent, the brains behind Courtney, or the representative of yet another party.

Today, she wore a formal dark blue tunic with a high collar that set off her high cheekbones and delicate features, and added an elfin edge to her image. He could almost smell the scent of oranges.

He shook his head.

"You seem most doubtful, Lord Whaler."

"More to everything on New Augusta is there than meets the eye." He smiled. "But I appreciate your interest, your concern, and your news, and hoping I soon will see you am I."

"I would hope that matters would work that way, Lord Whaler, but those determinations are over my head and with you and the powers that be."

Sylvia's control relaxed enough for a faint smile to escape onto the screen before it went blank.

The Ecolitan shook his head again, more violently.

Something more than trade was riding on the trade talks, at least for the Imperial players. The question was what.

He stood and looked down at the console, then turned away and checked himself. Dart tube and darts, belt fully charged, file folder on the trade talks . . . he was as ready as he could be under the circumstances.

He let the private portal to the corridor edge open, half-expecting to see the Diplomatic Police, an Imperial Monitor, or the Imperial Marines. With none of the agents of Imperial authority present, he marched out and down to the drop shaft and into the high speed descent lane. He had decided on a tunnel train, much as he disliked them, because there was less chance of either the Imperials tracking him closely or waylaying him.

"Still paranoid," he muttered as he waited in the concourse for the train.

Finding it hard to believe that it was still afternoon, he checked the time. 1550. Things were moving, probably too fast, and he wasn't having much of a chance to think them over. Neither were the other players, but they didn't have to. They just had to eliminate one Nathaniel Firstborne Whaler.

No obvious snoops or tails were planted on him, but after the day's events, they would be the best and virtually invisible, and he certainly didn't have the time to check out every speck of dust after every time someone got close to him.

Nathaniel had been trained for war—guerilla, conventional, and total—not for espionage. He felt more and more out of his element with each new addition to the cloak-and-dagger routine.

The tunnel train hissed up to the platform. The Ecolitan took a single seat in a row between the two doors. When the train had left the Diplomatic Concourse, half filled with what seemed to be Imperial supplied staffers to various Legations, he pulled out Sergel's report and began to read.

After the first quick skim, from what he could tell, at least three groups were involved. Sergel claimed he had been contacted by Sylvia Ferro-Maine's direct superior, Alia Herl-Tyre, because of the interest of the External Relations Committee of the Imperial Senate. Alia claimed that the Ministry of Commerce might act unilaterally on the Accord question and cut out the External Relations Committee . . . and the Senate. A Commerce agreement was not a treaty and did not require Senate approval.

According to Sergel, Ferro-Maine had previously been attached to the Imperial Intelligence Service. The I.I.S. was not under the control of the Emperor, but reported to the Senate directly. More precisely, to the staff of the Majority Leader, the Elected Consul. The separation was designed as a check on the powers of the Emperor and on the military branch.

At the first stop, the Ministry of Ecology, the Ecolitan took a quick look around the train. A few more junior bureaucrats climbed aboard, but the majority of passengers kept staring into space or reading folded faxtabs.

Sergel claimed he had not received anything for the routine information he provided to Alia and Sylvia, but did so to open up a "two-way communications flow."

Nathaniel didn't believe it. Sergel was about to get sent on a one way trip to Accord, provided Nathaniel survived the next few days to do the scheduling.

Courtney had hinted that there were two aspects to everything, and Marcella had told him to be careful. Both conversations would indicate that neither of those obviously powerful women were totally in control of the situation.

He shook his head. Despite his recognition of the female control angle of Imperial society, he still didn't have enough information. He doubted that Janis Du-Plessis would have any answers or be willing to share them, but he needed to complete the first round and to ensure all the players were fully involved.

The train hissed to a second stop—Ministry of Defense— where several nonuniformed types marched aboard with a bearing that contradicted their civilian attire.

For an Imperial capital, Nathaniel hadn't seen much evidence of the military, outside of the ceremonial Imperial Marine guards and the scattering of military types in the Emperor's throne room, receiving hall, whatever it was, when he had presented his credentials.

For an Empire with ten major fleets, and Forest Lord knew how many strike forces, it seemed odd that none of the military had surfaced directly on the trade questions. And odder still that so many indirect leads seemed to point to the scarcely visible Ministry of Defense.

The third train stop was the Ministry of External Affairs. A handful of passengers left with Nathaniel—a white-bearded man in a russet cloak, a pregnant woman in a ministry tunic he did not recognize, two youngsters in glittertights, and a man and a woman who appeared to be tourists from Sacrast, from the sticker on the carrying case the woman shouldered.

Nathaniel outpaced the lot to the lift shaft and took the high speed center lane to the two hundred and third level.

The Security Gate was just beyond the exit stage portal.

"It's after hours, citizen," announced the guard.

"I know. Nathaniel Whaler, Envoy from Accord. I have an appointment with Ms. Du-Plessis."

"They don't give appointments after 1530, citizen."

"I'm not a citizen, and I do have an appointment."

"I'm, sorry, citizen, but I'm not allowed to admit anyone. Orders, you know."

The Ecolitan studied the guard. Male, mid-aged, sagging slightly in the midsection, armed with both stunner and blaster, lounging back in the chair.

Nathaniel leaned forward so that he was half over the console, eyeing the layout.

"Quite a control board you have here," he observed, noting the open channel and input plates. The guard began to sit up and lean forward.

"What would happen if I," asked Nathaniel, as he reached over and tapped out Janis Du-Plessis' number, "called Ms. Du-Plessis to see if she were still here?"

The guard grabbed for the stunner. Nathaniel half vaulted, half circled the console and pinned the security man's arms in place.

"Why don't we just wait and see if she answers?" he asked as the guard began to struggle.

The screen unblanked and displayed the features of Janis Du-Plessis.

"Guard, what's going on?"

"This citizen—"

Nathaniel let go of the man with one arm, keyed the screen, then used his forearm to choke off the guard's response.

"I apologize for the direct approach, but this guard was

interpreting his orders so literally I found it impossible even to announce my arrival.''

The guard broke one arm free and grabbed for the laser blaster.

Regarding that as a uniquely unfriendly move, Nathaniel shifted his hands, caught the nerves behind the man's elbow and twisted.

"Yiii!" The laser skidded from the guard's limp fingers across the permatile.

The Ecolitan observed the surprise on Janis' face as she saw the weapon.

"Perhaps," gasped Nathaniel as he half lifted, half turned the guard from the chair and slammed a stiffened hand into his opponent's solar plexus, "I'm being over-dramatic, but I do believe that either you or someone else doesn't want me to see you."

"Not me . . . not—"

"Fine. Are you in room C-4?"

"Yes."

"I'll meet you there."

"What about the guard?"

"He'll be fine . . . at least for now," commented Nathaniel, looking down at the slumped figure. He hadn't hit the man *that* hard. "Now, would you send whatever signal is necessary to open the gate?"

"Oh, of course."

The gate opened. Nathaniel broke the screen connection, yanked the semiconscious guard out of the chair, hoisted him over his shoulder, and marched through the gate. It buzzed but shut behind him anyway.

C-4 was less than fifty meters away, but the guard's weight had the Ecolitan breathing heavier than he would have liked by the time he got there.

Janis Du-Plessis was waiting, open-handed, as he marched up.

Without a word, Nathaniel dumped the guard into one of the chairs. By now the man was nearly alert.

"I apologize, madam, but I need to ask this gentleman a question or two. While I do, you might want to study this folder, which someone doesn't want me to deliver to you."

He pulled the folder from under his tunic.

"I also apologize for its slightly bent condition, but I feared I might need two hands on the way over, and, unfortunately, I was correct."

She stood there, black hair slightly mussed, in her rust and tan tunic, as if she did not believe the spectacle of an Accord diplomat having to fight his way through her own guard for the sake of one thin file.

"I find this whole . . . episode . . . rather disgusting."

"So do I, madam. So do I, but apparently these trade talks have been escalated to a level beyond mere diplomacy."

He turned his full attention to the guard.

"All right, time for a few answers."

"Can't," protested the man.

"Who told you not to let me in?"

The guard just smiled. Nathaniel reached down and grabbed the nerves at the back of his neck, applying pressure. The sensation should have been acutely unpleasant.

"Who told you . . ." The Ecolitan stopped. The man was unconscious.

He shook his head and reached for the guard's belt stunner. Pulling it from the holster, he set it on mid-range.

"Strumm!"

"What happened? Why did you do that?"

"He's been pain conditioned. Any attempt to get information from him through tiredness, torture, pain, and he'll immediately black out. There are ways around it, but not without time or special equipment. It's very effective for this sort of thing."

He centered his attention on the Special Assistant to the Minister of External Affairs.

"Do you know most of the guards? Is he someone new?"

"I don't pay that much attention, but I don't recall seeing him before." ·

Nathaniel looked up to make sure the portal to the corridor was still closed.

Janis Du-Plessis had once been pretty. With her ivory complexion and long black hair, she was still attractive, but her cheekbones and nose weren't prominent enough for her to retain her prettiness as she grew older, despite the cosmetology of the Empire.

"Ms. Du-Plessis, as you may have noticed, my safe time in any one location appears to be limited."

"Why don't we go into my office?"

Nathaniel dragged the man in with him, laid him out by the doorway.

The woman was standing by her console, as if waiting for him to finish.

"Lord Whaler, I would appreciate some background. You place calls to me and to Minister Jansen but won't accept the return calls. All of a sudden, you claim it isn't your fault, give me some outlandish story about two attempts on your life, and insist on disrupting my private life in order to personally deliver what seems to be a quite routine set of terms for a trade agreement. It seems so reasonable on the surface that everything else seems totally unreasonable."

Nathaniel nodded, hoping she would go on.

"I decided to cancel my evening and see what would happen, but I certainly didn't plan on you attacking one of my guards, dragging him in here, questioning him, and having me cover up for you!"

"Madam, I don't expect you to cover up anything. I came to New Augusta assuming we had a mutual economic problem which could be solved. I have been assaulted twice, not counting the attempt by your guard to incinerate me when he failed to stop me from getting through to you. My calls to you—and I have called several times—have apparently not gotten through. In return, your calls to me were blocked when I was in my office waiting for them.

"Just this afternoon, someone successfully bombed my office. Fortunately, I was walking out the door at the time, but there were *two* explosions. Either someone, or several parties, is taking a great deal of explosives to warn me to depart, or they merely want to eliminate me. I care for neither possibility."

The hard expression on Janis' face softened.

"I can understand your concerns, but I don't understand why all . . . this . . . violence . . . is involved with a simple trade matter."

"I was hoping you could tell me. The Ministry of Commerce is interested. The Imperial Senate is interested, and for all I know, so are those planting the bombs."

"The Ministry of Commerce?" she snapped. "They don't have any business in trade terms with independent systems outside the Empire."

The pieces came together with a click.

"I think they're interested in the impact changes in the trade terms will have on Imperial commerce. What about the Senate?"

"That's got to be Courtney again, always wanting the last word on everything before the terms are even considered. I can take care of that." The fire in her eyes indicated she intended to try.

"I think you have everything in hand," he offered, rising from the pilot chair.

"Lord Whaler, you still haven't told me why your entrance had to be so violent."

"I don't know. One reason might be that the Commerce Ministry has no confidence in the process and would like different terms. That's one guess. But it is only a guess."

He frowned.

"Is there any way you could register our proposal in

your records, so that it could not be erased? Even if anything happened to you?''

''Are you suggesting something?''

''No. But I wasn't attacked for nothing, and you just told me that you did not know the guard who attacked me.''

''I see what you mean. If the effort was to cut us out, we really don't have it until it's in the data banks under seal. Certainly, registering it couldn't hurt and might well reduce the . . . uh . . . unpleasantness.''

She sat down at the console again, rapidly touching keys, placing the proposal facedown across the screen in order.

A soft chime sounded.

''We're done. Locked in and sealed.''

Nathaniel bowed.

''You have been gracious at a time when few have been and more helpful than you can possibly imagine.''

''You do me honor.'' She flushed, color momentarily replacing the flat ivory of her skin.

''No more than is your due.''

A long moment passed before the Ecolitan cleared his throat.

''We still need to deal with some leftover unpleasantness. I suggest two things. First, that you escort me to your private drop shaft. That way I can get to the tunnel train level without going through the main concourse. Second, that you return here and find the guard lying in the middle of the office. You will, of course, be most upset and call Imperial security.''

''I was coming back and found him?''

''Exactly. He'll be out for several hours. He can't possibly explain what happened without being probed. So he'll have to invent some excuse, which will say he was investigating something when he was stunned, and he doesn't know what happened.''

Nathaniel dragged the man into the middle of the reception area while Janis locked her console and office.

The rust and tan corridors to the private drop shaft of the senior staff and Ministers were deserted, the lights at half level.

"This doesn't go down to the tunnel train level, just to the Ministry vehicle concourse, you know." She touched the drop plate.

"Can I get to the trains?"

"Yes, but you'd have to walk back through the tower and another gate to catch the public shaft."

"Hmmm . . ." He pulled at his chin.

"Why don't I just send you back in a Ministry pool car?"

"That would be appreciated."

He couldn't see Janis doing him in, not when she had nothing to gain.

The electrocougar from the Ministry of External Affairs seemed identical to the one he had ridden in from the Commerce Ministry, with the same plasticloth hard seats, except for the colors of the car and the driver's uniform.

His driver was a petite black girl, perhaps the youngest driver he'd had.

He watched Janis standing at the dispatch point as the electrocougar whispered into the tunnel.

"Isn't she too old for you?"

The question jarred him.

"Oh . . . I suppose so . . . if it were personal."

"Business this late? You're an outworlder. You're used to working longer."

"How about you?"

"Way to get credits after classes. Besides, after-hours drivers usually just sit. Good time to study. Where you from?"

He wondered if she worked for someone. It didn't matter.

"Accord."

"Should have known from the black. Don't always

apply what you learn when you see it in real life. You don't look like you poison planets.''

"I never have. We haven't done anything that severe in centuries.''

"How come you're here?''

"Trade talks.''

"How come that's not in the faxtabs or casts? That ought to be big news.'' She grinned impishly, and Nathaniel caught it in the reflection from the front bubble. "Planet poisoners here to talk trade.''

She dropped the grin. "Guess that's unfair. Professor Ji-Kerns says we've done worse to some systems, but he's a man.''

Nathaniel ignored the slam to his sex.

"What are you studying?''

"Second year in law. Out-space legal systems. We haven't gotten to Accord yet. Working on Halston.''

"Why did you pick law?''

"Mother, she's the head of tactics at the Ministry of Defense, wanted me to go to Saskan, but I didn't like all the rules. Rather make them.''

"Saskan?''

"You know, that's the Imperial Space Academy where all the Fleet officers are trained.''

"I suppose she, your mother, I mean, doesn't like your doing this?''

"She doesn't mind. If I wasn't meant for the Eagles, I wasn't meant. This way, I can pretty much pay my own way. That's important. Lots of youngers don't, just collect basic and snerch. Guys are the worst, always talking about being Ministers, as if the Ministers ever did anything. Who does the work? You and me.''

Nathaniel nodded, although he didn't think she was really looking for a response.

"Bet you work for a fancy-pants Envoy. Here you are working, and he's probably luxing it up. First man I've seen working so late since I took the job, and you're an outworlder. Figures.''

She shook her head.

Nathaniel didn't bother to correct her misimpression. ''I wouldn't be surprised if anything and everything went on here. Or is it just boring because nothing happens after hours?''

''Pretty dull. Wouldn't dare to talk to any woman, and I don't rate standby for a Minister or Deputy. All of them sit and stare, or sit and read. Not like Perky. She's got the same job at Commerce. I got the idea from her, that is, driving after classes. She's Class I now, even got Lord Mersen last week.

''Told me the other day she drove three Fleet Commanders back from Defense to Commerce. Nothing like that happens here.''

The car slipped out of the tunnel.

''Want the public or private concourse?''

''Wherever I'm less likely to get noticed.''

''Public side, this time of day. Still crowded. Be like a tomb on the private side.'' A pause followed. ''What are you worried about?''

Nathaniel couldn't help laughing. The girl was one of the first real people, without a mask, that he'd talked to.

''Tell you when I get out.''

''Here you are.''

''Thanks for the ride.''

As he climbed out of the backseat, she poked her head through the top opening in the front bubble.

''You forgot to tell me.''

''I'm the Envoy, and someone keeps trying to assassinate me.''

Her mouth dropped open.

''Not everyone wants those trade talks.''

It was probably unfair to leave it at that, thought Nathaniel as he ducked away and into a public fresher stall on the concourse level.

With the belt detector he went over his clothes thoroughly for tracers or snoops. One minute speck on his collar registered, but it could have retained static charges. Otherwise he seemed clean.

He put on the rust film cloak over his blacks and left the fresher.

A woman talking to another woman on the far side of the corridor looked up as he passed, then looked back at the closing door to the fresher. She began fiddling with her pocket calendar, but centered her attention on the fresher, totally disregarding Nathaniel.

He took the lift shaft to the corridor for the private entrance to the Envoy's quarters. Under the cover of the cloak, he checked the entrance as he approached. The snoops had been replaced, of course, but they were standard. No energy links to the portal showed.

. . . XXIV . . .

Once inside, as he folded the cloak and surveyed the apartment, he swept the area again. The disabled visual snoop had not yet been replaced.

He marched into the study and eyed the comm unit.

With a sigh, he sank into the all too plush swivel and thumbed for the directory, keying up some background music at the same time. While whoever had links to the comm unit would know what he was asking, perhaps some of the other players wouldn't get all the information yet.

He tapped out the number for the Diplomatic Reference Library, assuming that it was either automated or operated around the clock. It was both.

"State your interest area."

"Interstellar law."

"Choose from among the following . . ."

The gist of the answer to his long question was that the Ministry of External Affairs had jurisdiction over trade and treaty matters involving nonempire systems.

"Query: authority of the Ministry of Commerce to enforce trade agreements within the Empire . . ."

The Commerce Ministry could request the Imperial Fleet to apply sanctions.

"Query: does an agreement between a former Empire system and the Ministry of Commerce constitute a legal basis for resumption of Imperial Jurisdiction?"

According to the library computer, there were precedents on both sides.

Nathaniel pulled at his chin, looked down at the screen. "Query . . ." What else could he ask? He signed off.

Leaning back in the swivel, he gazed out the window. Sunset would be coming soon, and for the moment he was going to watch it. Maybe think while he watched it, but watch it he would.

A few high and thin clouds dotted the sky, deep blue as he saw it through the panoramic window, and yellow white of the sun was turning golden as it dipped toward the tree-covered hills on the western horizon.

He'd seen the holos of the blighted forests created by the Secession, and the Terran casualty figures in the billions as the result of the ensuing starvation.

He'd also seen the slag that had been Haversol City and holos of the asteroid belt that had been Sligo before the Empire pulverized it.

Both sides were people, people like the girl who had driven him, people like Sylvia, like Marcella, even people like Janis Du-Plessis, who set in motion the bureaucracies that created the violence that appalled them.

The high flare of a shuttle in the distance over the port winked like an evening star early in the sky and was gone.

The shadows over the hills lengthened, and the lights in the other towers glowed stronger, and the sun dropped. He supposed he should finish what was necessary, what he could.

Some could wait until morning; some could not.

Seen in perspective, the whole thing was obvious. The Secession itself had created a terrible convulsion for the Empire. Fifty odd systems ripping themselves away, using the Accord grievances as an umbrella for a myriad of reasons, denying the government that had helped them stand alone.

In the beginning, the Empire had hesitated to use maximum force, planet busters, because of the closeness of the ties. It's hard to murder your cousin because he wants to stand alone, and the internal political outcry that had risen after the First Fleet had busted Sligo had rendered that option unusable.

Four hundred years later, no one thought in those terms. Accord's allies had gone their own way, some to their own small empires, big enough to give the old Empire pause. And Accord was considered Outie, an outland system. Relations were minimal, sometimes nonexistent, and the question of attacking "relatives" was moot. Twelve generations of Imperial schoolchildren had been raised with horror stories about Accord.

If the Empire decided to use force, no public outcry would be raised, and Accord could count on few allies. In return, the Institute could send out the death ships, and if everyone was lucky, perhaps ten percent of the population of a thousand systems might survive.

The Accord House of Delegates ignored the enormous growth in the massive destruct weaponry of the Empire. The Empire was totally ignorant of the potential biological and ecological disasters created by the Institute and already dispersed to where not even total destruction of the Accord Coordinate systems could stop the rain of lingering death.

From what he'd seen, neither side would believe the other's power, although Accord had acknowledged the Empire's fleets somewhat.

So what could he do?

He turned to the console and punched out the office number of Courtney Corwin-Smathers, leaving his own screen blank.

"Courtney here. What's wrong with your visual?"

"Whaler here. Call off the dogs, Courtney. You've made your point. The preliminary terms have been registered officially with External Affairs, and you'll have to coordinate with Janis Du-Plessis, but I think you can handle that.

"The other thing you should know is that Defense is also playing. We don't need that, and neither do you."

"Oh . . . ?"

"I still will have to stay around, making polite speech after polite speech, and committing Accord to nothing until you get your ions flared. Or do you have a better suggestion?"

"Your prudence is commendable, if belated, but Ms. Ku-Smythe might request a quiet elimination if the I.I.S. or the Ministry of Defense haven't already done so."

"That's a chance I'll have to take."

He tapped the stud and cut the connection.

His next call went to Marcella's direct office line. He got a recording with a smiling face.

"I am out at the moment. If you would leave a message, I will return your screen when I return."

"Whaler here. The Ministry of Defense has decided to shove Commerce directly out of the picture by eliminating me. You might also be interested to learn Alia Herl-Tyre paid off some of my Legation staff to stall you. At the same time, Defense exploded my office and removed one of my staffers. External Affairs thinks you played them for nulls."

Again leaving his own screen blank, he tapped out Sergel's private number, and got another recording requesting a message.

"Sergel. You'd better be gone tomorrow, or on your way, or have a damned good story. The External Relations staff knows you played them false, and the Ministry of Defense knows you failed."

He tapped out another number, with a blank screen. He didn't have a private number, but the External Relations Committee number for Alia Herl-Tyre. Another recording.

"Ms. Herl-Tyre. My name is Nathaniel Whaler, and we

haven't met. Sergel Weintre used to work for the Legation, until he claimed that you were paying him to spy on us, and we discovered that he was also being paid by the Ministry of Defense to spy on you as well as us.

"Under the circumstances, thought you'd be interested."

With a sigh, he leaned back and touched the wide belt, running his fingers along the side, splitting the layers and removing a thin flimsy.

The code system was crude, but unbreakable without either the flimsy, which would last for less than a standard hour after he touched it, or the Prime's personal diary, of which there was one copy. The system was one way, but that didn't matter.

After the ten minutes it took him to code what he needed, he picked up the draft and opened the door from his private quarters to his office. The walls to the staff office still were jagged and bulged in places, although the steel portal door remained untouched.

He palmed the plate, and the portal irised open. The deserted staff section had the lighting at half bright. He slipped behind Mydra's console, congratulating himself on his professional ease until he barked his knees as he pulled the chair up to the console.

The first job was to send the message to the Prime.

He accessed the direct comm line, feeling the charges ring higher and higher as the message ran out.

He hoped it would get there, and since the Legation was paying for the direct shot, it had a chance.

He staggered out from behind Mydra's console and back to his own office.

The next step would be trying to break the media blackout on the talks, which he suspected was due to their dull sound, rather than any conspiracy. After all, what self-respecting faxcaster in the capital of the Empire was interested in tariff and exchange terms negotiations between the Empire and a former colony, particularly when the Ministry involved hadn't told anyone and when the others didn't want anyone to know?

From the New Augusta directory, he got the numbers for Galactafax and Faxstellar.

"Greetings. I am the Accord Trade Envoy, Nathaniel Whaler. And a statement to make on the bombing of our Legation I have."

"The what?" asked the duty faxer at Galactafax.

"The bombing of our Legation by forces opposing the talks on trade—"

"Hold it! Hold it! Let me catch it all on flux. First, who are you? For the record?"

"Envoy Nathaniel Whaler, Acting Legate and Trade Envoy for the Legation of Accord."

He paused and cleared his throat.

"This very afternoon, my office was bombed. Two devices. Bystanders, several were hurt. Good faith we came in, but the Imperial Senate and Imperial Ministries respond not, but question who has jurisdiction. No one pays attention."

"Hang on there, Lord Whaler. Let me see if I have this straight. You were invited here for trade talks. The Imperial Senate and the Ministries are arguing over jurisdiction, and this afternoon your Legation was bombed, and people were injured. Is that the idea?"

"Essentially correct, that is. Diplomatic Police come, say they will look. Nothing happens."

"You mentioned a jurisdiction problem . . ."

"External Affairs should have control, but has done nothing. Commerce Ministry presses for answers but has no jurisdiction. Most confusing. Senate External Relations Committee staff is also interested, and Senator Helmsworth and the S.I.I. are involved somehow, I am told."

The Ecolitan wondered if he were carrying it all too far, but the young man on the other end was drinking it all in.

"The S.I.I. . . . S.I.I.? You mean the I.I.S., the Imperial Intelligence Service?

"That is what I understand."

"Lord Whaler, where can we reach you?"

"At the Accord Legation is where."

He gave the office and the private line, not wanting Mydra blocking the calls if the faxers waited until morning.

He repeated the process with the young woman who answered for Faxstellar. Her reaction was much the same.

Within twenty minutes, a distinguished-looking woman from Galactafax had gotten back to Nathaniel.

"Marjoy Far-Nova, Lord Whaler. I've seen the tape of your announcement, but I wondered if you could possibly supply a few more details for us about the trade talks and any possible connection this might have with the bombing."

"Connection I know not. Here I am, poor Envoy, wanting to ease relations with Empire. Here am I, empowered by my government to reduce some tariffs and eliminate others. But for this, right after we circulate proposals, my office is bombed. The situation is strange, but whom should I tell?"

"Let me get this down. After you circulated your trade proposals, your office was bombed. At the same time, no one in the Empire seems willing to act except those who you think should not be involved. Is that it?"

Nathaniel could only shrug and gesture to the bulging wall to his right.

Shortly thereafter, he went through a similar performance with the call back from Faxstellar, declining to speculate beyond the facts.

Once again, he headed to the deserted staff office and Mydra's console, this time not banging his knees as he sat down.

He set it for a voice scrambled tape and began to speak.

"To Scandalous Sam, the Gossip Man of New Augusta . . . Have you heard about the awful runaround they're giving that poor Envoy from Accord? They bombed his office, not once, but twice. And none of the Ministries will talk. His staff has been profiteered . . . and you should listen in on the snoop network, like Sylvia, Marcella, Alia, Courtney, and a few others do. One even we dare not name. His calls are blocked by his own staff. Call him, and they tell you he's behind in returning his screens. He doesn't know it yet. More to follow . . .''

Nathaniel wound it up and sent it off into the local faxdelivery.

A similar set of faxes went to other sources, as well as a scholarly letter under his own name to the pure print media.

That done, he closed down Mydra's console, trying to leave it exactly as he found it.

He was hungry, and officially and unofficially, all he had to do for a while was wait and play dumb.

He locked the portal into his private quarters and headed for the hygienarium, where he stripped and took a steaming fresher. He dressed slowly, choosing a dress green outfit and a rich, matching green cloak.

According to the belt multitector, the clothes weren't snooped or tagged, but the snoops outside his private entrance were fully functioning.

After a quick walk to the lift shaft, he took the slow outside lane all fifty levels up to the Legate's private dining rooms.

The head waiter was ready, this time.

"Lord Whaler . . . a pleasure to see you. Table in the main dining room or the portico?"

"The portico, if you please."

Through the wide expanse of unbroken permaglass he could see the shadows of the towers, their lights like beacons, and the dark outlines of the hills beyond. He was seated at a table for two at one end of the windowside tables.

Not much on the silver printed menu appealed to him, but he finally settled on the scampig with a salad, and liftea.

The liftea arrived immediately. Either he looked tired or

the staff had been briefed on the fact that liftea came first on Accord, not last.

He sipped the tea, watched the lights glitter, took in the occasional shuttle flare in the evening sky.

"I beg your pardon." The man's voice was lightly accented Panglais. Nathaniel pegged the speaker as Frankan.

He looked up to see a man standing by the table.

The Ecolitan rose, half bowing.

"At your service," he responded in Frankan.

"You honor me," replied the other diplomat in his own tongue. "Not many would immediately recognize my background or make the effort. But none of the formal nonsense. May I introduce myself?" He presented a diplomatic I.D. and miniature credentials identifying himself as Gerard De Vylerion, Legate of Frank. "Gerard De Vylerion, soon to be returning to Wryere."

Nathaniel sat and gestured to the seat across from him.

"Nathaniel Whaler, Envoy from Accord and acting Legate," he continued in Frankan.

"You do know Frankan. I must confess I knew who you were. After this afternoon, everyone wanted to talk to you, but your Legation indicated you were out of touch."

Nathaniel motioned for De Vylerion to go on.

"I've been here five standard years, full tour, and I've never heard of violence against a Legation. There aren't even any records. What did you do? Was it an accident?"

"Accident? No, I doubt it was an accident. I was leaving my office when they exploded. Two, one right after the other. We informed the Diplomatic Police, who came and went."

Nathaniel shrugged. "Nothing so mysterious was happening. We circulated preliminary proposals, and I felt that everyone who was interested should be informed. I did not want to say much about the explosions until I had a chance to think."

"I could not be that calm," answered the Frankan Legate, sipping from the glass he had brought with him.

"I waited to see if there were any reaction. But I will wait only so long."

"And?"

"I finally told the faxcasters. Was that how you found out?"

"No. My staff told me of an explosion on the three hundredth level, and I asked a friend of a friend. He told me an accident had occurred in the Accord Legation."

"No. Not an accident. Someone does not like what I am doing. Someone does not want, apparently, a peaceful trade treaty."

"Lord Whaler—a friend of mine, Lord Naguti, from Orknarli, is also interested." The Frankan gestured to his larger table where two others, a man and a woman, sat. "We could join you, but . . ."

"Alas, I see my table is too small."

The Ecolitan got up, beckoned to the waiter. As the man approached, he turned to De Vylerion, "Have you eaten?"

"Yes, but we would be honored. Have the waiter serve you at our table."

Probably a breach of etiquette, thought Nathaniel, but the chance to spread a little distrust of the Empire was too much to resist.

"Tables I will be changing," he told the waiter in Panglais, "and there would I like to be served."

The waiter nodded and retreated to his post.

The other two stood as the Ecolitan approached.

"Lord Naguti, acting Legate from Orknarli, and Lady Persis-Dyann. This is Lord Whaler, Envoy from Accord."

"I speak no Orknarlian," Nathaniel explained in Panglais, "but more fluent am I in Frankan, Old American, or Fuardian."

"We all understand Frankan," clipped Lady Persis-Dyann, who seemed too young and too sharp-featured to be an Imperial Lady.

"Then I will continue in Frankan," observed Nathaniel, switching languages with relief.

"It is a pleasure to meet you, Lady Persis-Dyann, and you, Lord Naguti, although under somewhat surprising circumstances."

"Lord Whaler has just informed me," added De Vylerion smoothly, "that not only was his Legation bombed, but that no one seemed terribly interested. He called the faxcasters himself."

"Oh?" asked the Lady.

"Most interesting," mused Lord Naguti.

Nathaniel took a sip of his tea.

"I'm puzzled," he began slowly. "I arrived thinking progress would be slow but steady and that a trade agreement could be worked out. It's not that big a problem. It deals with certain microtronics. But nothing happened. So I requested audiences and began direct contacts. Remember, the Empire requested us to come. I was perhaps too aggressive. Yesterday, it begins to appear someone does not want a treaty. Today, there is an explosion in my office."

He looked around the table. Naguti was nodding. Persis-Dyann seemed bored, and De Vylerion wore an expression of mild interest. He stopped and waited.

"If the treaty's so minor, why would anyone want to stall it?" asked Persis-Dyann.

"My thoughts exactly," answered Nathaniel. "That leads to an interesting point. Haversol came to New Augusta to negotiate and had the same trouble. Now . . . the similarity I cannot prove, but . . ."

Naguti nodded again.

"You men all talk in mysteries," observed the Lady.

"Not so mysterious, Lady Dyann," responded Naguti. "The Imperial Fleet attacked and reduced Haversol because Haversol refused to negotiate with the Empire. If what Lord Whaler says is true, negotiations were stalled by the Empire to give the impression of Haversolian recalcitrance and to give the Empire the option of using force."

"And because it was veiled in semilegality, the Federated Hegemony, the Accord Coordinate''—and there the Frankan De Vylerion inclined his head toward Nathaniel—''the Fuardian Conglomerate, and the other independent systems chose not to make an issue of a minor planet like Haversol.''

''That is true,'' added Nathaniel, leaning back from the table as the waiter delivered his roast scampig. ''Another disturbing thought occurs. Haversol was a minor system, and no one protested. Not even Accord, I admit, at least not beyond a simple protest. But Accord is not, shall I put it bluntly, the most admired of the smaller multisystem governments. And so, if the Empire creates a technicality on which to base the use of force against Accord, who will protest?''

Nathaniel cut into the roast scampig, wrinkling his nose as the steam escaped.

''Isn't that basing a lot on assumptions?'' cut in the Lady.

Nathaniel wondered which Ministry had bought her. Despite her sharp nose and piercing eyes, she was attractive and had a nice figure beneath the gold-trimmed brown tunic.

''Assumptions, yes,'' he continued after swallowing, ''but could you explain why there have been two attempts on my life, including exploding my office, and bribes to my staff?''

''Bribes to your staff?'' Naguti asked.

''A minor official, but I caught him and actually got a written confession that an Imperial Ministry was paying him to spy. Not unusual, I would guess, although since the Empire supplies most of my staff, I would question why they would need to approach him.''

''What do you think, Neri?'' De Vylerion asked.

''I think we may all have a problem. While I earnestly hope that the incidents which had befallen Accord and Lord Whaler are merely isolated coincidences, I have grave doubts that they are. You know, don't you, that the Fifth

Fleet was dispatched yesterday to reinforce the Sector Governor on our borders?''

Gerard took another sip from his near empty glass. Even Persis-Dyann was silent. Nathaniel took advantage of the lull to finish the scampig and salad.

''I regret my story has depressed you. Perhaps the lady is right. Certainly, there is no hard proof.''

''In our business, Whaler,'' said Gerard softly, ''and since you're still young, you may not always remember it, motivation and past actions are more important than scraps of proof. Hard proof often arrives just before the warheads.''

''Our debt, Lord Whaler,'' offered Naguti, rising, ''but I must be heading back to my Legation. May I escort you, Lady Dyann?''

''So far as our paths coincide.''

Nathaniel struggled to his feet as the pair left.

''Very nicely done, Whaler, but do you believe it?'' asked the Frankan as soon as they were alone.

''I've made it a bit more clear-cut than it really is, but, in essence, it's all true. True, but complicated, and the stakes are far higher.''

''I can guess why. Perhaps we are all fortunate Accord sent you and not another.'' He rose. ''I, too, must leave, but I appreciate your candor.''

The portico was nearly empty by then, with only two other tables occupied. The Ecolitan caught the eye of the waiter.

''All right is it if I return to my first table?''

''Yes, sir.''

''A Taxan brandy, please, and clear water.''

He sat down and stared out through the permaglass, watching the shuttle flares and the stars, so much thicker here than in the skies of the Rift planets, where an arm of blackness clove the center of the night heavens.

The brandy arrived, but he ignored it, still drawing in the stars.

It was like operating in a vacuum. Little or no feedback. Lord of the Forests! He didn't know whether he'd touched the people he'd met or whether everything he did was blocked just outside his ability to observe.

Perhaps the faxcasts or the morning faxtabs would show something. If they didn't, he wasn't sure what other studs he could press, what other people he could try to manipulate.

Destruction was easy. It was the refraining from destruction that was hard.

He picked up the brandy and watched the stars till past midnight.

He was cold sober and holding an almost full glass of Taxan brandy when he stood again. Every other table besides his was set in morning gold. His was still in evening silver.

As he strode back to the drop shaft and fifty levels down, he wondered, idly, whether he would find anyone waiting by or inside his door—whether an assailant or a Lady.

Finding neither Sergel nor Sylvia, or their like, he locked up and slipped into the large bed alone, and into sleep.

. . . XXV . . .

Nathaniel woke early, and gratefully, out of a nightmare where Imperial battlecruisers fractured planets and where Ecolitans on black wings sowed death down the Milky Way, turning the stars dark as they stepped from sun to sun.

A hot fresher helped begin to burn away the depression, as did the cup of liftea which followed from the tiny kitchen.

He had not been standing in the shambles of the Envoy's office, dressed in a set of crisp blacks he'd never worn before, for more than a few minutes before Hillary West-Coven scurried in from the front desk.

"Sir . . . Lord Whaler, there are two fax crews outside, and they say you personally called them. Ms. Da-Vios isn't here yet." Her tone conveyed that he was personally responsible for some catastrophe and that Mydra could have avoided it had she been present.

"Why, I did call them. Let them in, so fax the damage to our Legation they can. Talk with them I even will."

"Yes, sir. You *will* talk with them?"

"If they desire such."

"But . . . but . . ." Seeing Nathaniel's broad smile, she capitulated. "Yes, sir."

Nathaniel left his console to place himself firmly in front of the damage. The three women and one man who represented the media walked in. The two well-groomed women, with the hand-held directional cones and belt paks, were the commentators. The other two wore shoulder mounted fax units.

"You're Lord Whaler?" demanded the smaller of the two interviewers, who was dressed in a silver jumpsuit that flattered her slender figure and dark hair.

"Lord Whaler, I am." He beamed.

"Fine. Please stand over there out of the first shots while we get a panover of the damage. Marse, start at the right and sweep up toward that hole."

"Check-shot. Canning, two, three, and go."

The other interviewer nodded to her faxer, who followed the same pattern.

The once-over of the damage was followed with detailed close-ups of the two blast areas.

Nathaniel stood at one side, feeling somewhat neglected.

"Ms. West-Coven," asked the smaller interviewer, "can you tell us what happened?"

"One instant we were working. The next there was an explosion, and Lord Whaler came flying from his portal there. I remember seeing him standing there just before the blast, and I guess he was lucky. He was walking out when it happened."

"That was his office?"

"Yes."

Nathaniel cleared his throat, but no one was paying any attention. Both faxers were training their units on Hillary.

"How did it happen?"

For the first time, Hillary looked bewildered. "You'd better ask the Envoy."

"Lord Whaler. Stand right there."

The Ecolitan complied meekly. The media commentators were more peremptory than the bureaucrats.

"Do you know why the Legation was bombed?"

"Someone does not want the trade treaty. When I first arrived, attacked was I. Now comes the bomb."

"Isn't that stretching things?"

"Aren't you being overdramatic?"

Nathaniel shrugged as expressively as he could and pointed to the blast-torn wall. "That. That is not dramatic?"

The faxers were off Nathaniel.

The smaller commentator wound the segment up.

"That's the story at the Accord Legation. Trade talks, an explosion following an attempted assassination. Frian Su-Ryener for Galactafax at the Accord Legation."

The taller woman positioned herself by the worse section of the bulging wall and smiled.

"For the second time in as many days, violence in New Augusta. Yesterday, the I.I.S. refused to comment on why a fully armed agent was assaulted here in the capital. Last night, this explosion, and an Envoy who wears the diplomatic blacks. The rumored assailant of the I.I.S. agent also was reported to wear black.

"Now we learn that trade talks with the Empire are involved, and the Envoy involved has already been attacked once before. Why? Whatever it is, it's sparked the first bombing in New Augusta in three decades. This is Kyra Bar-Twyla for Faxstellar."

"Is that right about the I.I.S.?" Hillary asked.

"Worse than that," interrupted the other commentator, "if you believe the rumors. Defense had five agents in the area, and three don't know what happened and two are now walking nuts."

"No confirmation," clipped the taller one, "no story."

They both nodded to their faxers, and the four left as quickly and abruptly as they had arrived.

"What did they mean?" the Ecolitan asked Hillary.

"There's some rule by the Ministry of Communications. You have to have at least two witnesses to any rumor you fax, and three or two plus documentation if you present a fact and if it involves official Imperial business."

"You know that rule from where?"

Hillary was spared a response by the arrival of Mydra.

"Lord Whaler, do you think it was wise to let those . . . those . . . rumormongers in?"

"Wise, I know not. But what would they have said if I had said no?"

"You may have a point there, but sensationalism could affect the trade talks."

Nathaniel nodded politely and waited until the two were looking at him.

"Later, I think, we should talk. Right now, some communications I must make. Repairs, will they be made?"

Mydra retreated to her console without acknowledging the question.

The Ecolitan sat back down behind his own console and began to compose a faxletter for transmission to the Legations of the independent majors, the Federated Hegemony, and the Fuardian Conglomerate.

When it was completed, he buzzed Mydra.

"Yes, Lord Whaler?"

"In my console stored is a communication I need improved for transmission. As soon as possible in the formal way."

"I'll get right to it."

"See it I would like before you send it."

"Yes, sir."

As she was completing the text, he wandered out into the staff office and began to peer over her shoulder at the text screen. Much as he had suspected, the message bore little resemblance to what he had set out originally.

"Forgot you the part about Haversol."

"So I did. Do you think you should mention such an unpleasant incident so bluntly?"

"Find you a more politic way to express, and pleased I would be."

He waited as she revised the language.

"Need the part about the appearance of delay causing misunderstandings that could be avoided. Say it most politely, as you do."

Mydra nodded.

When it was completed, the faxtext from the acting Legate of Accord was a polite, understated account of the difficulties faced by one Nathaniel Whaler, with even politer implications about how precedents unfavorable to all non-Imperial systems could be set if current patterns continued.

It has to be good, thought Nathaniel. *Mydra doesn't like it a bit.*

"Show me, please, how it is sent."

Mydra touched several studs, and the dispatch plate turned red. She did not touch it.

Nathaniel bent over and tapped it.

"Do you not finish by this?" he asked naively.

"That's right, Lord Whaler."

He watched while she sent off the other twenty-three, knowing she was getting frustrated by the surveillance.

He retired to his console to authenticate the routine correspondence. The debris had been removed, but the repairs had not been started nor were any workers in evidence.

After running through the material, he decided to see if anything he had attempted to plant had showed up in the faxtabs. At the three buzzes from the console as it burped forth the faxtab, Mydra looked up sharply at him through the open portal. She seemed to relax as she saw him lean back in the big swivel and began to read.

The factual side of the news hadn't changed that much.

The First Minister of Orknarli protested the "maneuvers" of the Fifth Fleet. Repercussions of the synde bean shortage on Imperial trade balances. Ministry of Defense requests for greater funding. Prince Heuron dedicates H.M.S. *Gold Prince*, flagship of the newly dedicated Eleventh Fleet.

Scandalous Sam was at the end of the faxtab, and Nathaniel hesitated a moment before checking the gossip, not sure he wanted to see if any of the bait was there.

> Explosive news . . . should we tell you which diplomat had his office explode . . . after seeing a very special assistant . . . and yet he's so very hard to see . . . Which playboy of the court rolled his airchair over his chef? And don't forget . . .

Nathaniel let the flimsies drop. Unless the Imperials were onto every innuendo, Scandalous Sam's gossip needed a few more kicks to keep the interest in the Imperial treatment of Accord going.

At 1153, his private line buzzed, and out of the corner of his eye, he saw Mydra go bolt upright.

"Lord Whaler?"

"The same."

"Alexi Jansen, here, and my valued assistant for External Trade, Janis Du-Plessis. I understand there has been some confusion, some rather strange occurrences." Jansen was a big blond man with skin the color of leather, and he laughed as he finished the sentence.

"Of that, some," admitted Nathaniel.

"I do hope we can help."

"Our proposal submitted to Ms. Du-Plessis, and rapid consideration of those terms would be helpful." Nathaniel shrugged as dramatically as he could. "What can I say? Come for trade, get explosions. Come to talk, and . . ."

"Lord Whaler," commented Janis Du-Plessis, "we hope we can clear these up as soon as possible."

"Janis, here, told me about your visit. It seemed rather unusual, but she checked up on things, and that guard . . . he was wiped. Strange."

"Guard? Wiped? I had difficulties but did not understand the reasons."

Nathaniel shook himself and smiled into the screen. He went on, "Your courtesy I surely appreciate and look forward to hearing from you." The Ecolitan half bowed. Alexi Jansen bowed in return. "When we have finished an analysis of your proposal, Lord Whaler, we'll be back to you."

The screen images blanked.

Nathaniel cleared his throat loudly and thoroughly, stood away from the swivel, and strutted over to the open portal where he could peer down at Mydra.

"Mydra? Where is Sergel?"

"I don't know, Lord Whaler."

"He is supposed to be an Information Specialist, and never do I see him."

"I'll try to locate him, but I imagine he's quite busy at the moment."

"And busy doing what?" The Ecolitan turned and marched back to his swivel, clearing his throat again for effect.

He had decided he should be somewhat unreasonable, at least some of the time, and occasionally petty until he could see how things were shaking out.

Dropping himself into the swivel, the black and green swivel, with an audible thump, he twisted the chair to watch the low clouds swirl above the towers. At the angle he chose, he could keep an eye on Mydra without seeming to. The layout of the office had been designed to let her keep tabs on him, and the thought that he could reverse it gave him some small amusement as he saw Mydra keying things out using her console.

While he couldn't see the screen itself, she was faxing a number of individuals, from what he could tell.

At one point, her back stiffened, and he figured she'd been told something she hadn't expected. After that she made two or three more calls.

With a snapping movement that flipped out the back of her short black and tan tunic, she stood and entered his office.

Nathaniel returned his full attention to the storm clouds outside, watching the white-gray tops of the cumulus clouds race toward the patches of blue above.

"Lord Whaler?"

He swiveled back from his window view and put both feet on the floor directly behind his console.

"Yes, Mydra?"

"I can't seem to locate Mr. Weintre."

"Was he not in someone's custody the day before last?"

"You had him released."

"Fruit a little rotten can only get more rotten . . . it is hard to translate sayings into Panglais, but you understand?"

"A partly spoiled fruit can only rot? Is that what you meant? What does that have to do with Mr. Weintre?"

"Sergel has gotten rotten. First, a little trouble, now perhaps more trouble. Who guards troublemakers?"

"Here in the tower, the Diplomatic Police."

"Elsewhere?"

Nathaniel had a solid idea where Sergel was: in the hands of "specialists" at the Ministry of Defense who would be questioning him thoroughly, mind-probing him in depth. But the Ecolitan didn't want to voice that, just lead her along that track.

"The Imperial Monitors."

Nathaniel shrugged to indicate his ideas were exhausted and went on as if to change the subject. "All the difficulties we have, Mydra, and the Envoy from another system last night told me military people caused his problems. Is that possible?''

"Everyone likes to blame the Eagles, Lord Whaler, but they stay out of New Augusta for the most part.''

Nathaniel shrugged again. From the momentary gleam in her eyes, she'd gotten the thought he'd wanted to plant, the military aspect of Sergel's disappearance and the Legation's troubles.

"I understand. Force Command is strong on Accord, and I wondered if the military was also on New Augusta.''

Mydra gave him a smile that was equally warm and patronizing.

"The Empire's not quite like any place else in the galaxy, I suspect, Lord Whaler.''

"How true. Yet people are people.'' He looked out the window and leaned back again. "Not always do I say well what I think. Panglais is a lovely language but too flowery for a simple teacher of trade and economics. I came to New Augusta hoping people would see that agreement is possible always and that all lose when war comes.

"When the more powerful is stubborn, the small fight. Knowing they will lose, they fight, and before they perish, many would poison the water the victors would drink. Fighting is always so.''

Nathaniel looked at Mydra, efficient in her brown and tan.

"A scholar could express that better. The point is the same. Your Empire is . . . complex . . . many towers, many Ministries, many people, many battlecruisers, many troops. Accord is simple. Few people, few ships. The only defense we have is the power to destroy the ecologies of the galaxy, strewing death across the suns before we perish.''

He shrugged.

"Can I tell the Empire, with thousands of ships, that

little Accord can sow such vast death? Who believes? Can I tell our House of Delegates, who know they can sow such death, that the Empire does not believe? To prove our power, must millions die? And so, I sit and talk, sit and hope. Hope they have not forgotten.''

He looked blankly out the window.

The room was silent. The clouds swirled outside, and Nathaniel watched. Watched, hoping the snoops had gotten it all, hoping that Mydra had understood it all, and hoping that both thought he wasn't playing to the unseen audience.

"Lord Whaler," Mydra asked softly, "may I go?"

He nodded.

The waiting was the worst, whether it was waiting in the darkness of space, in a full-blanked needle-boat, knowing that another needle-boat waited, knowing that whoever moved first was dead, or whether it was lying flat in the jungle outback of Trezenia, listening for the slight change in pitch of the treehoppers' song to signify someone, something, was out there moving, or whether it was sitting behind a modernistic console waiting, debating whether to take stronger action, when too strong an action might unleash the disaster that needed to be contained.

He leaned further back in the swivel, half noting that the clouds were clearing, that the westernmost towers were glistening in the jacket of moisture lit by the noon sun.

The signs were there—the overt absence of military influence coupled with the continuing references to the "Eagles" and the large military bureaucracy; the gentle and total control of the population; the small stories about the use of the Fleets in pressuring out-systems; the dedication of the new flagship of the new Eleventh Fleet; the routine acceptance of the dispatch of the Fifth Fleet to intimidate Orknarli; and, of course, the example of Haversol.

The Imperials liked to play the diplomatic game as politely as possible, without overt violence, and using the threat of the immense force of the Empire as the major tool. The use of violence in New Augusta didn't fit, not unless Accord was a real threat to something being planned, not unless the conditioned fear of Accord ran deeper than he thought.

The intercom buzzed. He ignored it, trying to pin down the elusive angle of the bombings.

The intercom buzzed twice.

He wondered if Marcella had anything to do with the explosions. Why her warnings? Or Courtney's veiled references? And Sylvia . . . With that thought he wondered if he detected the faintest trace of orange blossoms in the office.

He shook his head.

His fingers headed for the console control studs as he swung back to face the bank of plates and lights. Finally, he touched the plates and tapped out the codes.

"Senator Helmsworth's office."

"Nathaniel Whaler for Sylvia Ferro-Maine."

"I'm sorry, Lord Whaler, but she and Ms. Corwin-Smathers are on the floor with the Senator."

Floor? Floor of what?

Charles caught the confusion on Nathaniel's face and flashed his professionally engaging smile at the Envoy.

"The floor of the Senate. The debate on the ad valorem tax changes has just begun." The receptionist paused. "Would you like to leave word that you called?"

"No . . . not right now. Thank you."

Nathaniel absently looked down at the console where the intercom plate still flashed.

Of course the lady was busy. Weren't they all? He shook his head again.

The intercom buzzed twice more, and this time he decided against ignoring it.

"Lord Whaler, the repair crews are here."

"Fine."

"They're likely to make a great deal of noise."

"Noise? Ah, yes, noise."

"Perhaps now would be a good time for you to eat?"

Nathaniel scratched his head, then nodded.

"Lunch, I suppose, I will have now."

He stood and looked out at the hills, now beginning to show a golden tinge. He wondered if the color shift were seasonal or merely the result of little rain.

. . . XXVI . . .

"He's a danger for two reasons."

"Two? The first is obvious. If he succeeds in getting that trade agreement, we lose the most favorable chance in generations to remove the Accord influence. But what's the second?"

Three officers sat in the small sound- and snoop-blanked room, and the special construction absorbed each word even before the next was uttered.

"His success fuels the myth of Accord's invincibility."

The third officer, a woman wearing the uniform of a Vice Admiral, frowned, tapped her fingers on the soft top of the table. "Can you honestly say that the average citizen knows, or cares, about whether Accord can hold us off? Who cares? When you get to that level of argument, it's a leadership discussion. The whole universe knows Accord is not an aggressive force. The more subtle danger is overlooked."

"Subtleties yet," snapped the First Fleet Commander. "How subtle is it that our traders are effectively blocked from the entire Rift? How subtle is it that fifty systems followed Accord into rebellion and still look to the black and green for leadership?"

The Rear Admiral shook her head. "For you, it's not subtle. But who in the Imperial Court really follows the trade flow on the Imperial borders? Who understands that Accord's example will leave us boxed on all borders? Or that stagnation is bound to follow? N'troya understands that. He should, since he's the Emperor, but he also claims that the use of force begets force, and that force will lead to the Empire's downfall."

"The Grand Admiral hasn't bought that."

"Not yet. That's the position her daughter is staking out at Commerce, and a successful trade treaty with Accord could bolster both the Emperor and young Ku-Smythe. Not incidentally, it would further strengthen Accord."

The Vice Commander spoke up.

"For generations, they've bluffed us, claiming their Institute could poison all the worlds of the Empire. It's just not possible, but everyone goes along with the blackmail bluff and nods."

The Rear Admiral looked at the two younger officers, the Fleet Commander and her Vice Commander.

"Bluff it might be, but if we get the go-ahead from the Grand Admiral, you'll have literally only standard hours in which to bake the entire system. Who knows what they have hidden on the outer planets, on asteroids, parked in orbit . . . "

"That can't be done, unless—"

"That's right. Even so, the nova front would take hours to get to the outer orbits, which means that you'd have to maintain a picket line until nearly the last minute."

Silence, deeper than before.

"But no one would ever challenge the Empire for generations . . . would they?"

. . . XXVII . . .

"Mydra, come with me."

"Lord Whaler, I couldn't."

"No?"

Mydra looked around the staff office as if for moral support, but Hillary had scurried out toward the front desk.

"I do have a great deal of work," she protested.

"Which can wait, can it not? Besides, the repair crews will make a great deal of noise, will they not?"

She almost smiled but managed to keep a straight face.

"Let me get my cloak."

He nodded, knowing she was surely going to do more than that, wondering whether the stops were for cosmetic touch-ups, snooper equipment, or to report to whomever she reported to, or all three.

Ten minutes later, she reappeared, wearing a deep brown cloak trimmed in cream, and with every dark brown hair in perfect place.

At the Legate's dining room, Nathaniel announced "the portico" and was rewarded with the same table he had had the night before.

"Have you dined here before?"

"Once or twice with Legate Witherspoon."

"A drink?" inquired the waiter.

Nathaniel inclined his head toward Mydra.

"Sperlin."

"Liftea."

"Do all Accordans like liftea?"

"A planetary vice it is, I fear." He gestured to the sweep of the windows and the towers. "Never would I tire of such a picture."

"I never do, either. You know. These are the only towers left on Terra."

"So was I told by someone."

"Tourists come from the underground cities all around the globe to see the views." There was an edge to her voice.

"They do?"

"The war with Accord, you know," she explained, "drove us underground. It's only been in the past century that any real aboveground excursions have been permitted."

"Not well liked are we, then?"

"I wouldn't say that, Lord Whaler, but Accord isn't the most popular system outside the Empire, either."

"That will affect trade talks, doubtless."

"It may, but that's your field, and I certainly wouldn't presume to guess."

The liftea and the white wine Mydra had ordered arrived with the menus.

As if to cover his confusion, Nathaniel immediately buried himself in the printed selections.

He'd already decided on a light salad after having checked his weight that morning. New Augusta was definitely too rich for Ecolitans, both in the complexity of the political systems and in the caloric content of the food.

He put down the menu and looked out the window, knowing as he did so that he was looking out windows far too much just in order to avoid talking.

"Lord Whaler?"

"Hmmm . . ."

"Earlier, you mentioned something about Accord and your worries. Are you still that worried?"

"Yes, Lady dear. Worried and a little tired. What can I do but wait? Terms have been suggested."

"I know that, but . . . "

The Ecolitan beckoned to the waiter.

"Yes, sir?"

Nathaniel waited for Mydra.

"I'll have the flamed shrimp, with the fruit salad."

"This salad here," added the Envoy as he pointed to the entree.

"Saying you were . . . " he prompted.

"I was wondering," she said slowly, "about what you said. You seemed so . . . weary . . . tired . . . and so sure that Accord and the Empire would end up destroying each other."

The Ecolitan let his shoulders sag slightly, then took a sip of the liftea.

"You know what I am. A professor of trade, an Ecolitan, and someone who is not a politician. Complicated diplomacy that seems separate from what I know to be true I have trouble with. A large Empire also needs many Ministries and people, but I understand not why they do not have the same purposes. But you have them and we, small system that we are, must deal as we can."

Mydra's right eyebrow twitched slightly.

As he paused, he could see the portico was beginning to fill with other diplomats and their guests.

"To us, we looked for simple negotiations. We proposed alternative terms—"

"I understand that, Lord Whaler. I do sympathize with the confusion which has occurred, and I suppose all Empires have problems with their bureaucracies, but that doesn't seem to be what bothers you. You seem almost haunted."

"Haunted?"

"Possessed. Bothered by an image of something terrible, as if the Empire were some ogre hanging over Accord."

"Did you not say that Accord was not liked? Should I not worry? Should we not worry? Should the people of Haversol not worry? Should the people of Orknarli not worry?"

He took another sip of his liftea.

Mydra followed his example and sipped her wine. He could sense the frustration she was feeling at his avoiding the real thrust of her question.

"You think I do not understand what you ask?" He shook his head. "I understand. Simple questions do not always have simple answers. Let me answer your questions with questions." He stopped to take another sip of the tea. "Is not the Empire more powerful now than before the Secession? Does not the Grand Admiral control more than ten fleets? Is not each of those fleets bigger than the entire Imperial Navy of the Secession time?" He waited.

"Yes. You said that already. You said that the Empire could destroy Accord. It was the other things you hinted at . . ."

"About the little people . . . about those who will not give in even though they would be destroyed?" He cleared his throat. "Accord did not win freedom with battlefleets, did we? Why does the Empire think we should turn to big ships and big fleets now? Why should we abandon our own ways of warfare? As the Empire has strengthened its weapons, would not poor Accord have done so as well?"

He shrugged, then finished in a lower tone. "Planets that cannot grow foods cannot support Empires. Any planet must support itself, except a very few, such as New Augusta. And to disrupt the balance necessary for such is not difficult for Accord, though the results would not be immediate. These weapons cannot be tested—not obviously—cannot be paraded through streets, cannot thunder through skies. Very quiet, and no one sees. The Emperor does not see the danger, nor does the Grand Admiral. And Accord does not understand that the Empire does not see. For me, it is dangerous even to hint at such, and dangerous not to.''

He forced a smile. ''We cannot dwell on this, but do our best to work it out.''

''Work out?'' stammered Mydra, her mind apparently fixed on the implications of what he'd said. ''You're not saying that Accord would literally wipe out life on hundreds of planets for better trade terms?''

''No. Accord does nothing first.'' He spaced his words firmly and deliberately. ''Remember. The Empire attacked Haversol over the terms of trade, not the other way. The Empire stalled trade talks, then used delay as an excuse. I see delay. I see me trying to get around that delay, and I see someone trying to kill me.''

He looked away from her and at the sunlit western hills. ''I have done what I can. You should enjoy the shrimp and the view.''

Nathaniel plunged into the salad which had been delivered during his monologue, discovering he was hungrier than he'd thought.

Mydra ate silently.

After he'd finished the salad down to the last morsel, including the bitter garnish, he straightened and studied the other tables.

The spacing became apparent. What amounted to a circle of empty tables surrounded his. Was he persona non grata, or did no one want to consort with the next victim of Imperial expansionism?

Even as he debated, a tall woman dressed in yellow stood up at one of the far tables and swiftly crossed the dining area toward him. A matriarch of Halston, he identified her, probably the Legate from her bearing and age.

He rose.

''Envoy Whaler? Berthea of Carthos.'' She spoke in Panglais.

With Mydra present, he decided against replying in Halstani.

"Your honor. May I present Ms. Mydra Da-Vios of the Legation staff?"

"My pleasure, and may I invite you both to join us?"

"Delighted we would be," Nathaniel answered quickly.

Three women, all attired in some shade of yellow trimmed with dark brown, and one man, dressed in a similar yellow tunic and trousers piped with the same dark brown, all came to their feet when Nathaniel, Mydra, and Berthea returned.

The women were Carin, Lynea, and Deirdre. The man, younger than Sergel, trimmer, blond, clean shaven, and regular featured, was Arthos.

Berthea wasted no time.

"Understand you're having trouble getting straight answers from the Empire."

The Ecolitan launched into his whole explanation, starting with his arrival, his meetings, and the ensuing strange events.

" . . . and I am waiting, hoping that the situation can be resolved."

All five of the Halstanians nodded.

"That's the story we'd heard, but I wanted to get it direct from you," snapped Berthea. "Sounds like a replay of the Haversol situation."

From the corner of his eye, Nathaniel could see Mydra sitting on the edge of her chair.

"Have you had any pressure from the Eagles?" asked Carin.

"Only that they sent a battlecruiser to escort me. Strange that none of the military have contacted the Legation."

"That fits," noted Berthea, gray eyes resting levelly on Mydra. "They stay in the background, just dispatch their fleets to do the talking. That Admiral Ku-Smythe, she's a cool one."

"Ku-Smythe? Special Assistant at Commerce, I thought."

"That's the daughter. Just as cold as the mother, I hear." That was Lynea's comment, who looked to be close to the same age as Marcella.

"Halston has had similar difficulties?"

"Not yet. We'd rather it didn't get that far. Orknarli's too close."

"Divide and conquer," chipped in Carin, who earned a frown from Berthea.

Nathaniel just nodded.

"For someone who's sitting on top of flamewasps, Lord Whaler, you seem rather detached."

"Not detached, just waiting, hoping that upon reflection the Empire will accept our very reasonable terms of trade."

"If they don't?"

"Then Accord will do what it must."

"I was afraid you'd say that," the tall Legate said softly.

Lynea flashed a puzzled look at her Legate.

"Check your histories, Lynea. Only fools, idiots, or men pick fights with the . . . with Accord."

The Ecolitan wondered how she had almost described Accord.

"My apologies, Ms. Da-Vios," added Berthea in a cold tone, inclining her head toward Mydra.

Nathaniel spread his hands in a gesture of appeal.

"In this, if you would convey our situation to any whom you think could be of value . . . " He let the sentence trail off.

"Will do. Understand your position. Probably would have to handle it in much the same way. Hope the Empire understands. Good luck."

Nathaniel understood as well and rose to his feet.

"Mydra, we need to return to the Legation."

Three strangers were working in his office when he returned. In the two plus hours since he and Mydra had been gone, plastic sheeting had been laid over virtually all the furniture and the carpeting. The workers were begin-

ning to cut out squares from the walls where the damage
had been the heaviest.

In passing through to his own private study, Nathaniel
saw enough to know the snooping equipment had been
replaced and improved.

Back in his quarters, he dropped into the smaller study
swivel and stared into space.

Finally, he turned to the screen on the comm unit and
began twisting through the public channels but only picked
up dramas, song and dance shows, music programs.

The fax channels had news somewhere. Was the two
position switch to the right of the selector for such a
distinction?

It was. The blue was for news and factual material, the
red for lighter fare.

After fifteen minutes of flipping back and forth, he
found one quick segment on the Accord–Empire situation.

A commentator in silver sat behind her console, green
eyes somehow enhanced, silver hair flashing, both professional and alluring at the same time, in a way that reminded him, distantly, of Marcella.

"Newest developments on the Accord trade talks."

Flash to a shot of the Accord seal on the Legation's
front portals, then to the tattered wall of Nathaniel's
office.

"Earlier today we showed you the bombing damage to
the Accord Legation and an interview with the Envoy
there, who insisted the Empire was stalling trade talks."

The screen shifted back to the commentator for an instant before displaying another scene, this time of a slender, gray-haired woman in brilliant yellow.

"The Matriarch Princeps of Halston today requested
that the Emperor favorably consider the terms of trade
offered by Accord and stated that delay would not be in
the best interests of either the Empire or other systems. No
amplification was forthcoming. Neither the Ministry of

Commerce nor the Ministry of External Affairs would comment.''

The screen flicked back to the commentator.

"In the meantime, Imperial Intelligence still denies one of its agents was injured while involved in the Accord case.

"Explanations are missing. The Accord Envoy has none, and no affected Imperial Ministries would comment.

"Next . . . a special report on the impact of the synde bean shortage—"

Nathaniel switched off the screen.

The media hadn't forgotten . . . so far.

He tapped the intercom.

"Mydra! Any word on Sergel?"

"No, sir. He doesn't answer, and he hasn't called in."

"Then please officially report that he is missing."

"So soon?"

"No. So late."

He cut Mydra off and accessed the Faxstellar number.

The receptionist was male, blond, regular featured, even if his chin was weak.

"Nathaniel Whaler, Envoy of Accord, this is. More interesting information have—"

"Yes, sir. Ms. Bar-Twyla said to put you straight through."

"Kyra Bar-Twyla . . . Lord Whaler. What a surprise! How can I help you?"

"Perhaps we can each other help. A person from my staff is missing."

"Are you serious?"

"Most serious. Mr. Sergel Weintre, my Information Specialist, is not in his quarters, has not reported to work, and was supposed to be here early this morning. Now is late afternoon and no Sergel. I would not worry about so trivial a matter, but after these past few days . . ." Nathaniel shrugged.

"Why do you think his disappearance is connected with the trade talks situation?"

"Suppose I should not say, but if you check with the Diplomatic Police, several days ago Mr. Weintre was found unconscious outside my quarters. He could not explain what happened or why. Now he is gone."

"Is Mr. Weintre a native?"

"Native?"

"Is he from Accord?"

"Yes. From Accord."

"That is very interesting. I appreciate it. Thank you."

Nathaniel was left staring at a blank screen.

The intercom buzzed.

"Lord Whaler?"

"Yes."

"I've just gotten a call from the Diplomatic Police. They've located Mr. Weintre."

"Where?"

"He was wandering around the Diplomatic Concourse, they said."

"Wandering?"

"Well . . . yes . . ."

"Why did he not come to the Legation?"

"He couldn't."

"Why not?"

"Because . . . because . . . he's been partially mind-wiped. He thinks he's eighteen standard years old and coming home from summer training. He doesn't understand how he ended up in New Augusta ten standard years older."

"I see. I see." He sighed. "Anything, anything there is that you can do, please arrange for Sergel." He swung his head from side to side.

"Yes, Lord Whaler."

Nathaniel shuddered. The Ministry of Defense did not like Accord, that was certain.

He faxscreened Galactafax.

"Lord Whaler at—"

"Yes, sir. Marjoy Far-Nova would like to tape you, sir."

"Lord Whaler, you have new developments?"

"Yes, Lady. Unhappily, I do."

"Unhappily?"

"My Information Specialist, Sergel Weintre, has been missing since yesterday. He has been found. Just found, but he thinks he is eighteen standard years, and part of his thoughts are gone."

"He's been mind-wiped?"

"That is the term."

"What did he know? Where can I confirm this?"

"I cannot say what he knew. I feared he was not to be trusted, and yesterday I ordered Mr. Weintre to see me this morning. I thought he might have been connected to some information losses, but he never arrived. Now the Diplomatic Police have him."

"Let me get this straight. You discovered, or suspected, that Mr. Weintre was not to be trusted, then the Legation was bombed. You tried to reach Mr. Weintre to question him. He disappeared and turns up mind-wiped?"

"That is essentially correct."

"Oh, sister! Will this . . ." she caught herself and turned her full attention back to the Ecolitan.

"Thank you, Lord Whaler."

With the blank screen again facing him, Nathaniel realized how secondary he was to the need for instant fax reporting.

He wondered belatedly if he were being strung out. What if Mydra had fed him a baited story?

He fumbled with the directory codes until he obtained the number for the Diplomatic Police.

"Lord Nathaniel Whaler," he announced.

"Yes." The cold-eyed dispatcher waited.

"Understand you have one of my staff, one Sergel Weintre?"

"No."

Nathaniel felt himself stiffen, even while trying to keep

calm. Had he been set up to be discredited? Left to hang himself with the media?

"Sure are you? Report had I that—"

"We did have Mr. Weintre, Lord Whaler, but on the instructions of your office, we have already begun the transfer to the rehabilitative center."

"Thank you. Thought I that you were not quite so quickly acting. That number, do you have it?"

He took it down, his heart still beating fast. He had to remember that he couldn't necessarily trust anyone. So easy to forget that in the isolated and pleasant surroundings of his quarters.

Then he called Kyra Bar-Twyla back and relayed the latest developments on Sergel.

She took the details quickly, and once she had the facts, cut him off.

He shrugged. Envoys didn't carry much weight with the Imperial media, that was for certain, nor with many others either. Not in New Augusta.

If the Empire didn't agree to trade talks, he hoped the stories in the faxcasts would have at least some of the independent systems asking questions and further doubting the Imperial good will.

The graceful way out would be negotiations . . . if the Ministry of Defense would accept a graceful way out.

. . . XXVIII . . .

The Ecolitan frowned, slammed his clenched fist into his right palm, once, twice . . . three times. Finally, he looked out into the darkness where the lights of the towers sparkled.

"Flame! Flame! Flame!"

"They want negotiations. There's every reason to have negotiations. But it isn't happening."

He glanced down at the small comm unit of the study.

"Why? Why doesn't anything happen?"

He should have been in bed hours earlier, but the sense of danger, the nagging, dragging tightness in his gut had not let him rest.

Instead, he had cleaned up and dressed, pulling on a green tunic and trousers, along with his belt and the rest of his easily concealed infiltration equipment.

He took a last look at the view from the small study at the lights of the towers and then tapped the lockplate on the portal into his Legation office.

The first sliver of light from the opening warned him. He drove through the portal even before it was open.

The four figures who seemed to turn in slow motion toward him all had masks slung around their necks, not yet

in position. Three were women. The fourth, on the far
right, leaning against the big official console, was a man.
All wore uniforms.

The first two women sprayed away from the Ecolitan,
slammed into the wall by his attack. The third Marine
went down as Whaler arced his elbow across her throat.

The man had a nerve tangler halfway from his holster
before the Ecolitan slashed it from his hand.

Seconds later, the man in green looked down at the
unconscious Marine and looked around the office.

Surprisingly, all four Marines were still breathing, and
one of the women on the far side of the office was
beginning to scrabble toward the stunner that lay about a
half meter from her outstretched hand.

Nathaniel reached it first, readjusted the setting from its
near-lethal level, and used it, first on the one conscious
soldier, then on the other three.

The masks meant that someone was about to gas his
quarters, and the fact that the Marines were in his
private Legation office meant someone on the Legation
staff, besides the unfortunate Sergel, had been in on
the operation.

He worried his tongue between his teeth for a moment,
tried to think, while moving toward the portal to the staff
office.

He had a stunner in each hand. While their high-pitched
strumm was noisier than he liked, they were quick. If
another crew were waiting, he would need all the edge in
time he could get.

Before activating the portal, he adjusted the stunners'
focuses to almost a point.

He looked at the portal, took a deep breath, shook himself gently, then tapped the lockplate.

Again, he came barreling through the portal, low and
fast, even before it was fully open.

His first shot dropped the single Marine guarding the

next doorway. His second paralyzed Hillary West-Coven's right hand before she could touch the console studs.

"You move, and I'll put the beam right above your heart."

She froze.

No one else was in the staff office.

"Stand up and move back from that console."

Nathaniel hadn't realized how olive her complexion was until he saw the whiteness beneath the skin tone.

"Lord Whaler, there must be some mistake."

"Right. I was mistaken."

Her left hand drifted forward.

"Strumm!" The needle width of the beam singed the back of her hand.

Hillary jumped backward a half step.

"Don't listen, do you?"

His eyes traveled the room. He didn't have much time. For all he knew, whatever Marines had been at the other door to his quarters were already inside.

Where could he go?

He smiled, and Hillary backed away yet another step until her back was almost to the wall.

"Sorry," he said.

"Strumm!"

The woman crumpled.

Nathaniel eased open the door to the hall which led to the reception area. It was empty, and he picked up Hillary and threw her over his right shoulder, stuffing the one stunner into his belt, leaving the other in his left hand.

Although Hillary was lighter than he expected, he set her down beside the portal to the reception area and took out the other stunner.

Shaking his head, he thumbed the portal access. Imagine, having to fight his way out of his own Legation!

This time he waited until the portal was three quarters of

the way open before snapping three quick shots. He dropped
both Marines who waited—one officer, one squad leader.

Once into the reception area, he made another check but
found no other employees or bodies. Hillary had to have
been the duty officer.

The reception console's screens showed that the exterior
corridor was empty, except for the two tunnel buggies that
bore the crest of the Diplomatic Tower, and except for the
two men dressed in repair uniforms.

Nathaniel snorted.

With a series of quick movements, he laid Hillary out
on the couch closest to the exterior portal and pulled off
the officer's tunic and beret. Both were too small to fit
him. He slit the tunic up the back and slipped it on over
his own. The beret came next.

He cradled Hillary in both arms, her weight on his
forearms while he still held the stunners, shadowed
by her.

He would not be able to carry her that way for long, but
long enough to do what was necessary.

He stepped outside and turned toward the ''repair''
buggies. Neither ''repairman'' looked up until he was
within five meters.

''Sss . . . what?''

''Have a problem?''

''*Strumm! Strumm!*''

Both crumpled, their faces blank.

He placed Hillary in the nearest buggy, climbed in, and
began to guide the vehicle toward the service shaft that the
maps had indicated was at the far end of the corridor.

He wondered if the level were temporarily blocked off
or if it were merely deserted in the hours between midnight
and dawn.

The service shaft was vacant, and he steered the buggy
onto the drop platform, setting the level destination for the
one hundred twenty-first level.

He hoped he could do what he wanted, since he in-

tended to get back to the three hundredth level shortly . . .
if he could.

Pulling Hillary off the buggy at the one hundred
twenty-first level, set it on remote and programmed a
course that would take it back toward the main lift shafts.

The service shaft took them another three levels down,
where he half lifted, half dragged Hillary out. There he
wadded up the beret and the tunic and let them drop into
the shaft.

Hillary was beginning to wake up. He used the stunner
again, at low power, to nick her larynx. While there was
some danger it might permanently damage her voice, at
the moment he felt less than charitable, and he needed
Hillary able to walk.

He gently tugged the gold film cloak from his belt and
let it billow around him and partly over Hillary. With his
arm around her tense body, he said, "You can't say a
word, but if you try to escape, I'll trigger the stunner
against your spine. You might not ever walk again, at least
not without a *long* rehab."

He gave her a gentle shove.

"Now, we're just a loving couple headed back for my
quarters . . . right?"

He could feel her reluctant nod.

"That's right, dear," he added.

They ambled toward the lift shaft. Once or twice, he bent
toward her, as if to embrace her, stopped, and looked
down into her eyes, which burned green hatred back at
him.

He smiled back at her.

They reached the lift shaft and slipped into the slow
rising lane.

The Ecolitan could see a few others in both drop and lift
shafts, which indicated that the tower had not been sealed
off for the attack on his quarters, which led to even more
interesting speculations.

As they stumbled off at the three hundredth level, Nathaniel checked the stages quickly but could see nothing out of the ordinary.

Sergel's quarters were even further from the shaft than Nathaniel's, but in the opposite direction. Once there, it took the Ecolitan less than a minute to manipulate the fields and slip inside.

The three rooms were a mess, everything totally out of order, with abundant signs that at least several intruders had pawed through the rooms.

Without warning, he pressed the nerves in the back of Hillary's neck and let her slump unconscious.

He needed the time to change the lock fields to keep anyone else from repeating his trick and to see what he could find, assuming the other searchers had left anything.

Point by point, centimeter by centimeter, he went through the three rooms—the living area, which had a small nook for food preparation; the sleeping room; and the hygienarium. The previous searchers had removed virtually all personal effects, outside of a few small console reference tape discs, clothing, four solidio cubes, some of Sergel's calling cards, and a package of blank and old-fashioned notepaper. Whoever had searched the quarters had apparently wanted every possible clue to the Information Specialist and to his psychology.

The Ecolitan finally straightened, pulled at his chin, and looked blankly at the wall. Sergel had not rated an exterior view, and the lack of windows made Nathaniel uncomfortable.

He sighed, checked Hillary, then stretched himself out on the other couch across from her, willing himself to wake in three standard hours or at the faintest sound.

In seconds, he was asleep.

When he awoke Hillary was still out. The Imperial standard time was 0700. He stretched and got to his feet, pacing back and forth in the cramped space for a few minutes. Finally, with one eye on Hillary he washed his face and cleaned up as well as he could.

Once he was fairly presentable, he moved back into the living quarters to keep a closer eye on Hillary, shaking his head as he tried to think things out.

Some things were clear. Some were not. The attempted "replacement" of the Envoy of Accord and the use of Imperial Marines in a clandestine attack on his quarters pointed toward a military involvement; and, to some degree, the fact that it was not being kept terribly quiet added to his concerns.

Yet it wasn't public, which meant that someone besides Accord wasn't supposed to know all the grisly details. Since the Terran public could have cared less about the fate of either trade talks or the Accord Envoy, the military didn't seem to want someone else to know, and if it weren't the head Admiral . . .

That left another question, which led to another answer.

He frowned. Who could he trust? Sylvia? Could he really trust her?

He didn't have much choice. He needed someone with the kind of access she could presumably provide.

With that, he tapped out the code.

"Senator Helmsworth's office."

"Nathaniel here, for Sylvia."

"Your business?" asked Charles, not really even looking into the screen.

"Personal."

"Thank you."

Sylvia's image snapped into place.

"Where are you?"

"Where I am, dear Lady. Two questions for you. First, are you loyal to the Emperor?"

"What does that mean?"

"It means what I asked. Whoever is after me isn't. That's why they're after me."

"Can you prove that?"

"Someone used a Marine detachment to raid my quarters. They weren't quite successful."

Sylvia's gray eyes widened. Nathaniel half ducked and turned, but Hillary was still out cold.

Sylvia drew in the chaos of Sergel's room and the figure lying on the stained scarlet couch.

Nathaniel shrugged.

"You've probably managed to trace where I am . . . which means I'll leave. So . . . where do I meet you?"

She laughed.

"The best place would be the Legate's dining room in the Diplomatic Tower. We could have a late breakfast there. That's possibly the one place where almost no one would dare to create a scene. If what you have to say isn't that compelling, however, you might have some trouble when you left."

Nathaniel shook his head from side to side. "So simple. I'm inclined to agree, and a friend will I bring, one with whom your friends might have much to say." He paused. "By the way, you never answered my question about the Emperor."

Sylvia frowned. "You know the answer, whether you know it or not. Otherwise, why would you have faxed me? Yes. Of course. How else could it be?"

This time, she waited to see what else he had to say.

"What can I say?"

He took a last look at the woman in the screen, who wore her hair down and swept back above a yellow and white tunic. Nathaniel decided he didn't like the yellow on her as well as the darker colors.

He smiled after the screen went blank. She would look good in either black or in the dark forest green of the Institute.

Once again, Hillary was beginning to stir, and he didn't really want to stun her another time.

He waited.

"Are you ready to head out?"

She jerked her head from side to side.

"You should be able to talk now, or whisper."

"No," she half croaked, half whispered.

"Why not? Just because you're part of this crew out to discredit the Emperor doesn't mean you aren't hungry."

"You men!"

He scowled. That was the second time around. First had been the agent who'd tried to zap him in the tunnel. Now Hillary was using the same phrase.

Stunner in hand, he gestured to the hygienarium.

"Clean up."

She glared at him but went ahead with her necessities, despite the lack of privacy, and finished up by brushing her short black hair.

The Ecolitan checked over his equipment a last time, then unlocked the door fields and ushered Hillary out before him. Although a few pedestrians strolled by Sergel's door, the area did not appear to be directly monitored, and Nathaniel and Hillary reached the main drop shaft without incident.

"Keep walking," the Ecolitan said lightly as they passed the drop and lift shafts.

Hillary only missed one step before continuing onward. "I thought we were going to breakfast . . ."

Nathaniel almost missed his step. He had not said anything about breakfast, except to Sylvia, and that meant Hillary had been feigning sleep. And that could mean trouble for Sylvia.

"I did mention that but not exactly when."

Nathaniel did not miss the newly stationed pair of Imperial Marine sentries before the Accord Legation, but since his destination was further down another corridor, he and Hillary only saw the pair from the far side of the shaft area.

At least one passerby gave the evening gold film cloak a strange look, but then shook her head and continued on. Possibly the Diplomatic Tower was the only section of New Augusta where outré clothing rated but a passing frown.

The Ecolitan could feel the tenseness mounting in Hillary as they began to circle back toward the private entrance to his personal quarters.

When he saw that there were no outside guards, he frowned. Were they inside? Would they expect him to strike back so quickly? Did he dare risk it?

He nearly laughed aloud.

Did he dare not to? Within hours, the omnipresent Imperial machine would have located him, and he couldn't keep dragging Hillary along.

He marched up to the portal and slapped his palm on the lock.

Even as the portal began to open, he tensed, then in a single fluid movement scooped Hillary up and tossed her through the portal.

He followed, stunner drawn.

"Strumm!"

"Strumm!"   .

Nathaniel was quicker, barely, and the single Marine pitched forward out of the stool and onto the tiles.

Hillary, who had absorbed the first shot, was flat on the tiles next to the Marine.

The Ecolitan felt sorry for her. Too many jolts to her system. But he had already left the entryway behind.

The bed was mussed, in the way that indicated it had not been slept in, but the quarters were vacant.

Nathaniel palmed the lock to his office and snapped a shot through the barely open portal to the spot behind the console.

He followed his shot, low and to the left, rolling and firing.

"Strumm!"

Another damned Marine!

"Strumm!"

A line of fire burned down his right arm.

The stunner dropped to the floor from his numb right hand. He shifted the aim of the stunner in his left hand.

"Strumm! Strumm!"

Nathaniel's first shot spun the female Marine to the carpet, and the second stilled her twitching.

He stood momentarily over the bodies, looking down at the second face of a man who looked like him. For a moment, he studied the patched wall, yet to be fully repaired from earlier explosive events.

He checked the portal to the staff office, decided that it would hold and took out the two small probes. The one he held in his right hand clattered to the floor. Even with full concentration, his pain conditioning could not override the jangled nerves in his right arm. With the single probe in his left hand, it took several minutes for him to lock the portal, though it would hold against anything less than a military laser cutter.

"Hope they don't have that handy."

"Strumm!"

He gave another jolt to the Marine before holstering the stunner and bending to drag his double back into his own private quarters through the still open portal.

He smiled as he glimpsed the ragged thunderclouds through the vista of the office window panorama.

Definitely prophetic. Definitely.

Back in the entryway of his private quarters with the three unconscious bodies, he knelt down, rolled Hillary over, listened to the heartbeat.

He was no doctor, but he didn't like the sound.

Still . . . he had to make a few changes.

First, he focused the stunner and burned out all four visual snoops. When he finished, he laid the stunner aside. The charge was exhausted.

With his good hand, he pulled the diplomatic blacks off his double and stuffed the man into the greens he had been wearing—minus the equipment belt and gear, which he retained. Then he hurried into a set of his own blacks, pocketing the I.D.s and other "official" credentials carried by the false Envoy.

Finally, he wiped off the useless stunner and tucked it into the other's belt holder.

The remaining stunner was down to about twenty percent charge, but he decided to keep it until he could replace or recharge it.

He straightened his stiff shoulders.

He hadn't been thinking clearly. Too long since he'd slept well. The easiest way out was the direct way.

After a sigh, he took a deep breath. With a grunt, he stooped and swung Hillary over his shoulder, lugging her through his quarters before setting her on the couch in his office.

Next, he dragged his double back into the office and laid him out in a position on the floor, and put the exhausted stunner in the unconscious man's hand.

Finally, he unlocked the portal and hit the emergency stud.

First through the portal from the staff office was Mydra, followed by another Marine.

"Whoever he is," snapped the Ecolitan, "he attacked through my private quarters, he used poor Hillary as a shield, and managed to get both guards as well."

He glared at the Marine. "Some protection you are!"

"But, sir . . . "

"But nothing. All's well that ends well, I suppose. Now . . . the woman . . . I mean . . . Hillary. She's in a bad way. Probably needs emergency medical care. Handle that immediately. Then there's the other Marine in my quarters, plus that one over there. You'd better post some guards *outside* my private exit this time. Damn the gossip. Enough's enough."

The Marine saluted and thumbed his belt comm.

"Lord Whaler . . ." began Mydra slowly.

He nodded at her.

"What do you intend to do with the intruder?"

"Take him to breakfast, of course. Under guard."

He could see the effort she was making to keep her jaw in place.

He chuckled, which he had never done in front of her before, and added, "Since I seem to require armed guards these days, they might as well carry my friend with me to my morning appointment."

. . . XXIX . . .

Sylvia, in the yellow and white that did not become her, was waiting for him in the outer lobby of the Legate's dining room.

Nathaniel watched her eyes widen as he walked in, flanked by three red-coated Imperial Marines, two of whom supported a semiconscious figure. The Ecolitan opened and closed his right hand several times, blocking away the pain. He had full control back, but it would be several hours before he would be able to relax his controls.

"I apologize for being late, dear Lady, but I had a great deal to accomplish since we talked, as I am sure you realize."

He gestured. "This gentleman might be of some interest to you, since he was attempting to be me."

He turned to the three Marines.

"Wait here with this gentleman. I fully expect you to be here when I return. Then we will deal with the problem."

"But . . . sir . . ."

"But nothing. I am certainly safe within the Legate's dining room, especially if you are guarding the entrance and exit. True?"

He offered his arm to Sylvia, faced the waiter, and nodded.

"Nathaniel Whaler, Envoy from Accord. A table for two on the portico."

The man's dark eyes widened fractionally, but his thin and clean-shaven face did not shift expressions.

Nathaniel turned his head toward Sylvia.

"And this time, dear Lady, I would appreciate it if you did not sneeze. To repeat our luncheon would create an additional strain I would rather not face—not right now, at least."

She stopped, right in the middle of the empty main dining room, and let go of his arm.

"I think you owe me an explanation."

"I do. You're right. I unreplaced their replacement of me, and I'm doing the best I can to get that replacement into your hands. So far, everyone either believes or is playing that I'm the replacement, rather than me. It won't last very long. So if you can have a team pick up that gentleman . . . fine. If not, then the Marines will take him away. They will interrogate him and discover he is indeed not me."

"How in Hades can I arrange that—right out from underneath the Defense Ministry—in the middle of the Legate's lobby?"

"I don't know, but the waiter is coming back, and we'd better get along to our thoroughly bugged and snooped table."

Sylvia smiled and the gray of her eyes seemed to lighten.

"I could make it so the snooping wouldn't work."

"Fine . . . and then they'll be even more suspicious."

Her face darkened.

"For Cloud's sake . . . you've already blown any cover I had. You think those Marines won't recognize me and tell the Admiral?"

His shoulders drooped slightly. "I should have thought

of that. Too much going on, and I'm not used to the wheels within wheels.''

She took his arm, and he could smell the faintest hint of the orange blossoms he had remembered. They strolled through the nearly empty outer dining room toward the waiter.

''If I hadn't recognized the risk, dear Envoy, I wouldn't have agreed to come.''

Sylvia disengaged herself from his arm and let the waiter seat her. Nathaniel pulled out his own chair and seated himself. His fingers flicked over his belt, and the readouts were clear. The table was snooped to the hilt.

The view from the portico was obscured by the swirl of dirty gray clouds that dipped below the tops of the towers, and the murkiness of the light reminded Nathaniel of the mountains of Trezenia. The tightness in his gut was the same, despite the opulence of the morning gold table setting, the white and gold dishes, and the gilded table utensils.

''Would you like menus, Lord Whaler?'' asked the waiter, hovering at the table edge between them, looking from one face to the other.

''Not I. I would like liftea, some fruit, if you have it, and any sort of breakfast pastry. Sylvia?''

''Just cafe, thank you.''

''Already eaten?''

She nodded, put her elbows on the table and leaned forward, her eyes studying his face intently.

''Yes. You're you.'' She leaned back. ''That's good, I think, but you realize we can't keep meeting this way.'' Again, he caught the glimpse of her smile, but only the glimpse.

''That, dear Lady, have I realized. And some plans I have to take care of that . . . if you would care to listen.''

''In a moment . . .''

''I see. In the meantime, what do you think of the view?''

"Frankly, I would prefer a few words on how a senior professor ever obtained the background to be able to have survived the amazing set of coincidences that have befallen you."

"We academics have hidden reserves, particularly when fueled by necessity." He paused, cleared his throat, and looked into the dark gray slate of her eyes. A moment later, he looked away.

"Most of us on Accord have taken early survival training through the Institute. I liked it, as well as the academics, and one thing led to another. Only the government or the Institute have the funds for out-system travel, and there was much I wanted to see. The comparative political economy and economic history which are my academic specialties do not rate field trips . . . meant that I had to maintain and upgrade my survival skills to obtain the Institute's backing for my academic studies . . ." He shrugged. "Call me the reluctant Ecolitan . . . or maybe the cowardly professor."

"Cowardly?"

"I'm afraid of everything. So I must prepare for everything."

Sylvia squinted and looked at her timestrip.

"In a few seconds, there will be a power failure."

His eyes darted toward the floor beneath the nearest table and back to Sylvia.

She nodded once, slowly.

"That seems a bit unusual for New Augusta."

"Even we have switching failures and equipment malfunctions once in a while."

"But—"

The entire room went gray, lit just by the light from the windows.

Nathaniel dropped and rolled under the table to his right in time to miss the bolt from the waiter's stunner.

He rolled further and yanked the man's feet from underneath him, but the waiter dropped like a dead weight.

"He lost his balance," observed Sylvia as Nathaniel looked up from the floor at her.

The Ecolitan scrambled to his feet and surveyed the rest of the portico. The other table in use was occupied by three Fuards, and none of the three—at the far end of the room—seemed to have noticed the disturbance, although all three were gesturing about the lack of lighting.

"Shall we return to our table, Lord Whaler?"

"If you so suggest."

Two new waiters appeared, gravely picked the figure off the floor, and disappeared.

Nathaniel shook his head.

"You do arrange things."

"I hope it's worth it. Now," and her voice hardened, "you have roughly five minutes to say what you need. Quickly."

He cleared his throat.

"Besides what you've already done, I need access to a console which can transmit messages directly to the Grand Admiral and to the Emperor. Second, I need to be able to walk through the most secret Defense sections you can get me into in the Defense Ministry Tower. Not any information—just walking the halls will be sufficient. The sooner the better. The longer it takes, the more likely the Admiral will think up something else, and I honestly don't know how many more of her traps I can avoid. They almost got me last night."

"You seem awfully sure that it's the Grand Admiral."

"Couldn't be anyone else, could it?"

Sylvia gave him a rueful grin, and he had to return the expression.

"No, but if you knew that, why did you ask me if I were loyal to the Emperor?"

"To let you know where I stood."

Her mouth opened in a slight O.

"You're more devious than I suspected, dear Envoy."

He looked straight at her, liking what he saw, but

pressed with the sense of the minutes ticking past, he raced on.

"Look. There's every reason for a simple trade agreement to be ratified. The credits aren't *that* significant. But it isn't. Instead, another fleet is building, and every time it looks like I move another step forward, someone with a military bearing or connection appears to stop me. When it gets right down to it, you can't trade with an incinerated system. That means only the military has a reason for stopping things cold, and they will, if—"

"You can't do something to stop it. What do you have in mind? Why do you need to walk through the secret sections of the Defense Tower?"

"To deliver a message that can't be delivered any other way."

"No other way?"

"This time, you'll have to trust me. Will you help?"

The Ecolitan became aware of how quiet the room was. Even the Fuards at the far end seemed to be conversing in whispers.

Sylvia seemed to be thinking over his request, but her face revealed nothing.

Finally, she looked up.

"I don't see how what you've asked is that unreasonable, under the circumstances. To set it up will take several hours, and you will have to leave with me. Right now."

"What about the Marines? Can I dismiss them and tell them to return? I'm a bit reluctant to disappear again so officially."

She frowned momentarily.

"That might be better."

He handed her a small capsule.

"Swallow that."

"Why?"

"Because the information in the Imperial data banks is

wrong, and because it will make your life a great deal more comfortable.''

"What are you planning? Not some sort of murder campaign?'' Her voice rose fractionally.

"Forest Lord, no. But a lot of people will be very uncomfortable, and I'd rather you weren't among them.'' He didn't like twisting the truth, even a little, especially when talking to Sylvia, but he didn't have time to explain. "Please.''

"All right.''

She swallowed the capsule with a gulp of water.

Nathaniel realized that their food had not arrived.

"No breakfast . . . ''

"I'll see you get something later—while we prepare.'' She rose, and added, "I'll wait here, while you dismiss your guards—or jailors.''

. . . **XXX** . . .

The Grand Admiral glanced back at the faxsheet that lay before her on the console.

For the fifth time in as many minutes, she picked it up again and read it through. Then she put it down.

Were her hands shaking? Nonsense!

She turned in the noiseless swivel and beheld the outer world. From her double thickness permaglassed view, she looked down and out over the golden plain, her eyes focused beyond the dome that contained the Imperial Palace.

Not looking at the words, she picked up the thin white sheet once more, and finally turned back to the console. She reached for the communication studs, then drew back her hands and read the fax message, this time slowly, and word by word.

J. KU-SMYTHE
GRAND ADMIRAL
MINISTRY OF DEFENSE
NEW AUGUSTA, TERRA
XVX-URG-CODE ONE BETA-SKV

YOUR INTEREST IN THE ACCORD ENVOY HAS BEEN

NOTED. THE ECOLITAN INSTITUTE UNDERSTANDS
YOUR INTEREST, AS DOES THE EMPEROR N'TROYA.

IN VIEW OF YOUR POSITION AS HEAD OF IMPERIAL DE-
FENSE AND SECURITY, THE SUCCESS OF ANY FURTHER
ACTS AGAINST EITHER THE EMPEROR OR ACCORD
DIPLOMATIC PERSONNEL WILL BE REGARDED AS A
PERSONAL FAILURE BY YOU TO CARRY OUT YOUR
RESPONSIBILITIES.

IN AN EFFORT TO BE HELPFUL IN THIS REGARD,
WE OFFER THE MOST RECENT PROJECTIONS AT
HAND. THESE PROJECTIONS INDICATE THAT MORE
THAN 80% OF ALL INHABITANTS OF THE MINISTRY
OF DEFENSE TOWER WILL SUFFER A LOW-GRADE VER-
SION OF GERSON'S DISEASE. FOR ROUGHLY 2%, THE
INFECTION WILL UNFORTUNATELY BE FATAL. NO
PRECAUTION YOU CAN NOW TAKE WILL BE EFFEC-
TIVE.

THIS TOTALLY SPONTANEOUS OUTBREAK HAS BEEN
PREDICTED BY THE EPIDEMIOLOGISTS OF THE IN-
STITUTE, AND WHILE TOTALLY COINCIDENTAL AND
WHILE WE REGRET IT IS TOO LATE TO PREVENT IT,
WE HOPE THIS ADVANCE NOTICE WILL BE HELPFUL
AND INDICATE OUR INTEREST IN FRIENDLY AND
NONMILITARY SOLUTIONS TO PROBLEMS, SUCH AS
TRADE.

WE ALSO HOPE THE EMPIRE IS NOT SO INDISCREET
AS TO BELIEVE THAT WAR IS THE MOST SUCCESSFUL
MEANS OF DEALING WITH ECONOMIC REALITY.

THEREFORE, THE SUCCESS OR FAILURE OF TRADE
TALKS WITH ACCORD WILL ALSO BE REGARDED AS
YOUR PERSONAL RESPONSIBILITY. IF YOU HAVE
ANY QUESTIONS, LORD WHALER, THE SENIOR ECOL-
ITAN AND THE ENVOY FROM ACCORD, WOULD BE
MOST HAPPY TO EXPLAIN. A COPY OF THIS MESSAGE
HAS ALSO GONE DIRECTLY TO EMPEROR N'TROYA.

No diplomat had written it, nor any functionary from any of the other Ministries. But how had the writer gotten her personal codes, down to the final and hidden authentications?

Not even the Emperor had those.

She did not doubt that the copy had in fact gone to the Emperor.

The fax was phrased as a public interest warning but was nothing more than a threat. And yet . . . even if she published the entire text as she had read it, who would believe it? If they did, wouldn't she be adding to Accord's credibility with the nonaligned systems?

She paused, then asked the console the question.

She returned to looking at the eastern plains, thinking, and waiting for the system to supply the answer.

Buzz.

"Gerson's Disease. Pathology. Informal name for influenza polioencephaliomyelitis (D-strain), an acute, infectious, virus disease characterized by inflammation of the gray matter of the spinal cord, and of the brain, coupled with respiratory inflammation, headache, fever, muscular pains, and irritation of the intestinal tract. Mortality in an untreated and susceptible population approaches ninety percent, but baseline T-type populations have normally demonstrated an immunity that approaches unity . . . immunization requires a series of injections . . . spread over roughly three standard months . . ."

The Admiral read the listing on the console screen twice, and the furrow between her eyebrows deepened into a gouge by the time she had finished.

The message was either a colossal bluff, or . . .

The Grand Admiral picked up the faxsheet and quietly tore the message to shreds.

Then she tapped out two instructions on her console.

If the fax had been correct, Accord not only possessed the ability to infect the most secure structure in New Augusta, but also to modify a disease in two separate aspects, a modification currently beyond Imperial medical technology.

Only time would tell, but at least for that time, any more of the attacks against the Ecolitan Envoy would have to be postponed. The risk was too great, even for her, particularly if the Emperor had a copy of the fax. If the Ecolitans had her codes, she had no doubt they had the Emperor's.

She repressed a shiver and turned back to the view of the plains, leaning back in the swivel. For a time she regarded the grass and the distant line of clouds above the horizon.

At last, she tapped a code, waiting . . .

"Marcella?"

. . . XXXI . . .

Nathaniel straightened his tunic in mid-stride, not pausing in his steps but matching his pace to Sylvia's.

"I'm still not sure why this has to be done," said Sylvia in a tone that was half statement, half question.

The Ecolitan inhaled deeply. The air in the corridor was still, with a metallic trace scent to it, the first hint of oil and machine he had smelled since he arrived in the indoor world of New Augusta.

"Metallic smell," he commented.

"The filters and recyclers are about ninety-nine and nine-tenths percent effective. The circulation here in the deeper parts of the tower isn't quite as effective as elsewhere."

"That's why we need to stroll through as much of the Defense Tower as possible. The relatively accessible corridors will do."

Sylvia straightened her own military tunic and frowned. "You still haven't elaborated. But not now."

Nathaniel sighed. "Have I asked you all your secrets?"

She laughed, a short gentle sound. "Touché."

The first security gate was staffed by a single guard, enclosed in a permaglass booth.

Nathaniel ran his eyes over the enclosure—guarded against energy weapons and projectiles, but not airtight.

"Let's see your passes." The woman's bored tone echoed in the emptiness of the deep corridor. Despite the standard lighting, the lack of ornamentation and the metallic edge to the air gave the area a tomblike feeling.

Sylvia placed two square cards facedown on the scanner.

"And your I.D.s and thumbprints," added the Defense sentry.

The three waited momentarily in the silence.

Nathaniel caught the green flash reflecting in the permaglass behind the sentry and almost shook his head. Bad design. A really alert intruder could take advantage of the warning.

"You're cleared."

The gate swung wide enough to let them pass through one at a time, then clunked shut. The sound reminded Nathaniel of a coffin lid falling shut.

He wondered whose coffin—Accord's or the Empire's?

"This way." The corridor branched, and Sylvia touched his hand, led him to the left.

Signs of greater activity began to appear as well as portals in the sides of the corridor and a military figure or two heading in one direction or another, some in uniforms similar to those he and Sylvia wore and some in the plain jumpsuits he had earlier suspected of being of military origin.

He nodded to himself.

Wheels within wheels . . . but all he had to do was to walk through the tower.

True—he could have planted the dispersers on Sylvia and asked her to do it, but that option bothered him. If Accord had dirty work, then he should be the one doing it. He knew his decision was irrational, and he hoped the Coordinate and the Institute didn't end up paying for it.

To be discovered as the Envoy from Accord within the

top-secret sections of the Ministry of Defense might be more than embarrassing. It might prove fatal.

He almost laughed, and had he done so, the sound would have been grim. Were he to be discovered, he wouldn't ever be found. The last thing the Empire could afford would be an admission that Accord could breach Imperial security at will.

After three more turns, the corridor, now more of a thoroughfare, widened further into a lift/drop shaft concourse.

"We're ordered to the fifth level," Sylvia said in a tight and controlled voice.

He nodded and followed, presuming, although she had said nothing on the subject, that every word within the Defense perimeters was monitored or at least computer scanned.

He straightened automatically, keying in a military posture, and let himself follow Sylvia. They had a lot of corridor left to cover.

. . . XXXII . . .

His feet hurt. He had walked further, hiked through the high plains of Trezenia, through the Parundan Rain Forests of Accord, and done it all with a standard field pack. He had forgotten how many extended marches he had led his trainees through, whether in rain, snow, or blistering sun. But now his feet hurt. And the muscles in his right arm still ached.

Nathaniel looked down at the omnipresent permaplast floor tiles. While they gave slightly under foot, they were hard, and he and Sylvia had walked more than ten kilos through the Defense Towers and the caverns beneath.

From the corner of his eye, he could see the portal to the Legation, and the pair of Imperial sentries.

"Here's where I leave you, dear Envoy. I hope things turn out the way you hoped."

"So do I." So do I, he added mentally.

Sylvia was gone even as he watched her melt into the passersby. He shook his head and trudged toward the portal, flinging back the film cloak to reveal his diplomatic blacks.

"Lord Whaler . . . we've been—"

"The same," he responded to the Marine with a smile, and he marched into the Legation.

"Lord Whaler, we've been a bit worried . . . what with the power failure and the disappearance of the man who attacked you. Then you dismissed your guards and went off by yourself." Heather Tew-Hawkes had moved around the reception console to greet him.

"How's Hillary?"

"They got her to the health center in time. It was close, but she should be back in a few days. She rambled a lot and kept insisting that there were two of you, and how she wasn't sure which one you really were." Heather smiled a tight smile, one obviously put on, and waited a moment before going on, as if to see whether Nathaniel would respond.

He didn't, just stood there, meeting her gaze levelly.

"She seemed more worried about you, but she's going to be fine."

"I'm glad of that." And he was. At the same time, the guilt and sadness rose within him.

Shortly, thousands of relatively innocent individuals would sicken, and some of them would die. Had there been a better way? Had he missed it?

He shook his head, forgetting where he was. How long, how long . . . ?

"Lord Whaler, are you all right?"

Heather's voice lost its tightness. Her tone of concern brought him back to the small Legation reception room with its mismatched lorkin wood furniture.

"Yes, Heather," he said slowly. "I'm all right. Tired, but all right." As right as can be, now.

He straightened.

"By the way, Heather, would you get someone to clean up my office. If I had an intact office, I might actually stay in it. Especially now, I might stay there."

A puzzled look flitted across the redhead's face, but she answered without questioning. "Mydra has already made the necessary arrangements. Maintenance has just about finished the repairs. They should be complete tonight, and your office will be ready in the morning.''

The Ecolitan shifted his weight from one sore foot to the other. Perhaps it had been the weight of the special heels on his boots. They might have changed the pattern of his stride just enough.

Shaking his head again, he turned toward the portal that led to his office and to his quarters.

"Lord Whaler?"

He turned back to the tentative sound of Heather's voice.

"Would you like me to order something for you to eat?''

"No, thank you, Heather. I appreciate it, but I'm not hungry right now. Perhaps later, perhaps later.''

He gave her a short smile that felt false, then went through the portal and down the hallway toward the staff office.

Mydra was standing by her console.

"The maintenance staff is finishing up the repairs to your office.''

"That's fine. I won't be using it tonight anyway. Where are the guards?''

"They're stationed outside the Legation and outside your private doorway.''

He nodded an acknowledgment.

"Lord Whaler, you look tired.''

"I am tired. Tired beyond . . .'' He broke off. Who would really understand?

Instead, he took a deep breath, inhaling the odor of wall solvent, and gathered himself together.

"You're right. I am tired, and I need a good night's rest. I will see you in the morning, Mydra.'' He paused, then finished in a softer tone. "And thank you for getting this mess cleaned up.''

He had turned even as she said, "That's only my job.''

The crew of three women and two men did not look up as he passed through his office. Thin blue plastic sheeting covered the carpet, the console, and the furniture. His boots left a line of tracks through the whitish powder that lifted at each step.

His quarters were empty—and clean. Even the private entryway tiles had been repolished to a beige glaze, with all the scuffs and bootmarks removed.

He took out the two probes from his belt and began to work on the portal controls. After several minutes, he stopped. The newly replaced control units were more complicated than the originals. His right hand was trembling too much to finish the alignment he needed.

Putting down the probes, he sat cross-legged on the tile next to the wall portal, concentrating on holding back the waves of fatigue, while trying to let his arm and finger muscles relax.

At last, he got back on his knees and completed the changes.

With a sigh, he closed the access panel, leaned to his feet, and trudged back through the quarters to the exit portal between the private study and the office.

Again, he changed the fields to lock totally the portal. This time he had to stop twice to rest.

Finally, with another deep breath and a sigh, he headed to the sleeping quarters, forcing himself to take off his clothing piece by piece before collapsing onto the bed.

Just before the darkness washed over him, he wondered if he had smelled orange blossoms.

. . . XXXIII . . .

The console buzzed.

"Admiral, there's some disturbing news you ought to know."

"Such as?"

"Well . . . it's hard to explain," stammered the Commander on the other end of the screen. "It looks like an epidemic, but there hasn't been one . . . here . . . in ages . . . not with the air recirculators and purifiers." Her eyes dropped along with her voice.

"What sort of epidemic? How widespread? New Augusta? Planetwide?"

"Not exactly, Admiral. Not exactly. So far ninety percent or more of those reported cases are Defense Ministry personnel."

The Admiral looked squarely into the screen. The indirect lighting of her office had gradually brightened as the day had waned. The touches of gray in her dark hair looked silver, simultaneously gave her a harder appearance.

"Let me know if anything changes or if the outbreak should spread."

She broke the connection.

The most senior officer of the Ministry of Defense of

the Empire of Light stood away from her console, away from the five banners fanned on the inner wall, away from the gilt-framed honors on the side wall, and turned to look at the horizon to the east.

She wondered if Accord's sun, invisible to the best of Terran optical telescopes, including the orbital observatory, would be above or below the visual horizon, were it visible.

"Accord . . . one man," she whispered softly. "One man."

The goal of a lifetime was gone. Perhaps she had never had it. Perhaps her daughter had been right all along.

She studied the plains grass below, then the darkening sky to the east.

Finally, she squared her shoulders and turned back to the console.

There was more to the Empire than the Rift, and more to the Ministry than the Eleventh Fleet.

Her fingers unstacked the messages, and she began to scan them as they flashed across the screen.

. . . XXXIV . . .

The Ecolitan Envoy stood by the swivel and studied the plush office for at least the tenth time in the last hour.

The day had been long. No one had faxed. No messages on trade had arrived. No fax commentators had followed up on any previous events. Perhaps all the quiet had been for the best. Just in the past few hours had reports of a mysterious illness at the Ministry of Defense begun to surface.

The fax commentators had announced the tower was closed until the entire structure could be totally sterilized, and that all victims were being treated in isolated facilities. So far, there had been nearly a hundred fatalities, out of ten thousand cases discovered.

Nathaniel shook his head.

It had been so easy, and the Empire had been so secure in its smugness . . . and would probably continue to be—except for the few who knew. Knowing the ways of empires, he wondered if that knowledge would die with its possessors, until a generation from now no one would remember and Accord would again be faced with the same dilemma. Why did it always take sheer power?

Restraining power was always the hardest part. It would

have taken far less effort to have decimated the entire population of New Augusta than it had to engineer the limited impact on the Ministry of Defense.

The private line buzzed, interrupting his self-probing.

He jabbed the accept stud.

"Lord Whaler." He hated using the "Lord," and it was all he could do to refrain from the simple "Whaler" he would have preferred.

The caller was Marcella Ku-Smythe. Nathaniel had never given her his private number, not that he recalled, at least.

"Lord Whaler?"

"Yes."

"I was wondering, upon reflection, how you saw the trade talks progressing."

He shrugged, wondering what she wanted. "I have done what I could do to persuade the Empire. I hope those who count are persuaded, but after the strangeness with Mr. Weintre . . ."

"What strangeness?"

"Mr. Weintre, the Information Specialist, disappeared some days ago. When he was recently found, his memories were gone."

"All of them?" Despite the question, her inquiry was matter-of-fact, as if she knew the answer and wanted to get to something else.

"He thinks he is eighteen standard years."

Marcella's always perfect hair was not, but slightly disarrayed, and a faint smudge showed beneath her left eye.

"I see." She stopped, and the tip of her tongue touched her upper lip. "Lord Whaler . . ."

"Yes?"

"I feel that there may have been some misunderstanding. In no way would the Ministry of Commerce wish anything but a speedy resolution to the trade talks, and one which would be of mutual benefit."

Nathaniel almost whistled. He was getting the closest

thing to an apology possible from the always-efficient Marcella.

"Dear Lady," he lied, "no misunderstanding. Your position and your efforts toward meaningful trade agreement have always been recognized, and for that I thank you and wish you well."

While her face remained composed, the Ecolitan could sense her relief through the screen.

"At the same time," he continued, "so far have I not seen any movement from the Empire." He shrugged again. "And without such movement . . ."

"While I cannot promise anything personally, Lord Whaler, I would suspect that your terms are being studied carefully and that within a short time the Empire will respond positively and much along the lines you originally suggested. You have been most persuasive, I understand. Most persuasive."

"Dear Lady, I do appreciate your call and your courtesy in keeping me informed."

"Thank you, Lord Whaler."

The screen blanked.

The Ecolitan frowned. Beneath the facade, the Lady had been upset. Upset indeed.

Then it clicked. Obviously, her mother the Grand Admiral had briefed her on the warning and on the ensuing epidemic. Perhaps the information would last more than a generation. Perhaps . . . but all he could do was wait. Wait and hope.

He decided against any more great debates, mentally filed the information, and locked up his office to retire to his private quarters.

Dinner would be whatever he could get out of the tiny kitchen, followed by a full night's sleep. Sleep he was shorter on than food.

Still . . . after he finished the small salad and meat patty smothered in a too-sweet sauce, he sat and watched the tower lights from the small and private study, punctuated as they were by the occasional shuttle flare, until he was tired enough to head for his bed.

He woke refreshed, despite the recurrence of the nightmares about the death ships and the Imperial fleet.

This time, the Imperial Fleet Commander had been Marcella Ku-Smythe, except she'd been older and black haired. Doubtless, his subconscious was picturing her mother, Admiral Ku-Smythe.

What was her father like?

He dismissed the question as he got out of bed and staggered into the kitchen for a cup of liftea.

A melon supplied by hidden means followed the liftea.

Next came the hygienarium and a complete fresher.

After dressing, he settled behind the small console in the private study of his quarters, turning to watch the early morning clouds scatter and the golden sun lift a silver dew off the towers. As he looked out through the wide window, he marveled at the fact that the day was basically his.

No matter how he'd gotten steamed up about things, the Empire was on its weekend break, and negotiations would not be held. Period.

At the Institute, somehow, he'd never gotten into the habit of a regular division between work and play.

Still . . . his time on New Augusta would be limited. Should he go sight-seeing?

Alone? With whom?

Would Sylvia consider showing him some sights?

He recovered her card from his pouch and studied it, checking the time on the console.

Too early to call anyway.

He passed the next hour by studying the figures on the trade balances, mentally calculating the amount of increased Imperial tariffs Accord could absorb and which of its own tariffs Accord could realistically drop below the levels in the proposal to the Empire.

The parameters were simple enough, but he'd have to wait for the actual negotiations to see what the Empire might accept, assuming that Marcella was right and that he would see some progress in the next few days.

He put the papers back into his datacase and stretched.

Finally, after letting his fingers stray toward the console and onto the keystuds and pulling them back twice, he punched out the New Augusta directory on the screen, requesting the listing for Sylvia Ferro-Maine.

A single number was listed, Private Tower Orange.

He tapped out the number, wondering if she would stay on the screen once she saw his face.

The faxscreen chimed four times, but there was no answer and no recording.

Could she actually be at work?

He tried the Senator's office.

"Senator Helmsworth's office."

The face that appeared on the screen was another woman, black, with curly brown hair, strong nose, and flashing teeth.

"Lord Whaler, from the Accord Legation. I was looking for Sylvia Ferro-Maine."

"Just a moment, Lord Whaler."

Sylvia appeared shortly, wearing her casual yellow-striped tunic, the top two buttons undone, and with her dark hair loose.

"Working are you?"

"We work most days, Lord Whaler."

"Is there any chance that I could persuade you otherwise? To show me a few sights later in the day?"

"I'll be tied up until early afternoon."

"That would be fine. Early afternoon, I mean. Should I meet you somewhere?"

"Why don't I meet you at your Legation around 1400. You have a duty officer who can call you?"

"There is one. Always," he added ruefully.

"Then at 1400, dear Envoy."

Nathaniel found himself staring at a blank screen.

He leaned back.

In the meantime, what could he do? Why was he so restless?

He let his eyes traverse the console.

Stir the pot with a few more anonymous tips?

He smiled. Snooped or not, his hidden watchers couldn't stop his communications.

"Sam," he began on the keyboard, "have you heard the latest about the Envoy from the black planet? His staff is losing their minds. At least one did, wiped all the way back to age eighteen, poor fellow. He's the one who visited the Envoy's office just before the fireworks exploded. Rumor has it that he was on three separate payrolls, and only one was Accord's."

Nathaniel knew it was weak, but it would keep Sam's mind on the Accord issue and might get a phrase or two in the gossip section. He sent it off and found himself pacing around the study, which felt too small, looking at the time on the console, wanting 1400 to arrive.

He debated running through a workout but rejected the idea.

Compromising, he sat down back in front of the console and accessed historical information on New Augusta, deciding to see if he could learn anything new while he waited.

Surprisingly, the Empire apparently had no problem with open library files. The index alone was massive. That whetted his interest and encouraged him to dig in.

"Buzz!"

He barely resisted the urge to jump before tapping the plate on the screen.

"Lord Whaler?"

Heather was on the screen.

He looked for the time. 1407.

"Yes?"

"A lady in the reception area says you are expecting her."

"Ms. Ferro-Maine? Ah, yes. I'll be there shortly."

He shut down the screen. So far he'd gotten through the founding of New Augusta and the events leading up to the creation of the Empire from the wreckage of the Second Federation.

Realizing he was still in a set of undress greens, he retreated to his bedroom for a quick change to a tan tunic and matching trousers.

Sylvia rose when he entered the reception area. Since the morning, she had changed into a short-sleeved, dark blue tunic trimmed with white, with corresponding slacks. The color imparted a fragile, almost elflike cast to her face.

"I understand you were hard at work."

"Just background research. Not work."

"Please don't tell Courtney that," she mock-pleaded.

"Our secret." He looked over at Heather and shrugged. "When I will be back, I do not know."

"Don't worry, Lord Whaler." The redhead smiled. "You need to enjoy yourself."

As they stepped out into the corridor, he turned toward Sylvia. "Where would you suggest we begin?"

She came to a stop and faced him.

"What do you have in mind this time?"

He ignored the hint of bitterness in her tone.

"To look, to sightsee, perhaps to have some dinner at a place you suggest. Just to enjoy the afternoon. Or did I not make myself clear?" he asked.

"I wasn't sure. Wanted to know where we stood. Have you seen the fire fountains at the Gallery?"

"I knew of neither. Where?"

"Let's go. We'll take the drop and the tunnel train. The Gallery is where the most noted art from all through the Empire is displayed. They change exhibits almost daily, and some of it is fascinating. There's also a section of pre-Imperial art dating back to the dawn."

She reached for his hand and half skipped, half ran down the corridor toward the drop shaft.

With the pace she set, it seemed only minutes before he was being dragged into the Gallery.

The circular main hall was larger than the receiving hall where he had met the Emperor and more than twice as high. In the center a bronze wall, fully three meters high, circled an area fifty meters across.

Behind and above the wall the fire fountains played, colors interweaving, shimmering, rising, falling—the rough image of a dying angel, superseded by the angry red bursts that suggested the usurpation of grace by a demon and the fall of the demon in turn.

Green, green, the first real green he had seen inside the corridors and tunnels of New Augusta, showered up in the eternal triumph of spring, measured in instants, followed by the darker green of summer and the red and gold of fall, the gold fading into the dead white of winter.

Standing there, entranced, the corners of his eyes filled with his reaction to the green images and the flow of seasons.

"You miss Accord?"

"Yes. You have so many endless tunnels and walled-away vistas from the towers where one can see, but not touch."

She reached over and touched his hand.

"Let's go see the old Hall of Sculpture."

Again, she skipped off, catching him off balance as he watched her dancer's gracefulness leaving him flat-footed.

He had to remind himself that she had once been and still might be an agent of the Imperial Intelligence Service.

No, he corrected, doubtless still was. How else could she have gotten the materials which gained them access to the Defense Tower?

"This one dates from before the age of atomic power. It's called the Thinker."

"They had trade negotiations then, I see."

"Less of the diplomat, dear Envoy, and more of the artist."

"I cannot draw even straight lines."

Sylvia drifted toward the next sculpture, a representation of a man breaking out of a sphere. Nathaniel studied the markings on the sphere momentarily before understanding, belatedly, that the sphere was Terra and that the markings were the outlines of the continents.

The sculptor had captured a steely look of determination, one that the Ecolitan had seen more than once on the faces of his Institute troops, along with the hint of hope, a suggestion of something faraway and unattainable.

"*Flight*, circa 100 A.E.F.F. Sculptor unknown. Recovered from ruins at DENV."

The Ecolitan nodded. Sylvia, on her way to the next figure, didn't fully appreciate what the artist had meant. He did. Maybe that was the problem between the Empire and Accord. The Empire stood for containment, whether in New Augusta's corridors or within the sector boundaries drawn from star to star.

He left *Flight* and rejoined Sylvia at the next statue, a dancer poised on one toe, impossibly balanced on that single point.

"You miss the dance?" he guessed.

"You don't ever get it out of your blood."

"Why did you not continue?"

"I wasn't good enough. Not for the Imperial Court, with its pick of the best from hundreds and hundreds of systems. Oh . . . I fought it, but in the long run, you accept the decision of the Arbiter."

"Arbiter?"

"The Arbiters of the Arts, who judge who gets into the artistic professions."

"That is important?"

"Dear Envoy, for an artist, it's everything. If you aren't accepted by one of the Arbiters for the arts or for a profession, you've got two choices—emigrate or join one of the services."

"I see. And you?"

"Foreign Service . . . barely." The undercurrent of bitterness was there.

"Why did you not emigrate to where you could dance?"

"It doesn't work that way. Emigration is randomly assigned. Otherwise the children of the well-connected would all end up on places like Calleria and Einstein, and the unknowns and those out of favor would be out on the worlds of the Alparta. The one thing that's been kept absolutely fair is the emigration lottery."

Nathaniel doubted that, but kept his mouth shut. How the Empire kept order on New Augusta was becoming much clearer. He changed the subject.

"Do you still dance?"

"As a hobby, a spare-time pursuit, but enough of that, dear Envoy."

He patted her shoulder, not sure exactly what else he could do.

She walked out from underneath his second pat, touched his hand, and was on her way to the next exhibit.

The rest of the Hall of Sculpture was a blur. His thoughts kept going back to the statues of the man emerging from Terra and to the dancer.

As they emerged from the Gallery, Sylvia halted in mid-skip, and pointed to the miniature garden they had passed on the way into the main hall.

"Are the flowers on Accord much like that?"

"Those few we have are from Terra, but there aren't that many except for the fruit trees."

He hoped she would let the statement go, knowing at the same time she wouldn't. How was he going to explain, without lapsing into pedantry, that while Accord was a product of parallel evolution, the principal plant families were more like the year around, nonflowering gymnosperms than the deciduous trees of Terra. After two millennia, the imported Terran stock was beginning to predominate over much of the Accord native flora. The hardier breeds and the crosses developed by the Institute could hold their own against the Terran plants, and, in some cases, were reversing the trend.

The drier high steppes were totally indigenous and would remain that way since Terran cacti and plains grasses had not been among the original imports.

"No flowers? Except on fruit trees? We're limited because of ecological problems. You're free to walk your planet, but there's nothing bright to see?"

"Not exactly. The finger tree, with green and yellow striped fronds, can be spectacular in the dry seasons."

"But what about flowers? Just plain old flowers beautiful to look at?"

Nathaniel shrugged. While he enjoyed the finger trees and the spring greenbursts of the corran forests as much as anyone, he hadn't placed the need for a large variety of flowers at the center of his aesthetics.

"Maybe that's why," she mused.

"Why what?" He was annoyed, not knowing why.

"Why you don't understand the starkness you present, why the black and the dark forest green you wear so often fit you so well. Flowers and dance go together with sunshine and open air. You have the open air but not the flowers. We have the flowers." She looked down at the blooms. "Now's not the time for any more philosophy. You need to see more before you go, and I can't imagine you'll be the one to stay and sightsee once your talks are complete. And it won't be all that long now."

She started off, with more a brisk walk than a skip.

"Next, you ought to see the Maze of Traitors."

He repressed the urge to ask her how she knew the talks wouldn't last too long and clamped down on his tongue. Sylvia seemed to flit from point to point and subject to subject with annoying rapidity, not ever quite finishing anything.

Maze of Traitors? he wondered.

Sylvia was still moving quickly, and he had to quickstep to catch her.

"Can tell your military background, dear Envoy, you know?"

"Military?"

"You don't ever amble or skip or run. You march or quick-step, and if you really got behind, I'd bet on a military jog or a flat-out sprint."

"Maze of Traitors?" he asked, not wanting to touch on the question of his background.

"Dates from the First Foundation. Legend has it the Directorate built it under Alregord. He called the fallen oligarchs rats, but any rat who could run the maze could emigrate. We can get there from the Concourse at the Ministry of Defense."

The history of New Augusta hadn't mentioned the Maze of Traitors, and the rise of the Directorate under Alregord had merited two brief paragraphs.

Sylvia flung herself into the drop shaft and assumed he would follow, which he did but without the same reckless abandon.

The Maze of Traitors had been sanitized and covered with permaglass, on which tourists could walk and trace the paths beneath the transparent flooring. The Maze was deserted, only a man and two children wandered ahead of them.

Each of the hazards beneath was marked with a plaque and announcing stand.

"Station six," declared a disembodied voice as Nathaniel approached. "This is the delayed drop trap, which was counterweighted so that it did not drop until the body weight was a full meter onto the surface. According to the records, less than twenty percent of the criminal victims ever escaped this section.

"Station nine. As you can see, this appears to be a gentle incline which leads to a cul-de-sac, but the surface is specially treated to be directionally friction sensitive, making a return climb back up the ramp impossible for all but the fastest."

Nathaniel did not ask what happened to those who could not make the climb. The two paragraphs about Alregord had been specific enough.

"Station thirty-six. This is the false exit, identical to the real exit except for the seal of the Directorate beneath the lettering. Each victim was shown a picture of the real exit before being placed in the entry area, but no special emphasis was placed on the need for absolute identity. As a precaution, the incinerator units in the walls, like the other weapons in the Maze, were disconnected when it was restored by the Emperor H'taillen."

Fast as he'd been in touring the maze, Sylvia had gone ahead and was waiting.

"Why did you think I should see this?"

"Just did. Call it for my own reasons. No more questions, dear Envoy, please. Now, how about the observation platform at Tower Center?"

He'd heard of that—the circular permaglass platform on the tallest tower in the center of New Augusta where it was rumored that you could see three hundred kilometers. Unless the towers were taller than he suspected, three hundred kilometers seemed a bit far. He supposed he could have figured out the math, but assuming that the earth was flat, technically a two-kilometer tower would have allowed a look at flat ground more than six hundred kilometers away, although the angle would be so flat as to be useless. Probably the maximum distance would be closer to one hundred kilos. In any case, the view might be worth it.

As at the Maze of Traitors, he and Sylvia found few tourists or others on the observation platform, even though there were no restrictions on entry, no cost for entering the high speed lift shaft, and plenty of space atop the tower.

As the morning had promised, the sky was clear. In the growing dusk of the late afternoon, the shadows of the towers spilled over the Imperial Palace to the east. The western mountains were black, the sun behind them, with sparkles of light flashing from behind them.

"You can see the glitter from the ice," he observed.

"I like to see the shadows across the plains grass," Sylvia answered.

He eased his way around the absolutely clear walkway to the eastern side and looked at the Imperial Palace again. Seen from the tower, it was a low mound of lusterless gray metal anchored by five squat golden towers, none of which reached half as far into the sky as the lowest tower of the city.

Somehow, Nathaniel would have expected the highest tower of all to have belonged to the Emperor.

"On stormy days, you can see the plains grasses dancing with the wind, and the patterns change as the winds play through the towers."

Sylvia must have used a scope. Either that or she watched from a lower vantage point. His vision was supposed to be excellent, but he could only make out the general bending of the grasses from his office.

"After the Ecologic Rebellion, all of this had to be restored square by square. Just a hundred years ago, my mother said, there were bare patches you could see from the towers."

Sylvia twirled and looked up at him.

"I'm hungry. What are you in the mood for?"

"Something simple . . . something you like . . . something . . . somewhere an Envoy would not discover."

She grinned, and there was a hint of wildness in the gray eyes.

"But not too dangerous," he added quickly. "Food and danger don't mix. Not without poor digestion."

As they dropped down the shaft, he wondered if he had let himself in for more than he should.

After a long tunnel train ride, well past the Port of Entry, and a long walk, punctuated with a drop shaft, followed by another long walk through the first angled and jointed corridor he'd seen on Terra, he was certain of it.

He kept his fingers playing over the detectors in his belt, but no energy foci were registering.

At irregular intervals, hallways joined and branched from the main corridor, and a few local residents hurried on their ways, not bothering to look at either the Ecolitan or his escort.

The flooring was harder, and the sound of footsteps echoed more than in the tower corridors.

"This is one of the older residential areas. People who don't like the towers, mainly. It dates back to right after the Rebellion."

Sylvia led him off the main corridor and around a gentle curve in the hallway to a dead end, but it took him a moment to realize it.

At first glance, he thought it was a garden plopped into the middle of the rabbit warren they had scurried through. His second look took in the umbrellaed tables under the low trees and soft lighting. People were seated at most of the tables, but Sylvia led him along a gravelled path through a hedge and to a table for two, set by itself.

"Astounded . . . amazed . . . speechless . . . almost," he muttered, "but not quite."

"I hope so." She laughed.

"Whatever you say, dear Lady. I am in your hands."

And he was, because as flighty Sylvia had flitted through the afternoon he had lost sight of the fact that she was a perfectly competent intelligence agent.

She pointed to the table. "A seat?"

He sat, and she settled herself across from him, taking the napkin, real cloth, Nathaniel noted, and putting it in her lap.

"I would like to set the record straight, dear Envoy." She looked squarely at him, and the scatterbrainedness was gone, her eyes cold like slate.

"One, I understand the impossible situation you face. Two, you have behaved like a perfect gentleman while being a total bastard. Three, you asked me to trust you, and I did, and a lot of people died. It was necessary, but I don't like it. Four, I helped you do it, but I don't want to talk about it. Five, I can't help liking you. Six, dinner is my treat.''

The Ecolitan managed to keep his face nearly expressionless, even with the sinking feelings that settled in the pit of his stomach.

Sylvia smiled. The coldness was gone, as if turned off by a switch.

"This garden was planted blade by blade, stem by stem, by the owner. It's unique in Noram, maybe anywhere on Terra. And the food is as good as the atmosphere."

"May be the only one in the galaxy," commented Nathaniel. "Never seen one like this with such flowers, paths, trees, especially totally indoors."

A young woman, black-haired and black-eyed, edged through the hedge and looked at Sylvia, who nodded.

The waitress departed, to return with two slender crystal glasses filled with a golden liquid.

"Sniff it first," urged Sylvia.

He did. He couldn't place the bouquet, but the warmth of it recalled a summer's evening and seemed to relax the tension in his back and legs.

Sylvia took a sip of hers. After a moment, he followed. The taste was stronger than the delicacy of the bouquet suggested, but the warmth of the trickle that eased down his throat was totally without a sting or hint of bitterness.

"Arranged everything, have you?"

"Absolutely everything. Memories are the most important thing you'll take back to Accord. I want you to remember this dinner."

"And the Empire, too?" he queried, teasing.

"Empires are people, as I think you once said, and we all share the same stars."

"With such artistic interests and concerns, how did you get from the study of dance to the Foreign Service and to the Senator's office?'' And to the Intelligence Service along the way? he wondered as well.

"That's a long story, and not one to tell tonight. Let's just say I don't like doing the same thing for very long, except dancing, which I can't for reasons we've already discussed. So I change as I can. Maybe I'll emigrate, but emigration is a one-way ticket. You don't do that without a good reason.''

The waitress reappeared with two thin china plates, each containing a salad. Nathaniel touched the edge of the plate.

"Real china,'' confirmed the dancer/intelligence agent/ woman across the table from him.

The lighting dimmed in the garden, and the small lamp on the table came to life with a flame of its own.

Nathaniel took a last sip of the liqueur. Sylvia had already finished hers and started on the greenery. He followed her example. The small salad was as good in its way as the drink had been.

"Lord Whaler?''

He started.

"What do you really think of the Empire? In your heart of hearts?''

"That you ask of a diplomat? Or an Ecolitan?''

She just looked at him.

"It's difficult to put the feelings of a lifetime into words, and not in my own language, but I will try.''

"Take your time. I'll listen.''

"The Empire is different, so different. It's large, always pressing at Accord. Some fear the Empire because it is big. Some wish it would go away. Some want to destroy it . . .''

"You?''

"The Empire is dead at heart, I fear, although no one, or few except the Emperor himself, knows it.''

He took another bite of the salad before going on.

"Dreams, aspirations, are the shadows of the future.

Art, also. At the Hall of Sculpture, there were only a few people. You saw the dancer. I wondered at the man breaking free of the earth. But where were the other dreamers? The Emperor's Palace does not soar to the skies but buries itself in the earth.''

"But what about the growth, the new systems, the explorations, the success in battles?"

"They are not from the heart of the Empire. The young of the outer systems bleed and strive. Like Accord, they will some day want to dream their own dreams. I hope the Empire is wise enough to understand when that time comes. But I doubt that.''

She shivered, though the air was warm.

"You paint a dark picture, and your words are compelling. I suppose that's why—'' She broke off as the waitress came through the hedge to remove the small plates.

He wondered where she'd been heading, but before he could ask, she threw another question at him.

"Why did you take the job?"

"I was asked by the House of Delegates."

"Were you required to accept?" Her tone was dry, a slight curl at the corner of her mouth. In the dim light, he wasn't sure if she was masking lightness, a mild skepticism, or out-and-out disbelief.

The slight breeze carried the faintest hint of orange toward him as he waited. Finally, he spoke. "No. But duty, responsibility . . .''

"Does everyone on Accord take duty so seriously?"

He laughed. With her put-on seriousness, it was impossible not to.

"Does everyone here take duty as seriously as you do?" he countered, hoping for a laugh in return.

He got it.

"Touché, dear Envoy. I suppose I deserved that."

Another set of china plates appeared from the hands of the waitress, as if by some sort of magic.

The main course was equally simple, a single slice of

meat under a golden sauce, and a side dish of long slice beans, sprinkled with nuts and a clear sauce.

"What is it?"

"My secret."

He waited until she started before venturing a bite. Like the salad and the liqueur, the meat was excellent, with an almost cristnut flavor that lingered after each bite.

"Gentle men are the most dangerous, don't you think?"

"What?"

"They give the impression of weakness, of confusion, and they often let themselves be pushed on minor matters because they're only willing to fight for the most important things."

"Perhaps. But is such a person gentle?"

"Would you consider yourself a gentle person, Lord Whaler?"

"In those terms, no. I would not."

"I would, I think," she mused, looking, but not really looking, at him with an unfocused expression.

He waited, not willing to commit himself.

"Why?" She paused. "Because power is only a means to an end, rather than the end." Her eyes focused on him, but the seriousness was gone. "How do you like the food so far?"

The Ecolitan couldn't answer, his mouth full, and finished the rather large bite he had taken.

"Delicious."

"The dessert is heavier. But I do admit to a sweet tooth, and I've selected an old favorite."

The dinner plates disappeared at the magic hands of the waitress and were replaced with crystal bowls filled with a brown pudding like substance topped with white fluff.

The taste was distantly familiar . . . chocolate. He'd had it once before, years ago when he and Raoul had done student drops on Fioren. A real luxury, chocolate, at fifty Imperial credits a gram. His estimation of the cost of the dinner rose further.

Whatever it cost, he was enjoying it.

The chocolate dessert was followed with two small snifters of Taxan brandy.

"Never have I been so royally treated."

"I hope not. I hope not."

Over the low hedge, he caught sight of sparkles in the air. Sylvia glanced in the same direction, then back at him.

"Marchelle can overdo it. Replica fireflies. Real ones can't be brought into the tunnels."

He sat there in quiet, the subdued hum of conversation from other tables barely audible, wondering why Sylvia had gone to such lengths. Wondering if she had set him up for a rude surprise.

"Time to depart," she announced. "Time to get you back to your Legation and me back to my cubbyhole before I turn into a scull again. Ci'ella complex, you know."

Not understanding a word, he nodded, his fingers dropping to his belt and still finding no energy fields, no snoops, no other devices in the vicinity.

Nathaniel left the grassy lawn, the hedges, and the tables with a feeling of regret, not sure why.

"Always hate to leave," Sylvia murmured, "but there's a purpose for every time."

Pleasure or not, dinner or not, Nathaniel forced himself into combat alert, mentally ticking through the checklist. If ever there were a time to be alert, now was that time, when he didn't feel the slightest bit like it.

He stayed next to Sylvia, through the curves and lift shafts back to the tunnel train, alert for any deviation from the route by which they had come.

The train was almost empty, and that worried Nathaniel.

Sylvia wore an amused smile but said nothing.

"Few use the train," he commented halfway back toward the Diplomatic Tower, feeling the silence weigh on him.

"Right now. Too late for most and too early for the real carousers. Aren't many of them any longer."

With his newfound understanding of the Imperial population control techniques, he understood why.

He lapsed back into silence. Never had he mastered the art of small talk while keeping thoroughly alert. That was for espionage types, not Ecolitans.

A few souls were in the concourse of the Diplomatic Tower when the two of them swung off the train, but, again, he could find no trace of either tails or energy concentrations.

Finally, they reached the portal to the Legation, which was opened by the duty officer as they approached.

"Here's where we part company, dear Envoy." She took his hands in hers.

He stiffened, unsure of what to do.

"You're expecting the worst, have been all afternoon. You're too ethical. Even when you play dirty, you play fair."

Turning to face him full on, Sylvia stood on her tiptoes, brushed her lips across his forehead and stepped back, still holding his hands.

"Good night."

She was gone, gliding toward the drop shaft before he could open his mouth. When he did, he left it open because there was nothing to say.

What could he say? Obviously, he was more transparent than he thought.

He closed his mouth and turned toward the still-open portal.

Heather stood inside behind the console.

"Still here, Heather?"

"All day, Lord Whaler. I trust you had an enjoyable outing."

"Enjoyable but puzzling. Most puzzling." He shook his head as he started toward his private quarters, still alert, still checking.

Neither his office nor his quarters had been touched, further snooped, or otherwise tampered with so far as he could tell.

He was still shaking his head when he finally climbed into bed. Another social encounter with the women of the Empire was unlikely, for a while at least. Another might well undo him totally.

The faintest hint of orange blossoms drifted into the room as he closed his eyes, but when he looked, the space was empty. He turned over and willed himself to sleep.

. . . XXXV . . .

Even after a full day more of studying the history and development of New Augusta from the viewpoint of the Imperial historians, followed by another night's sleep, Nathaniel felt he had only a slightly more than superficial grasp of the motivations of the people with whom he was dealing. He understood better some of the phobias of the Imperial citizenry, such as the dislike of the color black, which, interestingly enough, had been the color adopted by the Directorate after Alregord.

Perhaps Accord had been wrong to let the Institute choose the combination of military expert/scholar. Were his well-intentioned machinations leading the way to disaster?

Despite his elementary precautions, Sylvia could have set him up for assassination or an incident which could have totally embarrassed him or reduced his credibility. Instead, she had treated him to a charming afternoon and evening, while making clear she knew exactly what he was up to. But she hadn't explained her reasons. Maybe they were supposed to be obvious, but to him they certainly weren't.

He shrugged as he donned his blacks. The week ahead

was going to be interesting enough without adding worry
on top of worry.

Should he get into his office early? Too early, and
Mydra would be suspicious. Too late, and she'd glare.

He laughed at himself for the thoughts. Like the generally unseen Imperial men, he was reacting to the pleasure
and displeasure of the Imperial women.

The hell with it! Forest Lord take the foremost. He liked
being at work early, and he was going to enjoy it.

He took a cup of liftea in his tiny kitchen and eased
through the apartment quarters into his office. The shadows of the westernmost towers reached the foothills below
the mountains, but the rational side of his mind questioned
what his eyes told him. Were the towers that tall?

The sky was cloudless, as it was so often, and he
enjoyed the blue heights. The skies over the Institute
displayed clouds more often, in keeping with the generally
wetter weather he was used to.

He leaned back in the swivel, debated whether he should
try to finish the Imperial version of the history of New
Augusta or enjoy the view.

The view won.

"Lord Whaler?"

Mydra stood in the open portal from the staff office.

"Beautiful morning, Mydra, is it not?"

"If you say so." She looked at his console. "I'll be
feeding some communications which need authorizations
into your console. If you could take care of them this
morning, I'd certainly appreciate it."

"Fine. Will do them as soon as they're ready."

So much for the history of New Augusta and the view.
Duty called. He drained the lukewarm remainder of the
tea.

With a touch on the power stud, the second faxscreen lit
and projected the first communications.

Most were either letters back to students, supplying
information or referring them to the Institute for more

detailed studies. Another batch was composed of routine denials of emigration requests from Terra to Accord.

He found himself amused that the facsimile of his signature remained as the principal validation of communications after centuries of electronic transmission methods.

"After all this thinking machinery, someone still has to read and authorize this junk."

Midway through the program stack, the intercom buzzed.

"Lord Jansen for you."

Moderately surprised that a call through the main office was actually being routed to him, he jabbed the stud.

"Lord Whaler."

"Alexi Jansen, Lord Whaler."

"Good it is to hear from you."

"We've had a chance to go over your proposal, Ms. Du-Plessis and I, and I was wondering if you and your staff could talk over some of the points raised."

"Most happy to do so."

Jansen cleared his throat and waited.

Nathaniel waited also, then realized that Jansen was in a difficult position. The Minister couldn't really demand that they meet over at the Ministry of External Affairs, nor did he want to talk in the leaky confines of the Accord Legation.

Nathaniel cleared his throat in return, gestured around his office. "Alas, not terribly suited are my spaces, but pleased would I be if no other space is available."

The Ecolitan could see the relief on the Deputy Minister's face.

"Our offices are not that much more spacious, but if you would like to come here, I would be more than pleased to send Ms. Du-Plessis and put a tunnel limousine at your service."

"That would be most gracious. I regret our situation, but you know the damage we have suffered."

"I understand, Lord Whaler. I certainly understand."

"A time we have not agreed upon."

"There is a saying about striking while the iron is hot," responded Jansen.

"Cancelled my appointments because of the damage, since I knew not when it would be repaired. I am free today."

"Right after midday? We could meet and settle some of the points."

"That would be fine."

After another ten minutes of phrases within phrases, it was agreed that at 1230 Janis Du-Plessis would arrive to whisk one Nathaniel Whaler off to the tower housing the Ministry of External Affairs.

The Ecolitan leaned back in the swivel momentarily. Then he leaned forward and began to rummage through the remaining datacase, the one that hadn't been blasted to shreds by Sergel and his friends. Enough files and holo slides remained for his purposes.

He went back to the authentication of student comms, obviously foisted off on him by Mydra. Envoys weren't supposed to look out windows and enjoy the views.

A standard hour later, he'd finished and turned the screen back to his history studies of New Augusta. Before he reached the last few centuries of the glorious and stupendous history of the capital of the Empire of Light, the intercom buzzed.

Nathaniel shook his head. The closer to the present the text got, the preachier it became.

"Ms. Du-Plessis has arrived."

Nathaniel did not acknowledge the announcement but picked up the datacase and marched to the portal door.

"Where is she?" he asked Mydra.

"At . . . the main desk."

"See you somewhat later."

He interrupted a conversation between Heather Tew-Hawkes and Janis Du-Plessis at the front desk with his sudden appearance.

"Ready to go?"

"Uh . . . is anyone else coming?"

"Not immediately," lied Nathaniel.

"Later?"

"Later," lied the Ecolitan, "and shall we go?"

"Yes, Lord Whaler."

As he left for the drop shaft with Janis, he could see the puzzled look on Heather's face from the corner of his eye.

Janis Du-Plessis did not make a single comment during the drop to the concourse level or on the way to the External Affairs electrocar, except a curt, "This way."

The driver was not the black youngster he'd had before, Nathaniel observed with regret, but an older woman with short cut black hair flecked with silver.

He couldn't tell whether the color was natural or applied.

Janis sat on the far side of the rear seat of the limousine and pointedly stared out the window at the murals as the electrocougar dipped into the tunnel.

"Amazing it is how things are governed by impressions and appearances," mused Nathaniel. "Sometimes, the slave is the master, and sometimes the master is the slave, and sometimes both master and slave think they are the master."

He wasn't getting a reaction and didn't expect one. He just waited.

"How did you get selected as Envoy, Lord Whaler?"

"That is a rather long story. An authority on trade was required, but one not indebted to the bureaucracy or to either political party. I was available. The Empire indicated the matter was urgent, and I was sent."

The Assistant shifted her weight and turned to face him, her face pale in the dim light of the electrocar.

"Always, it seems as if Accord is cloaked in mystery."

"It is not that mysterious. I am concerned. One of my staff has been mind-wiped. I have been attacked and bombed."

Nathaniel cleared his throat, pulled at his chin, and said nothing further.

The car hummed onward through the tunnel.

"You indicated your staff would meet us. How can we finalize the agreements?" Her voice rose slightly as she finished.

"Staff is a luxury."

"A luxury?"

"Does the lion tell the owl his business? Does the star-diver instruct the glide-ringer?"

Janis displayed the puzzled look he had seen all too often over the past few days. He wondered how she had gotten as far as she had. Was her mother a General of the Marines?

He let the silence draw out, wrapping the stillness around him like a blanket.

The official electrocar began the climb out of the tunnel and into the concourse area of the Ministry of External Affairs.

"What will I tell Lord Jansen?"

"That everything is under control. That you have the situation in hand. That is true . . . is it not? Of course it is."

Four ceremonial guards in rust and tan, three women and one man, waited at the private concourse entrance.

Alexi Jansen stood by the door of the conference room on the one hundred forty-first level. Through the portal, Nathaniel could see a projecting faxscreen and two technicians.

"Greetings, Lord Whaler."

Jansen looked at Janis, who returned the glance without expression, then back at Nathaniel.

"Will . . . uh . . . others . . . be joining us?"

"I fear that some misimpressions may have been conveyed. While others might wish to be here, I am indeed the expert on trade, and we can proceed, I assure you."

Jansen raised both eyebrows.

"Do you think that wise . . . that is . . . without supporting technical staff?"

"Lord Jansen, I am empowered to act solely, if I so

choose. Let us go ahead, and we shall see what we can work out.''

The Ecolitan marched around Jansen and into the conference room. Janis looked at Jansen with a look that said, Don't blame me.

Nathaniel placed his case on the table in front of the chair that was his, letting the case push a green and black name placard into the middle of the polished wood surface. He opened the case and removed four of the files, snapped the case shut, and put the datacase on the carpet next to his chair.

"Shall we begin?"

Jansen, who had followed the Envoy into the room but still stood, opened his mouth, shut it, opened it. Finally, he closed it and nodded.

Janis Du-Plessis handed a card to Jansen and sat down.

"The first item," she announced in a businesslike tone, "is the proposed schedule on microminibits."

The technician fiddled with the controls of the projecting faxscreen, and a holo of the list appeared above the end of the table.

"That is the schedule as it presently exists. You will note the Imperial tariff is the highest on the combined minibits, though still very low under the circumstances—around eight percent of assessed valuation—and decreases with complexity to a low of four percent on the single minibit."

The holo projection changed to show a second set of figures, displayed in green, next to the first set.

"The green figures represent the change suggested by the Coordinate of Accord. Those maintain the present rate of graduation, but increase the top rate to ten percent and the lowest rate to around six percent."

The Ecolitan looked at his file and checked his figures against those on the screen. They matched. He'd known that immediately, but if he hadn't made the overt comparison, his lack of response would have been misinterpreted as knowing the numbers inside out. He knew all the figures cold, and the real and allowable leeways, without consulting the folders, but Jansen and Du-Plessis wouldn't have believed it. If they did, they would ask rather embarrassing questions.

"Correct those figures are," he announced in a self-satisfied tone.

"External Affairs," continued Janis Du-Plessis, "would like to suggest a further change, increasing the rate of graduation and raising the base scale to eight and a half percent so that the full rate of twelve percent is first assessed on quintuple units, as is now the case."

The latest projection added a set of figures in red beside the green figures that had bordered the original tariff rates in black.

Nathaniel pointedly looked at the holo chart, then bent down and retrieved his datacase, from which he extracted a miniputer. He began entering figures into the instrument, either frowning or nodding as the results came up.

He stopped for a moment and let his eyes flick around the room, from the rust hangings to the nondescript tan fabric-covered walls to the rich dark wood of the conference table, then back across the faces around the table.

Lord Jansen wore a politely bored expression, sitting back with no real interest in the various projection figures.

Janis Du-Plessis twitched as his eyes crossed hers. Nathaniel realized she had been studying him. The other staffer, not the fax technician, was running numbers through a small console, which had to be linked with the main External Affairs data banks.

The projection tech's expression matched Jansen's, but on her the boredom looked contemptuous as well.

The Ecolitan glanced back at the figures. The Empire, or External Affairs, reasoned the more complex the minibit, the greater the advantage that Accord possessed, the reason underlying the graduation of the tariff schedule. A twelve percent tariff rate effectively meant a fifty percent increase in the rate.

"A twelve percent rate means, dear friends, an increase of fifty percent in the tariff rate."

"These figures were developed after long consultations with the affected Imperial industries and with regard to the calculated rate of return to Accord's suppliers."

"A twelve percent rate will reduce many imports to nothing, and the purpose of the talks was to further trade, to make it fair, but not to stop it."

Actually, Accord's industry could make money so long as the top rate stayed below fifteen percent. In any case, the minibits were important but not the entire battle.

"Lord Whaler, here are the supplementary figures. Chart One B, please, Devon."

Chart One B appeared in place of the microminibit tariff schedule. On it were the volumes of Accord exports to Terra, the existing tariff rates, the revenue to the Empire, followed by a second column showing the volume of imports from Accord projected under the External Affairs proposal.

"As you can see, even with our proposal, the volume of imports from Accord will decrease only ten percent, but the increase in the effective price will give our manufacturers enough leeway to compete."

The problem with the External Affairs proposal was that it put too much duty on the more complex minibits, where the emerging and continuing market was likely to be, and too little on the simpler, lower profit minibits. Plus, accepting the idea of a more steeply graduated schedule left the door open for further steepening and set a dangerous precedent.

Nathaniel dug a memorandum from his datacase. Stripped of all the technical nomenclature, it basically stated that the Accord microprocessing industry had developed the capability of producing triple minibits which could do the work of Imperial quintuple minibits produced by the Noram microprocessors. The terms triple and quintuple were misnomers, since a single minibit referred to a million gate choice, and each level multiplied by ten.

He handed the memorandum to Janis.

"As this indicates, there is likely to be a problem of description."

He sat back and waited for her to read the two page technical summary.

After Janis read it, she passed it on to the console staffer, who scanned both pages into the data banks and passed it on to Lord Jansen.

"He's right," announced the data tech after several minutes at the console.

Jansen, beginning to lose his bored look, started to lean forward in his swivel.

"This could set us back to square one, Lord Whaler. Why did you even bring it up?"

"Several reasons. First, not to bring it up risks the Empire declaring that we have bargained in bad faith. Second, the information points out the error in using a graduated tariff based on an artificial distinction. Third, the problem has to be resolved."

"See your point," observed Jansen.

"So what do you suggest?" snapped Janis. "You brought the problem to our attention. You must have some suggestions."

"Already, it appeared likely some questions were arising over the point at which the maximum level of the tariff should be assessed. Is that not true?"

"That's true. That's a question on any graduated schedule. What does that have to do with this?"

The Ecolitan shrugged, as if the answer were obvious, even to a dullard like the Envoy from Accord.

"Simple Envoy that I am, it seems obvious that the problems lie not in the articles being taxed but in the tax structure. If the schedule is not graduated, then using different names for equipment all doing the same job will not matter.''

''Are you suggesting a flat rate for all minibits?''

Nathaniel avoided a direct answer. ''What would be the average of costs to Accord, given a flat rate of nine percent?''

''That's low,'' answered Janis, ''but let's see it, Devon.''

Nathaniel already knew the answer. Under the current trade flows in microminibits, a nine percent rate would reduce the tariffs Accord paid the Empire by about two percent. Assuming a decrease in Accord exports to the Empire of ten percent, a tariff rate of nine and a half percent would give the Empire a comparable increase in tariff revenues.

The numbers flashed up into the midair holo display.

''You'll get even more of a break at nine percent,'' protested Janis, ''and the present situation is already unacceptable.''

''Nine and one half,'' offered Nathaniel.

No one said anything until the next display appeared, showing the figures outlining the results of his suggestion.

''That would be somewhat of an improvement, but I hope that Accord would be somewhat more flexible,'' said Jansen, ''particularly given the higher volume of trade in multiple minibits.''

Nathaniel began to play around with his computer, finally threw up his hands.

''What about ten percent?''

At the ten percent rate, the Imperial figures showed close to a twenty percent reduction in imports from Accord, and slightly more revenue to the Imperial treasury.

Nathaniel's estimation of the economists at the Ministry of External Affairs took a nosedive. No commodity was that price-elastic over a half percent. Plus, it was apparent that no one had calculated the impact of technological change.

He frowned.

''Nine and three quarters as a final offer?'' he asked.

"Ten!" Jansen declared before Janis could say anything.

"But the loss! A true increase in tariffs . . . this represents nearly forty percent . . . but—" protested Nathaniel.

"Lord Whaler, for several years now, many of our microprocessors have been suffering because tariffs were too low. It's not just the present situation the Emperor must consider. There are many other factors . . ." Janis let her voice trail off.

"Ah, yes, I understand 'other factors.' While I would prefer the nine and three quarters rate, for the sake of agreement, we will accept ten percent. What else can I do?" The Ecolitan shrugged.

"For the sake of making progress, let us close the discussion on this item," suggested Jansen. "Of course, we will have to clear this with the Emperor and the full Ministry staff."

Nathaniel made appropriate notations on his file.

"I will also check."

"The next item," droned Janis Du-Plessis, "is . . ."

Nathaniel fumbled through the files again. It was going to be a long afternoon.

. . . XXXVI . . .

The negotiation sessions went on and on, with weekend interruptions, scattered breaks for "clarifications," then, like everything else in New Augusta, ended abruptly on a mid-week day.

The whole agreement had been packaged and readied for transmission to the Imperial Senate and the tender mercies of Senator Helmsworth and his colleagues.

Nathaniel found himself behind his Envoy's desk with a full day looking at him. After more than a standard month, Marlaan was still on vacation, and Witherspoon, reputed to have just finished his "consultations" on Accord, was planning to take home leave before returning to Terra.

"They certainly gave me enough vine to swing cliff clear," he muttered to no one in particular.

He glanced out the wide window at the clear sky, absently wondering why the Imperials had preferred to negotiate in a windowless room, then looked back at the faxscreen and the authentication lists for the outgoing communications. He suspected that Mydra piled up the lists whenever she thought he spent too much time staring out the permaglass.

The intercom buzzed.

Nathaniel looked up from the second faxscreen, punched the accept stud.

"Marcella Ku-Smythe for you, Lord Whaler."

"Thank you."

He jabbed at the flashing plate.

"Ms. Ku-Smythe?"

"Yes, Lord Whaler. Let me be among the first to congratulate you on the progress I hear you have been making with External Affairs."

"Only talks, dear Lady, long and involved, wherein everyone must check with everyone." He shrugged. "And progress? Who can tell?"

"You're too modest."

"A mere fumbler with numbers am I."

Nathaniel glanced up at the bare wall, out through the open portal to the staff office, looked back at his fingers, and finally clasped both hands before looking back into the screen.

Marcella dropped her eyes for a moment.

"How long do you think it will take you to complete the talks?"

"If nothing unforeseen arrives, if no further difficulties are observed, then most of the work is done," he hedged. "But for your sake and mine, I hope nothing unforeseen occurs."

"For my sake?"

"We are what we are, Lady, not what we would like others to see or what they would like to see. Me . . . a mere fumbler of numbers, a professor doing what he can. You . . . a most competent Special Assistant."

"Were the Commerce Department to take a more active role?"

"I defer to your superior knowledge and to that of your associates and family. Doubtless you know best. For my part, humble as it is, so long as the talks result in the mutual agreement of Accord and the Empire on tariffs and the continued independence of Accord, your presence would always be welcome, whether in an official or in an unofficial capacity.''

He half bowed to her image on the screen.

"Thank you for your graciousness, Lord Whaler. While I could not accept under the circumstances, I appreciate your understanding."

He looked at the blank faxscreen for several minutes, shook his head. Desirable woman but definitely the strong-willed type.

He shook his head again, violently. Enough wool-gathering. Getting involved with anyone, Sylvia or Marcella, at this stage of the game, while the final terms of the agreement were hanging before the Senate, could be highly counter-productive, to say the least.

He flicked back to the scan screen and the list of authentications Mydra had dredged up. They had helped fill the hours, not necessarily pleasantly, while External Affairs had wrangled with the staff of the External Relations Committee to ready the package for full Senate consideration.

He tapped on the intercom.

"Yes, Lord Whaler."

"Sergel? Isn't he due for release shortly?"

"I checked this morning, and he could be sent back to Accord any time now."

"Would you make the arrangements? For later this week?"

"I'll take care of it and let you know."

The Ecolitan froze the seemingly endless stream of authentications on the second screen, putting them in temporary storage, and flicked on one of the faxnews channels.

". . . in one of the more surprising developments during the hearings on the Purse, Senator Helmsworth proposed close to a fifty percent increase in the budget for the Imperial Intelligence Service. Helmsworth, when questioned, cited reasons of Imperial security and offered to display evidence in secret debate. For the first time in more than a generation, public debate was halted for the secret session. The sole outsider present was Grand Admiral Ku-Smythe. After the presentation, the chamber was opened, and the motion passed unanimously."

The screen switched from a view of the Senate chambers, hung in shimmering red and paneled in dark wood, to a mid-aged woman wearing the cream tunic with the red slash of an Imperial Senator.

"Senator Re-Lorins, before the secret session, you questioned the need for such an increase in funding. Yet you voted for the increase. Why?"

"Both the Senator from Noram and the Grand Admiral showed evidence of a persuasive nature. Rather startling and shocking evidence, I might add, even to me."

"Can you reveal the nature of that evidence?"

"No. I cannot."

The screen cut back to the commentator and her studio console.

"That was the only statement from Senator Re-Lorins, Chair of the Intelligence Committee. No other Senator would comment, including Senator Helmsworth."

The screen filled with a panorama of dying plants in their fields.

"The synde bean virus is still on the move. These bean fields on Heraculon are the latest victims of the gypsy virus which seems to appear at random. Botany pathologists are puzzled at the spread of the resistant species of the virus, which was formerly controlled with a derivative of antoziae."

The next scene was an empty warehouse.

"At this time of year, the warehouses on Heraculon are normally beginning to reach full capacity. As you can see, that's far from the situation now.

"Bryna Fre-Levin on Heraculon."

As the screen switched again, this time to an orbit scene centered on an Imperial battlecruiser, martial trumpets blared in the background.

"Admiral of the Fleets, Jorik Ypre-Tanelorn, transferred his flag to H.M.S. *Gold Prince*, which will lead the new Eleventh Fleet through its shakedown cruises before it takes station.

"Admiral Ypre-Tanelorn," and the screen featured a still shot of a black-haired, thin-faced man with a pencil mustache and black eyes under bushy eyebrows, a picture of perfect formality with the Admiral in his dress red and gold uniform, the starburst of the Empire above his left breast. "The Admiral declared the Eleventh Fleet will serve as the vanguard for continuing peace and stability for the Empire and its allies."

The screen dropped back to the studio.

"Back in New Augusta, the Empress welcomed an unusual delegation, a talking centaur troupe from Alpha Megara—"

Nathaniel flicked off the faxnews and leaned back in the swivel.

He wondered if he should let the media take another shot at Sergel's situation. They'd probably take it, but he shook his head.

Sergel's example was tragic but not permanent. And Sergel might well turn out better the second time around, in any case.

The late afternoon sunlight through the filtered permaglass warmed his no longer quite so crisp diplomatic blacks, yet the selective polarization let him see the golden disc of the sun hanging over the western hills without requiring him to squint.

The other towers rose, dark gold, before the western hills, like so many obelisks, or so many pillars of dark fire shedding flickers of reflected light.

He put his feet up on the console, leaning further back in the chair to watch the play of light over the towers.

The intercom buzzed, and he sat up quickly, realizing that over an hour had passed as he had let his thoughts drift.

"Ms. Corwin-Smathers for you."

"Lord Whaler."

Courtney was wearing a cream tunic with rust piping and banded scarlet flecks at the cuffs.

"My pleasure, Lord Whaler."

"And mine also, to hear from you, although I am puzzled at the reason for your courtesy."

"No real reason, Lord Whaler. Senator Helmsworth would have liked to call himself, but right now things are rather hectic over here."

"I heard about the Intelligence Service . . . "

"That was just another incidental, for which, by the way, we thank you. Your actions were most instrumental in helping the Senator, though not in the way you probably intended. That and the synde bean problem . . ."

"Coincidence has been helpful to many throughout history."

"But that was not the reason I called on behalf of the Senator, you understand. He did want me to convey our appreciation for the way in which the trade negotiations have been handled and to let you know that we look forward to an early ratification vote in the Senate."

"Only doing my humble best, dear Lady, and without the help and advice you and others have provided, indeed I would have been lost. You are most kind, and I look forward to a successful vote."

"Lord Whaler, you are too unassuming."

He shrugged his now-habitual shrug. "We do what we can, and hope for the best for all."

"The Empire is doing its best also, Lord Whaler, and Senator Helmsworth and I, and the Emperor, I'm sure, look forward to the successful and peaceful resolution of the trade talks in the weeks ahead."

"Your concern and reassurance lift my spirits."

"That's all I really wanted to say. The Senator wanted you to know that the agreements will be coming before the Senate shortly and to convey that to your government. We all understand your talents and your sense of restraint, and wish you well.''

''Thank you.''

Courtney nodded, and once again, Nathaniel was left looking at a blank screen. One thing he'd never get used to, no matter how long he stayed in New Augusta, was the abruptness with which most friendly fax calls were terminated.

The synde bean thing . . . was that something the Institute was involved with? If it were, he'd be the last to know, sitting on Earth. Certainly, that sort of mutation was well within the capabilities of the Institute. If it had been the work of the Ecolitans, and the Emperor thought so, so much the better.

He wondered if the offhand reference he'd made to the synde bean situation had been construed to mean more by Courtney. Not beyond the realm of possibility.

With a quick tap, he called Mydra on the intercom.

''Why don't you finish up the authentications tomorrow, Mydra?''

''All right, Lord Whaler. If you say so.''

''Is there anything special I should do?''

''No. Not really.''

''Then to your superior judgment I defer.''

Nathaniel turned back to watch the late afternoon change into evening and to watch as the evening crept from beneath the hills toward the base of the westernmost towers like an incoming tide of darkness. So unlikely his return to New Augusta would ever be that he wanted to fix the spectacular images firmly in his mind.

. . . XXXVII . . .

Nathaniel took another look around the Envoy's office. His three bags and datacase were stacked up by the exit portal, ready to be picked up.

The signing ceremony at the Emperor's Indoor Garden had gone off without a hitch, although he'd been surprised to find himself greeting Lord Fergus, rather than Lord Mersen or Rotoller. For whatever reason, neither Janis nor Marcella had been at the Indoor Garden. Nor Sylvia, though there was no reason why she should have been.

For that matter, neither had the Empress, which probably reflected her feelings about provincials from Accord.

"Lord Whaler?"

He turned.

Heather Tew-Hawkes, Hillary, and Mydra were standing in the doorway.

"The Marines will be here in about an hour for you and your luggage," said Mydra. "May we come in?"

"Of course, dear ladies."

He gestured to the chairs and couch.

The three women walked into the office but did not sit down. Mydra, in the center, had her hands clasped behind her back.

"Lord Whaler," began the office manager, "I have a confession to make."

Nathaniel nodded.

"When Legate Witherspoon left and when Mr. Marlaan abruptly took leave, I was deeply concerned about the continued effectiveness of the Legation—"

"As you had a right to be," interrupted the Ecolitan gently.

"And I couldn't help but wonder how an inexperienced professor from an out-planet university was going to deal with a complex set of negotiations. When you first came in, I thought my worst fears had been realized." Mydra paused.

"Mine too," chimed in Heather.

Hillary smiled a shy smile of agreement.

"After your arrival, things just got worse. The violence, the bombings, and all the strange goings-on, not to mention the dreadful thing that happened to poor Sergel, all of those were enough to make me want to leave."

Nathaniel nodded again. "But you did not, and stayed to help me through the difficulties."

"You were so calm, even when you were certain the Empire was courting disaster, and so determined to work things out for everyone." Mydra gave a sheepish grin.

Heather was smiling also. "I heard from my friends who work in some of the other Legations how much people who really count were impressed with what you did in such a short time. I don't think any of us here really understood all that was going on."

I hope not, thought the Ecolitan as he listened. I hope not.

"At first," Mydra went on, "I wondered why no one had been sent to check on you. But that became obvious later on."

"When you were the one who stayed and picked up the pieces," added Heather.

"Especially after the bombing and when someone tried to kidnap you," added Hillary.

"Do what we must."

"That's true, Lord Whaler, but we did want you to know that we, all of us on the staff, understand how difficult your job has been and how careful you had to be. We wanted to give you this before you left." Mydra brought her hand from behind her back and opened it. On her palm was a small black box.

"But . . ." he protested.

"Go ahead. Open it," prompted Heather.

"It won't explode." Mydra laughed.

He opened the jewelry case gingerly. On the green velvet was a collar pin, done in black and green, a miniature of the formal crest of the Ecolitan Institute.

He studied the pin, realizing that it was not enamel or lacquer, but that the colors came from the depths of the two metals themselves.

"Beautiful . . . but . . . I don't deserve such . . . such a magnificent . . . not I . . ." he stammered.

"Everyone here chipped in," said Heather.

They had to, and then some, realized the Ecolitan. The pin was solid lustral.

"For doing my duty, I could not accept something like this. Not something so beautiful."

Mydra gave him an even broader grin. "You can't refuse it. Gifts of personal jewelry authorized by the Emperor are acceptable. Failure to accept such a gift would amount to an insult to the Imperial Court."

Nathaniel turned the pin over.

"From the staff, Accord Legation, and from His Imperial Majesty. J.L.M. N'troya, in sincere appreciation."

A tiny imprint of the Imperial Seal appeared beneath the inscription.

Why would the Emperor add his name in "sincere appreciation"?

"Why would the Emperor . . . ?" he asked out loud.

"That's the second part of my confession," admitted Mydra. "That afternoon when you were so depressed, when you were talking about how the Empire didn't understand Accord and its abilities, and how Accord couldn't understand how the Empire didn't understand . . ."

"Yes?"

"Well . . . I recorded it. I couldn't say it the way you did. So I recorded it, and I sent what you said to a friend who has direct access to the Emperor." She spread her hands. "I know I shouldn't have, but you wouldn't have admitted it in public, and if you'd said it straight out, no one would have believed it. And you were so right and so depressed."

"Don't be either. Just accept it," advised Heather.

"We wanted you to have something, and it almost wasn't ready in time," added Mydra.

"Go ahead. Pin it on," insisted Hillary.

He started to, but his fingers felt a meter wide.

"Here," said Heather, "let me help."

"Looks good on your blacks," observed Mydra as Heather stepped back.

"Bet it will go with his greens, too." That was from Hillary.

"He's blushing, Mydra. He's really blushing." Heather giggled.

Nathaniel shrugged, knowing he couldn't do anything about the flush that spread across his face.

"What can I say?"

"Nothing. Nothing at all," answered Heather. "Just enjoy it."

"You deserve some recognition, Lord Whaler. I doubt that Legate Witherspoon, Mr. Marlaan, or anyone on Accord will fully understand all you did for them, and the rest of the Empire certainly won't either."

The Ecolitan stood there helplessly.

"Come on, ladies. We've still got a Legation to run. For once, we've left the Envoy speechless."

All three were smiling self-satisfied smiles as they marched out of his office.

Nathaniel collapsed into his swivel, wondering how much they really knew, and more important, how much anyone else knew. The answers would be largely academic, since the trade agreement revisions had been signed and approved by the Empire, and the House of Delegates wasn't in the mood for suicide by refusing to hold up Accord's end.

He switched on the faxnews. One channel was discussing the synde bean shortage. He flicked the selector.

". . . in a quiet ceremony at the Indoor Garden, the Emperor signed the new trade agreements with the Accord Coordinate. While observers termed the agreements 'routine,' the talks literally exploded earlier this year when the Accord Legation was bombed.

"Although the investigations by the Imperial Intelligence Service and the Ministry of Defense failed to uncover the reasons for the bombings or the individuals involved, the evidence uncovered led to a revamping of the Intelligence Service and the resignations of Lord Rotoller and Lord Mersen from the Commerce Ministry . . .

"The revised tariff and trade terms are expected to benefit the Imperial transport and microprocessing industries—"

Nathaniel flicked the newsfax program off the console. Time to go. As soon as the Marines arrived, he'd be on his way to the port and the shuttle that would carry him to the Accord courier that waited for him. Three subjective weeks, and two objective days, and he'd be home, along with the agreement to be ratified by the House of Delegates.

He fingered the collar pin, possibly the most expensive personal possession he'd ever owned.

The private circuit on his console chimed. He debated not answering, but touched the plate with his forefinger.

"Lord Whaler."

The caller was Marcella Ku-Smythe.

"Congratulations, Lord Whaler."

"The same to you. All is going well with you?"

"I think it will. I'm working with Lord Fergus now, and I learned a lot from watching you."

Very convenient system, reflected the Ecolitan. Change the figureheads and leave the structure, with the women still in control.

"You're leaving soon?" She pointed through the screen toward the bags behind him.

"A short while."

"I'm very glad I reached you. You know, I'm scheduled for a trip to Accord later on to close down our section of the Imperial Legation in Harmony and to make a final evaluation. Perhaps I could look you up."

"Anything is possible."

"And," she looked straight at Nathaniel, "I expect some explanation of your specialties."

"My specialties?"

"How to sell nonexistent tariff reductions, for one. I just finished analyzing the final terms. You eliminated the Accord duties on all Imperial microprocessors. Very generous, but how will that help? We can't compete here on Terra. Then there was the increase in Imperial multichip duties to ten percent. The market is so competitive that nothing less than a fifteen percent rate would offer any real protection. All two hundred plus reductions and changes follow the same pattern."

She smiled and waited for his response.

"You do me far too much credit. I only followed my instructions to the best of my ability. You are far more expert than I am."

"Perhaps I am overstating the case. But I really do admire you. There's always the tendency to underestimate men these days, no matter what we say, no matter what I told you about not underestimating you. But no hard feelings—you did what you had to, and as delicately as possible, all things considered."

"I fear my understanding is limited."

"Oh, Lord Whaler, you're still the cautious one. I can't

blame you. If there was a lot you didn't know about us, there was more we didn't bother to look up on you. A senior practicing scholar of the Ecolitan Institute, flawlessly fluent in at least five languages, including Panglais. A man considered one of the brighter economists on Accord and who is a trained military specialist who normally spends an hour a day practicing hand-to-hand combat. No wonder you looked bored and restless! We had it all in the file and didn't bother to notice the inconsistencies once you blundered in, stumbled over your tongue, and bored the devil out of us all.''

She grinned at him, and there was no mistaking the openness of the humor.

''Before we could figure that out, you make fools out of some very competent security agents, among others, and the media starts asking us very embarrassing questions.

''Lord Whaler, loyal and obtuse, stumbles along trying to explain that 'he is trying to help,' but no one is interested. The faxhounds keep asking about bombings, secret agents who failed, jurisdiction, and why the Empire can't get its act together when Imperial industries are suffering. Now we have a trade agreement which gives the Empire sufficient short-term gains to quiet everyone, while reinforcing Accord's long-term position and independence.''

Nathaniel cleared his throat. Loudly. ''Too kind, much too kind, gracious Lady—''

''And,'' Marcella plunged on, ''since the treaty doesn't cost the Empire too much and avoids the possibility of getting involved in another ecological war, no one is about to admit that a bumbling and stumbling Envoy from a third-rate system is really an extraordinarily capable agent from the only independent, first-rate power of a nongovernmental nature. Besides, and this is strictly personal, it serves Janis right.''

The Ecolitan relaxed fractionally. Marcella wasn't talking about the real military aspects behind the treaty, but she'd definitely picked up on the power of the Institute, which was interesting since most of Accord's House of Delegates didn't understand that. And since Marcella didn't have to bear the final responsibility, as Janis might, she would let things slide.

"I guess that's it, Lord Whaler. Don't be too surprised to hear from me."

The screen blanked.

Nathaniel shook his head.

He supposed he ought to feel sorry for Janis Du-Plessis. She was outclassed by virtually everyone, from Mydra to Marcella to Sylvia, who, in her own quiet way, was the class act of the lot.

Sylvia!

He glanced around the console, then jabbed at the controls, letting his fingers flicker over the keyboard to pick out the information he needed.

He smiled as the screen printed up the answers he was hoping for.

While he waited for the system to dredge up the last responses to the questions he had posed, he looked out again through the wide window, out at the mountains in the distance, at the blue of the sky, and at the thunderclouds piling up over them.

The intercom buzzed.

He ignored it while the screen scripted out the last of the clearances he had requested.

"Whaler," he muttered, "you're assuming a lot."

He shook his head.

"You're also being impetuous, which is not at all healthy in your line of work."

Having refused to persuade himself, he committed the clearance numbers and codes to memory, then, as an afterthought, jotted them down on a note sheet, which he folded carefully and placed in his belt pouch.

That done, he stabbed the intercom stud.

"Lord Whaler, the Marine Guard will be arriving shortly."

"Thank you, Mydra. I'll let you know the final arrangements shortly."

He tapped out another number, one he wasn't supposed to know.

"Ferro-Maine . . . Lord Whaler!"

"Nathaniel," he corrected softly, taking in Sylvia's face, the wide clear gray eyes, and the strand of dark hair dropping over her forehead.

"What . . . can I do for you?"

"Where are you?"

"At the office . . . you know that . . . that's where you called," she stammered. "I thought you were leaving."

"I am. That is, I may be shortly. Please stay where you are, dear Lady." He grinned happily and broke the connection. On the screen he could see the confusion running across her face as her image faded.

"Mydra, please have my luggage delivered to the shuttle port by the Marines and tell them that I will meet them there."

"But . . . Lord Whaler! You can't do that!"

"Dear Mydra . . . I have to . . . but don't worry. Not this time."

He was already moving toward his private quarters and the outside exit when he tapped the intercom stud.

By the time he raced through the quarters and into the corridor toward the drop shaft, he was nearly running. He slowed only after he was actually dropping toward the concourse and the tunnel train station below.

The platform concourse at his destination station—the Imperial Senate Tower—was moderately crowded but melted away from him as he marched toward the lift shaft.

"Seem to draw back from an Ecolitan on the march," he mused as he watched a number of citizens edge away from his path.

Sylvia's office was only fifty meters from the exit stage.

"Lord Whaler, how good to see you," burbled Charles,

the friendly receptionist, half rising from his chair and leaning toward a small panel on the console.

Nathaniel reached the man before Charles' hand could hit the warning plate.

"This is a friendly visit, Charles," announced the Ecolitan as he hoisted the other away from his console.

"Friendly?"

"As a matter of fact," noted Nathaniel, he tapped the flat plate labeled, F-M.

"You're here? Here?" asked Sylvia on the small screen.

"Nowhere else. Do you want to come out or invite me in?"

"I'll be right out."

Nathaniel returned his full attention to Charles and set the receptionist down in a swing chair away from the main communications console.

"Lord Whaler?"

"Yes, Charles."

"Why . . . I mean . . . to what do we owe . . . ?"

"To a happy occasion, I hope."

Nathaniel kept his eye on the console and on the portal from the staff offices, wondering if he should have charged all the way through, hoping that Sylvia wasn't ducking out whatever back ways existed.

"Happy time?"

"I hope," the Ecolitan added under his breath, wondering what he was doing literally hours before he was to catch his shuttle home.

His head snapped up at the whisper of a portal.

Charles looked at the console, then at Whaler, and decided to stay put.

Sylvia was wearing the same blue and white trimmed tunic she had worn when they had gone sightseeing together. Did he smell the faint tang of orange blossoms? What was he seeing in those gray eyes?

He shook his head.

"I'm impressed. You came to say good-bye in person."

Her voice was polite, but he could sense an undercurrent, exactly what he couldn't identify.

He shook his head again.

"No. I didn't."

"You didn't?"

"Not to say good-bye." He shifted his weight, looked at her for a long moment, then at the floor, before finally taking the slip of notepaper from his belt and handing it to her.

She unfolded it.

"This is supposed to mean something, dear Envoy?"

"Nathaniel," he corrected automatically. "Sylvia, you know I'm not good at speeches . . . and there's not much time—"

"So don't deliver a speech. Say what you have to and go."

"Those codes represent your visa, your clearance, and your immigration permit to Accord."

From the corner of his eye, Nathaniel could see Charles' mouth drop wide open.

"Me . . . an ex-Imperial agent?"

"No. You . . . the person . . . the woman . . . Flamehell! We've got less than three hours to catch the shuttle."

"For what?"

"For Accord. For us."

Sylvia smiled, and her expression was guarded. "Why us?"

"Because I want you to come with me!"

The guarded look was replaced with a fuller, yet somehow more tentative smile.

"You haven't asked me."

"Would you please come with me?" He finally managed to grin himself. "Even if you hadn't planned to emigrate for a few more years yet?"

"But I'm scarcely—"

"Sylvia."

"Yes."

Without realizing what he was doing, Nathaniel reached for her, only to find she had the same thing in mind. They collided in mid-step, grabbing at each other to keep from falling.

"I think this time you beat me to it," he murmured in her ear.

"Not now. We've only got three hours to catch the shuttle."

She kissed him slowly full upon the lips and then stepped back from his arms.

Charles shook his head from side to side as the tall man and the dancer walked from the office, hand in hand.

TOR
BOOKS The Best in Science Fiction

LIEGE-KILLER • Christopher Hinz
"*Liege-Killer* is a genuine page-turner, beautifully written and exciting from start to finish....Don't miss it."—*Locus*

HARVEST OF STARS • Poul Anderson
"A true masterpiece. An important work—not just of science fiction but of contemporary literature. Visionary and beautifully written, elegaic and transcendent, *Harvest of Stars* is the brightest star in Poul Anderson's constellation."
—Keith Ferrell, editor, *Omni*

FIREDANCE • Steven Barnes
SF adventure in 21st century California—by the co-author of *Beowulf's Children*.

ASH OCK • Christopher Hinz
"A well-handled science fiction thriller."—*Kirkus Reviews*

CALDÉ OF THE LONG SUN • Gene Wolfe
The third volume in the critically-acclaimed Book of the Long Sun.
"Dazzling."—*The New York Times*

OF TANGIBLE GHOSTS • L.E. Modesitt, Jr.
Ingenious alternate universe SF from the author of the *Recluce* fantasy series.

THE SHATTERED SPHERE • Roger MacBride Allen
The second book of the Hunted Earth continues the thrilling story that began in *The Ring of Charon*, a daringly original hard science fiction novel.

THE PRICE OF THE STARS • Debra Doyle and James D. Macdonald
Book One of the Mageworlds—the breakneck SF epic of the most brawling family in the human galaxy!